Boomerang
When Life Comes Back to Bite You

Also By
Marcia Fine

*Stressed in Scottsdale**

Gossip.com

*Paper Children – An Immigrant's Legacy**

*The Blind Eye**

*Award Winning

Boomerang

When Life Comes Back to Bite You

Marcia Fine

L'IMAGE PRESS

Scottsdale, Arizona

Boomerang
When Life Comes Back to Bite You

ISBN#: 978-0-9826952-1-0

$14.95
ISBN 978-0-9826952-1-0
51495>

9 780982 695210

L'IMAGE PRESS

Scottsdale, Arizona

FOR SKIP, MY PARTNER IN LIFE.

1

IN THIRTY MINUTES I'VE EVOLVED FROM disheveled professor to well-groomed lunch lady, my abandoned Birkenstocks slapped against the baseboard of my bedroom closet, jeans skirt on the floor and standard oxford shirt draped over a hook. I'm meeting Glee and April and I haven't seen them in ages.

Of course the transition is a miracle of make-up and clothes. I'm ready with foundation, lip liner, mascara and three colors of eye shadow, which I hope I've painted in the right places. *Fapitzed*, a Yiddish word for showing off everything you've got, means make-up, hair, nails, fancy clothes, jewelry, high heels, all the girlie stuff that requires a commitment of time and supreme effort. My mother thinks I should be look like this all the time. If she saw me today, she'd say, "Jean, you look stunning. Just stunning. Like Debra Winger in *Terms of Endearment* before she got sick."

Maybe I look better, but I don't feel it. Megan, my department head, has given me an ultimatum that swims in my swamp brain. I adjust my steel-jawed push-up bra with a snap and a wiggle, catching a glimpse of myself in the mirror. I haven't worn heels this high since Glee had a boudoir party and we had to dress as whores and pimps.

I leave Tempe, home of Arizona State University where dudes with spiked blue hair sail by on roller blades, their cappuccinos held high, for Scottsdale, Land of the *Fapitzed*. My gnawing thoughts about Megan will have to wait until later.

Instead of the 101 Freeway I negotiate traffic through a grid of streets (Thomas Jefferson's idea), L-shaped shopping centers and beige developments with red tile roofs. No ethnic neighborhoods with bustling outdoor café's and funky boutiques like other big cities. It's all new. The older places left fight for survival against urban blight.

An interest in aesthetics dictates that the architecture and colors remain true to the desert that's been mowed down to put the buildings there. No Miami art-deco hues, only sand, dusk, adobe, and Navajo white. Few green lawns either. The barren landscape of gravel and sand on miles of tract homes are dotted with compass cactus that lean toward the southwest, their circumference design reflecting the sun. They even make candy from the pulp that's reminiscent of strawberry jam. We used to send it to our friends, a home-grown novelty like taffy from the Jersey shore or coconut patties from Florida.

Palo verde trees grace many lawns with waxy leaves and needle-like stems that sprout tiny yellow flowers. Desert plants are hearty because they don't require much water, but it takes a while to get used to beige everywhere. Not a blade of grass in sight.

My Volvo slides into a space under covered parking at Fashion Square, mall extraordinaire. The restaurant Glee has picked for lunch is an upscale, pseudo-Chinese/Thai place. My heels keep me unbalanced as my fashionable purse swings from my shoulder, one that doesn't hold my wallet, keys or glasses, but matches my outfit.

Glee waits for me in the entrance, her wild dark hair, in an I-just-fell-out-of-bed look. A some-time yoga instructor and erotic artist, Glee dresses in costumes, a capricious gypsy with wild taste. Usually, she's in something provocative, willing to turn the world on, but today she's covered. A hand-painted orange and pink scarf winds its way around her neck, ending in tassels with gold bands--a stripper during Mardi Gras who forgot to take her clothes off.

I love her because she makes me laugh and has a good soul, but I know she's crazy. Of course Maury says we're all nuts, but Glee's truly a pleasant dysfunctional. Her mission in life is to take enough workshops to grow and experience everything. Fortunately, she's married to Ted, the condo king of Scottsdale, who finances the search for inner peace and outer beauty.

Glee and I greet each other with hugs and air kisses, making sure not to smudge the delicate lip lines we've painted with precision. Her tattooed lips are more pooched and redder than mine since she had fat removed from her thighs and pumped into them. In fact, she grabs my shoulders to assure we air kiss on both sides of our cheeks, a habit she brought back from France years ago along with a ceramic bidet.

"Jean, you look fabulous! I haven't seen you looking so glamorous in ages!" cries Glee as we pull apart.

An older couple in Bermudas stares at us. The wife whispers to her husband as she places her hand on top of his, "They're so *fapitzed*."

Our hostess seats us at a table that faces outward so we can watch for April. I remove my sunglasses. "Look at this," Glee says as she lifts her top above her waist.

"What is that? Are you wearing a girdle?" I reach over to tap on the pink corset wrapped around her waist.

"No. This is the undergarment you wear for two weeks after liposuction. Dr. Reingler did me a few days ago. I'm going to have the midriff of a twenty-year old."

"Didn't you already have liposuction?"

"Yes, but that was for my drooping ass and sagging thighs. This is different. We've got to keep everything up and flat, except the breasts, of course." She shimmies a little and the tassels shift.

When Glee starts on her plastic surgeries, I envision her surrounded with before and after photos, gauze and ointments. I can't imagine going through the pain and inconvenience, but she says everyone is addicted to something and hers makes her look good.

Most people here come from somewhere else. Glee's a rare Phoenix native whose upbringing was steeped in economic turmoil. Usually her mother divorced well, but the fourth one plunged them into poverty. The country club membership evaporated, the Mercedes was confiscated, the horses disappeared, and Glee bounced from boarding school back home. Her insecurities still boil under the surface. Since she found Ted and his congenital bucks, she works on herself inside and out as though she's one of his building projects.

We spot April teetering behind the hostess, her Versace glasses hiding her aquamarine eyes. In a tight red dress that outlines her model's figure and zebra Jimmy Choo's, her hips sway like a fifties movie star. It's the kind of walk that used to make men drop their dangling cigarettes from their lips and fan themselves with their hats. April looks fantastic. It's her job.

Tables of businessmen, their silk ties a panoply of blues, purples, and muted reds, stop their conversation, forks held midway to their mouths as April passes their table. She's a gorgeous sea creature floating through an ocean of attention, queen of the mermaids. I'm sure they're in agreement with Maury that her heart-shaped tush is a number ten. Mine's only a mushy six.

Glee pushes back her chair so they can air kiss and then I do the same.

"You look smashing," says Glee.

"Thank you. What a long line at valet!" she grumbles placing her Kate Spade tote near her red toenails. April pulls out her chair. I notice the men return to their conversations. "The market is taking another dive. The tech roller coaster ruins my day."

April's married to Steve Lefkowitz, a personal injury attorney whose advertising includes the jingle, *You can bet, we'll get them upset. Call Harding, Collier, Smith and Lefkowitz.* She reaches for her water, the grape-sized diamond on her finger sending out sparks.

After we've pushed a few noodles across the plate, laugh about some gossip--a local society woman who's experimenting with cybersex—-I share my outrage at Megan, although I don't know if either of them will get having a boss since they don't work.

"'You are bringing ruin to my department,' she says to me." I imitate Megan's voice with its uppity accent, a residue from her

Boston Brahmin family. "She's in this regulation six-by-eight community college office, windows shut against an October breeze, that she thinks is an English woman's home. It's all chintz and ruffles, rose slip-covered chairs and English country prints. It smells musty. Remember I caught her once with a powder puff half-way to her armpit? She loves talcum powder!"

Glee frowns and April giggles. "Doesn't she know there are carcinogens in it?" Glee asks me. "You should tell her it could cause Alzheimer's." Glee takes her organic information very seriously.

"Glee, please. I think she's already got it. Anyway, the woman's a drama queen! I'm sitting there with my pits sprouting water with my body in a full-blown hot flash trying to figure out a way I can hijack some of the talcum from her drawer. By the way, the plant estrogen you gave me doesn't work."

"I told you to see my herbologist. You need a full work up," says Glee. April nods in agreement because she's younger and doesn't have flashes yet.

I put my sunglasses on to imitate Megan and the way she lifts her chin for a power peer-down over the top of her readers. I move forward in my chair.

"She stares hard into my eyes. 'Did you assign *Women as Lovers* in your Women Lit class last semester? After the trouble with your curriculum choices a few years ago I thought I had made my position clear.'"

April says, "Jean, you're too funny. Why don't you just bag the job and play with us full time?"

"April, I couldn't keep up with you. Anyway, I told Megan it was on my list of reading materials and she tells me the book is outside the approved college curriculum. All I could do was stare at her bountiful bosom of uncooked muffin dough, the rest of her covered in large purple violets more appropriate for the upholstery. I explained to her it's an optional choice. I want to give the students exposure to all kinds of ideas while they're in an educational setting."

"Then she lays it on me. 'Do you remember a student named Tiffany Gorden?' My mind scampers through names on my computer sheets for Women and Literature, Women and Mythology, and Feminist Expression. Of course it doesn't ring a bell."

I go back to my haughty accent as April and Glee lean in. This is not of their world. "I'll refresh your memory. She was in your morning section last semester and she picked the selection I just mentioned, which I might add, is only available at the gay and lesbian book store off campus." I raise my voice an octave on the last few words. The table of men next to us glances in our direction.

"How am I supposed to remember one Tiffany among all the other Tiffanys?" That's my synonym for the blonde sorority types who always sit together. The students who stand out are the ones who participate in class discussions. She must have been one of those back-row silent-sitters.

"She tells me this young woman failed my course and was traumatized by going to a gay book store. I couldn't believe it. She didn't have to pick that selection. There were other choices. Besides, only two books had a gay theme. Then I remember the Tiffany who sat near one of my favorite students, Doris. Anyway, Tiffany claimed she was ill when the books were assigned.

When are we going to stop coddling these kids? No wonder they don't accept responsibility. Of course, that's an absurd thing for me to say when Michael just moved out a few months ago, but I never said I was consistent."

"How is Michael?" asks Glee, changing the subject to our often un-employed son.

"He called yesterday and he wants to bring over his girlfriend," I share. Glee and April have known our son, a sweet, albeit lazy child, since pre-school when we all lived in the same neighborhood. The lettuce wrap I'm attempting to eat falls apart mid-air, most of it hitting the plate but not all. I swipe at the tablecloth and my lap.

"What happened to Cashmere?" asks April, putting a fork with a miniscule amount of food between her red lips.

"You mean Velvet. This is a new one. What a party boy he's been, more interested in beer and broads," I say using a term I abhor for women. It's the first time he's wanted me to meet one of his girlfriends.

"Is it serious?" asks Glee.

"I don't know, but I can't wait to see who he thinks is presentable enough to bring home."

"Oh, don't worry. He's maturing. College has probably made him appreciate you and Maury more," says Glee, ever the positive soul-searcher.

Glee knows our disappointment when my underachiever had to take a year of classes after graduation to qualify for graduate school. How can two driven parents create such an unfocused kid? Anyway, his grades have improved so maybe he's on the right path.

"So what happened with Tiffany?" April asks me.

"She didn't want to read the book, especially after her visit to the bookstore. Megan told me the women in there had mannish haircuts." I self-consciously pull the back of my hair down toward my collar. Mannish haircuts? The woman is out of touch.

"She applied to drop the class too late in the semester so she flunked."

"I don't see that you did anything wrong," says Glee.

"Neither do I but Megan said they don't want to make their campus a hotbed of liberal thought." I move back into my Julia Child voice. 'Alternative lifestyle discussions breed controversy, especially with funding under review. Remove that or any other selection dealing with that topic immediately. And change Tiffany's grade to an incomplete.'"

"I swear, defiance burned in my chest. I told her in an educational setting students need to be exposed to ideas. Besides, I never change a grade." Megan rolled her mouth into a disapproving, pinched "O", swiveled her chair back to the desk and reached for her reading glasses. I was dismissed."

I didn't verbalize it to my friends but when I headed for my Last Legs Volvo in the faculty parking lot that morning, each flop of my Birkenstocks making me angrier, I kept thinking: What kind of academic freedom is this? Telling me what books to use and to change a grade. I've tolerated Megan's autocratic, high-handed style in the past, especially when my salary helped defray some of Lara's wedding expenses, but now she's too demanding. Do I fight back and unleash her wrath or do I give in? My car started with a cough and a screech from the fan belt. On my ride home while my head pounded a steady African beat, I forced myself to bury the problem for the afternoon.

My longtime friends take me out of my world, one of community college students who can't read and barely write past seventh grade level, an ailing twenty-year old house, and a husband and two grown kids who still need me.

We depart after the check arrives, sailing through the restaurant, an aquatic parade with April as the homecoming mermaid on the front float and then Glee. I'm in the rear. No matter how *fapitzed* I get I'm still Jeannie, a band nerd in my cardboard high school uniform stuck behind the horses in a parade. We repeat our air kissing routine outside. Glee reminds me to embrace whomever Michael brings home. "She might be his soul- mate," she says, twirling the tassels on her scarf.

Probably more like a crotch-mate, knowing my horny son.

"Don't forget about my art opening in a few weeks," Glee goes on. "You've got to meet Tuni and Ellis Sterling. They just moved here from overseas." She leans in closer to kiss me and says, "They've got a terrific business idea and Ted says we're all going to make a lot of money!" She waves as valet pulls her black Mercedes sedan up under the *porte cochere*.

As if Glee and Ted need any more money. April continues into the mall to shop, a contact sport in Scottsdale. I hike to the Volvo with a slower gait to accommodate my crushed toes.

Next to my car a woman on a cell phone, her fingers splayed with wet nails, says loud enough to echo in the garage, "Isabella, *este es senora. Como es bebe? En casa en diez minutos*." She drops her keys. I pick them up for her as she mouths "thank you" taking them with two French-manicured fingers.

I slip off my heels and unhook my bra at a red light. I can breathe at last, a fading supermodel returning from the Land of the *Fapitzed*.

2

THE PHONE RINGS, EARLY FOR ANYONE TO CALL ME.

"Mom?" says Michael, his voice a bit hoarse. "I want to bring my girlfriend over to meet you. Okay?"

Michael calling me? Usually, he bursts through the door, dragging his dirty clothes behind him. I don't wash his clothes, but he likes the convenience of the detergents, bleaches and softeners waiting for him. Maury says I shouldn't let him bring his laundry home. But ever since he went back to school, moved to his own apartment and has gotten decent grades, I support his efforts. Besides, it's a chance to chat.

This is a first. Ever since Velvet or as I called her, Velveeta Surprise, disappeared into the dancing nightlife of Tucson, Michael hasn't shared much of his social world. This one must be presentable or at least have a name that doesn't invoke lurid comments and smoky bars.

"I'll be home. Don't you want to bring her over when your Dad is here, too? He won't be home until after office hours."

"I want you to meet Rosa now." His voice sounds edgy, but I dismiss it.

I glance around the kitchen. Not exactly clean, but the white

Mexican tile counters are clear and I can get rid of the few breakfast dishes in the sink. It's nice having an empty nest--when you clean up, it stays that way. With Lara and her husband, Gus, living out of town, Michael is the only kid around to mess things up.

I spring into action, changing into a fresh white shirt I bought at Dunn Edwards because I liked the rainbow logo over the pocket. I load the dishwasher. I barely have time to finger-comb my unruly hair before the door opens. I check the mirror near the front door. I look like a mom. Michael's mom.

* * *

Rosa Abulafia Chavez oozes Latina sensuality when she walks through the door--flawless face, even white teeth, full lips, and a beauty mark suspended near the corner of her mouth. Her long lashes and arched brows frame large coffee eyes. They remind me of the exaggerated ones we used to draw as children. Smooth café au lait skin and high cheekbones hint at an Indian ancestor. She's beautiful and a bit cool.

In denim shorts and a tight yellow camp shirt tied in the front to expose a piece of tan belly, she removes a black baseball cap, the beak curled into a half moon. She fluffs her hair with her fingers. A Widow's Peak crowns her smooth forehead. Rosa and I can't shake hands because she's holding a giant Slurpee cup from 7-11, condensation dripping down the side onto my Oriental runner.

Michael introduces us and she smiles. He hugs me awkwardly.

My son, with his close-cropped dark hair, the front sticking straight up, has been sitting in the sun. Never a fashion plate, he wears shorts and a T-shirt with faded writing. Must have been too much bleach.

"Welcome, Rosa," I say. She nods at me.

He squeezes his thumb and forefinger over the bridge of his nose when I question him about his coloring. "I've been studying outside on the patio," he says. I frown and he looks away.

"How 'bout a snack?" I offer.

"Okay. I'm hungry," he says. When isn't he?

"What would you like?" Michael, who's behind Rosa, moves to sit down in the family room. It's the room we live in, a hodge-podge of rattan furniture, TV, bookshelves, a multi-colored Oriental rug on the wood floor and a comfortable sofa that needs re-upholstering, a project I need to tackle someday.

"What do you have?" Rosa asks as we remain in the foyer.

I move into the kitchen to rummage in my refrigerator. "How 'bout hummus? Or grape leaves? Or maybe salsa and chips?" Whoops. Did I offend her? I grab a bottle of pomegranate juice and a stack of glasses.

"Salsa and chips would be great."

Rosa joins Michael on the couch, snuggling against him.

We gather around the small table dipping into the salsa, holding napkins to catch the drip. I pour juice for us. Michael leans back, eyes closed. He drops his head into the cushions with a sigh.

"Tired, honey?" I ask him. I lean over to pat his leg. Maybe I can prod him to tell me why he was in such a rush to come over. He rubs his eyes again, pulling his head upright and shakes his head no, sucking in his lips. Rosa looks at him as though she expects him to say something. I'm getting nowhere so I turn my attention to Rosa.

"Where are you from?" I ask. Michael groans. One of those, Mom, *you-ask-too-many-questions* noises.

What else am I supposed to talk about? I don't think Rosa heard me. I take a different tack.

"What are you studying?"

She crosses her long legs, feet dark from our desert sun, the nails a berry-red. "Social sciences," Rosa answers as she adjusts a throw pillow into the small of her back. Then nothing. I flounder.

"Do you like to travel?" I ask, searching for a thread, a string to connect.

"I've traveled through Central America. I love the Mayan ruins."

"We went to Chichenitza years ago," I offer. "The kids called it Chicken Pizza." No laugh of acknowledgement. "A fascinating culture."

"My family is descended from the ancient Mayans." As she speaks Michael watches her lips.

"Where are you from?" I ask again.

Michael moves forward on the sofa to reach for more chips. He gives me an encouraging look. I can tell he wants this to go well.

"Originally, Mexico City," she says pronouncing it Me-hee-co, the Latino way, "but my family's business is in Guadalajara."

I don't understand. Rosa has only a slight hint of an accent. She picks up on my confusion and adds, "Oh, my parents sent me to boarding school in California."

Rosa leans into Michael with an encouraging look, but whatever the hint is, he doesn't take it. He slaps his hands on his knees and gets up.

"Mom, we've got to be going." He reaches down to help Rosa who's sunk into the cushions. "I wanted you two meet. I'll check with you and Dad in a couple of days."

Rosa gives him an exasperated look, rolling her eyes. I'm not sure I like her. She's impatient with Michael and not too friendly.

I walk them to the door, puzzled. "Thanks," says Michael. He gives me a quick kiss on the cheek. Thanks? For what? That was quick. What was the purpose of the visit?

I glance at my watch and realize it's time for me to leave for a meeting with Megan and my class. On the drive over to the college I think about why Michael wanted to bring Rosa over today. There must be more to it. If he's serious about her, he sure didn't look happy. I hope it's not one of those tortuous relationships.

Megan's office door is open when I arrive. Her back to me, bent over, she searches in a desk drawer, probably for an emergency powdering. I knock to let her know I've arrived. She whirls around, her purse draped on her arm, the kind with two sets of handles.

"Oh, Jean. You're late and I'm on my way for an appointment with the dean." Her mouth turns into a flat line of disapproval. A small puff of talcum hangs in the air.

"I'm sorry. My son stopped by and . . ."

I can tell she's impatient with me from her body language, feet apart and folders waving in her hand. Her briefcase sits open on her desk. I clear my throat. "Megan, I've decided I'm not going to change Tiffany's grade. It's not fair to the other students or to my principles. She never started the assignment or tried to communicate with me. She doesn't deserve to receive an incomplete."

"That's your final answer?" she asks. The unused shoulder strap from her purse drags on the floor. Only a compulsive would buy a purse with two sets of handles.

"Yes, I'm firm in my decision."

Megan sighs, looking at me as though I'm a child who doesn't understand the rules of Red Rover. In her most uppity accent she says, "I'm warning you. Your course is not a requirement. It's an elective. This recalcitrance on your part will cost you my support and the dean's. I'm on my way over there to discuss the matter with him right now. Quite foolish of you." She snaps her briefcase shut and pushes by me muttering, "It's beyond me why anyone would be so stubborn."

Why should I change Tiffany's grade? I explain my course requirements on the first day. The students know exactly where they stand. Miss Powder Puff Phd. will adjust. I'm left with a whiff of powder and the job of closing the door without a free hand. I make my way down the hall and through the double glass doors with a fast clip.

One of my former students waits along the outside walkway. Doris, a big-boned blonde from Texas with a tattoo of a snake that starts at her ankle and wraps itself around her calf, curls up her leg, and disappears into the hemline above her skirt. She clutches a pile of university catalogues to her chest. Even though I feel rotten instead of elated that I've taken a stand with Megan, I put on a cheery front.

"Doris, how's it going?" I set my briefcase on the ground between my feet so I can push a persistent curl off my forehead.

"Miz Rubin, it's going great! Since I took your class last

semester, I've changed from business to pre-law." She smiles with the exhilaration of a trick-or-treater holding a bag stuffed with sticky chocolate and bubble gum instead of apples.

"That's terrific. You were always enthused in class, asking questions." One of the few with any intellectual curiosity. "Why'd you change?"

Doris moves closer to me, her expression serious, her blue eyes wide with conviction. "Miz Rubin, your women's class gave me confidence. When I finished reading some of the selections, I thought I could do anything. I felt so empowered. I mean, I never thought of myself as a feminist before, and growing up in a conservative small town that thinks libbers are bra burners . . ."

She stops, her earnest gaze grasps mine. "Your class made me see my potential." She lowers her head and then lifts it. Her eyes swim with moisture. She touches my arm, her wrist encircled with tattered thread bracelets of purple and red. "You made the difference, Miz Rubin."

I'm so moved by what she's said. "Thank you. I needed to hear that. Especially today," I say. "Call me Jean."

"Miz Rubin sounds better to me," she says, doubtful.

We pause for a moment. I grapple with my stuff to hug her and then head for class, my mind ricocheting between Doris and a disaster. It's s good thing this is a lesson I've taught before. I can't wait to head for home, my refuge.

It's a family trait to tear up the newspaper. My mother cuts out articles with a cuticle scissors, leaving a strange scalloped edge on everything she deems important. When I was away at college, she sent me ones on virginity. A little late I thought. Anyway, Maury, my overworked and underpaid slave to our health care system, is short on time so I clip articles and he reads my censored version of world events. Mostly he peruses a motley mix of golf magazines, medical journals and outdated *Newsweeks*. My hero bungles through his mental machinations in semi-narcolepsy.

The paper's my comic relief, especially when I'm on edge.

After dinner I glance at an article with a picture of a legislator, her hair in a Marge Simpson beehive. In Arizona we've got some strange elected officials: a mayor who got lost and called 9-1-1, a government official who slept in his office, and a state representative who claimed UFOs graced our western sky and sued the federal government claiming a cover-up. On David Letterman she waxed poetic about lights in the sky, a true sign that extra-terrestrial beings picked our Valley of the Sun for their conclave. That is, until the Air National Guard released records of training exercises that utilized parachute-borne flares. "Third Rock from the Sun" meets the Land of Cactus and Kooks.

Later, I snuggle next to Maury in our king-size bed. He reaches his fuzzy arms around me for a hug. We kiss on the lips, a dry one that allows me to look in his soft eyes.

"How was Michael's girlfriend?" he asks me.

"I don't know. Beautiful but not too friendly."

"Think it's serious?" Maury strokes my hair off my forehead.

"God, I hope not." I change the subject to Megan and our meeting.

Always my champion, Maury's my lovable, patient supporter.

"Forget Megan. She can't do anything. It's your perogative not to change a grade." He reaches for the nightstand. "Hey, I read this article you left me."

Legislative Profile

Rep. Flora Boudreaux

Representation: District 423

Born: July 25, 1950

Hometown: Bisbee

Occupation: Homemaker/activist

Education: Bisbee Union High School; Concho Community College; Beaver College

Family: Divorced-4; children-2.

Party: Republican

Years in legislature: 2

Political Hero: Phyliss Schlafly, founder of the Eagle Forum

What you should have been voted by your high school classmates: Most Likely to Succeed

Favorite quote: "Abstinence is a virtue." Reverend Cornelius Shoup

What are the most important issues facing the legislature? Put Bible values back in our schools. Teaching abstinence.

What major bills did you introduce in this session? A ban on lap dancing at strip joints; a ban on gay and lesbian groups utilizing meeting rooms in the colleges; books with offensive material

removed from school libraries; funding
to find the link between breast cancer
and abortions.
What do you want written on your tombstone?
"She gave our kids traditional values."
If state government could only do one
thing for the people, what should it be?
State government should be responsible
for the moral fiber of its people. We
need to set a precedent by cleaning up
the smut in our own backyards.

"This woman's an idiot." He waves the article in the air. A born liberal, the caliber of people in public office usually gets a rise out of Maury. "How can the constituents vote for someone who thinks there's a link between breast cancer and abortion?" I pat his chest to calm him down.

"Ah, what's the use?" He crumples the article into a ball and drops it off the side of the bed. Amber, our golden retriever, jumps down, picks it up in her mouth and returns it with her tail wagging, a chance for a game. "No, Amber, not now," says Maury as he switches off the light.

We wrap ourselves back into a hug that gets uncomfortable in a few minutes. Separated, we fluff our pillows.

"Why do you think Michael was in such a rush to bring over Rosa?" I ask in the dark.

I wait for Maury's response, but I'm answered with the sounds of steady breathing. Gone again.

3

THREE DAYS AFTER I MET ROSA, MICHAEL shows up without a laundry bag close to dinnertime. It's when we share what happened with our day. He pulls out a chair across from Maury. I remember when he first moved back from Tucson to live with us, he shattered our household serenity and destroyed any fantasies we had about romping nude. Well, actually those ended a long time ago. Anyway, we're lucky Arizona State accepted him with his mediocre grades. They must have seen some potential in his LSAT scores. Maury shook his head in dismay when Michael confessed a lack of goals. Law school presented a good option. It gave Michael more time to decide what direction to pursue.

"Whatever you do, a law degree will help," lectured Maury. He thinks business or finance would be a better choice for our less-than-stellar student. After a semester of improved grades, we set him up in an apartment with the directive to apply himself. My soccer playing, rock fan, somewhat lethargic *Star Wars* freak has followed the rules so far.

"Dad, I need to talk to you. It's serious."

Maury drops his paper, ending our conversation about the Scottsdale housewife who tossed her husband's headless torso into a dumpster and left the scene in a blue Jaguar wearing red leather gloves. He peers at Michael over his reading glasses, the 'yes?' look in his eyes.

"Mom, Dad, I have to tell you something." Michael drums his fingers. His dark brown eyes bounce back and forth between Maury at the table and me near the sink. Stalling, he gets up for a glass of water, then returns to the table to sip it.

I wait. If he can't get this out, how's he ever going to argue a case in court? Maury, his usual placid look on his face, blinks his eyes expectantly.

Michael clears his throat.

"This isn't easy and I know you're going to be upset, but accidents happen." He moves the glass aside and folds his hands on the table, his eyes opened wide.

Accident? This had better not be what I think it is. Did my baby get himself into a mess? My heart begins a slow thump. Later Maury confessed he thought it was the car, but my female intuition told me it wasn't. I leave my post at the sink and walk over to touch Michael's shoulders. "Just get it out. Whatever it is, tell us. We've always been supportive."

"Rosa's pregnant." Michael's head falls forward over his clasped hands. I drop down on a chair at the table, speechless, which is a rare occurrence for me, the original motor mouth.

The words lay there on my chili pepper placemats like unexploded grenades.

Maury's quiet, his eyes boring a hole into the top of Michael's head. Then his cheeks turn red, the newspaper falls to the floor. He pulls off his reading glasses and flings them onto the table. I rarely see my teddy bear husband angry, but his eyes flash thunder now.

"For chrissakes, Michael, are you an idiot? You were thinking with the little head instead of the big one. How many conversations did we have about using protection? Weren't you using contraceptives?" His voice escalates.

"Some of the time," answers Michael like a little boy, the one I remember before his voice changed.

"Some of the time?" Maury bellows. He pounds a fist on the table. Michael and I jump.

"Dad," Michael pleads. His face crashes into an expression of fear and disappointment, a fallen clay mess.

"Maury, there's no need to raise your voice. Let's stay calm and figure this out. What's done is done."

I feel awful for Michael. He looks so pathetic, but I'm more concerned about Maury. His blood pressure must be sky high. I've never seen him this upset. He's usually the voice of reason while I get excited.

I'm getting angry. Did this girl get pregnant on purpose? Or is she looking for a meal ticket to stay in the States? Or, worse yet, does she think we have a lot of money because Maury's a doctor? Boy, is she in for a big surprise.

My stressed husband takes a deep breath and looks down at the table attempting to calm himself. But the little artery on the side of his head pulses, a chugging train moving along the tracks. "I don't believe this," Maury yells, slamming his hand on the table again. The ceramic bowl in the center shakes. His glasses fall off the table.

My heart picks up to a trot. Maury might explode. Michael's eyebrows criss-cross into a "V", his mouth turned down. "Dad, it was an accident." He looks smaller than his six-feet, hunched at the table, and sounding so pathetic.

I'm too numb to even cry. All the dreams I had for this kid crash into a heap. Some girl stole them away. Maury pushes his chair back and stands up.

"This is the behavior of an irresponsible *schlepper*! You know better than this."

Then he sits down again. The storm is over and Maury becomes the clinician.

"What trimester is she in?"

"She's about two-and-a-half months."

"Are you sure?"

Glum, Michael replies, "Yes."

"What are you going to do about it?" Maury bends over to pick up his fallen glasses.

Michael, defeated, puts his hands over his face and shakes his head. The part of his hair that sticks up in the front with gel doesn't move. "I dunno. I have a paper due for submission to Law Review tomorrow and I've been worried about telling you for weeks."

"Michael, would she consider termination?" I'm not pleased at having to ask about that alternative.

He looks up, his dark eyes so much like mine, and drops another bomb. "Mom, she's Catholic."

Oy. This is getting worse. My movie mind envisions large bosomed Spanish women dressed in black taffeta dresses that rustle when they walk, a few wearing mantillas like black crowns. Mega-sized crosses of the dying Jesus, his limp arms resting in their cleavage, twinkle in the light. Their dour expressions of disapproval match hair pulled into severe gray buns. Milling about, rosaries in hand, their dry lips repeat incantations. Rosa's mother supported by two priests is hysterical with grief, her face hidden by a black veil, her mourning dress trails the floor.

"Ay, mi Dios," I imagine her screaming. She falls to her knees, prostrate on the floor. The priests and women rush to lift her, as she collapses yet again.

My watery eyes bring me back to reality. Okay. So I'm a little melodramatic, but I bet they won't be thrilled on their end either. This is complicated. "Are you in love? Lifetime kind of love?" I ask.

"I adore Rosa." He looks at me and knows that isn't a satisfactory answer. "I love her with all my heart and soul. She's the brightest, most beautiful girl I've ever met." A plea for me to understand his passion.

"Are you planning to marry her?" My heart rate changes from a horse at full gallop to a scalded cat taking off.

"I don't know." His answer's fraught with pain, possibilities, and reality. His face, usually one of twenty-something skepticism, looks sad. I notice a pimple on his neck, a remnant of his adolescence.

"Michael," Maury says, "this is very serious. What do you and Rosa want?" He sounds calmer.

"I'd like to marry her, but she's Catholic. Day-of-the-Dead Catholic. Never-miss-a-mass Catholic."

"What does she say about you being Jewish? "

"She likes it. I mean. It's okay. Actually, she's been asking a lot of questions," says Michael, his hand wandering to that pimple.

I call my friends on our conference line the next morning after my herbal tea.

"Glee? You there?"

"I'm here," she says.

"April, you there?" I ask.

"Ready, roger and over," she says being cute.

"Remember at lunch I told you Michael was bringing over his girlfriend?" They murmur in agreement. I play this for dramatic impact with my voice calm, except then I lose it. "She's pregnant!" I scream.

"Jean, oh my God, no!" April cries out. "What are they going to do?"

Before I can answer Glee interrupts. "Are they getting married? If they are, you know April and I will have a shower for her." Glee and her priorities. A celebration, no matter what.

"You don't understand," I shout. "She's Catholic. From Mexico."

"Don't worry. It'll work out. Steve and I aren't of the same faith," says April.

"And I believe in everything," Glee says to console me.

"When is the baby due?" asks April, a bit more grounded than Glee.

"In seven months," I say, my voice ripe with disappointment.

"Look on the bright side," says Glee. "You're going to be a

grandmother. We can shop for the baby. The outfits are darling."

"Yes, there's going to be a baby out of all of this. But there's a lot of other stuff to get by first. What if she wants to name the baby Jesus?" I ask, pronouncing it Hey-sooz. I can hear my parents who lack any knowledge of foreign languages yelling for him on the street, "Jesus, where are you? It's time for dinner."

"Jean, you worry too much. Michael's sensible," says April. "But, Jesus Rubin does have a ring to it."

"What's happening at work?" Glee asks me.

"Today's the day Megan tells me what the dean said. I don't know him well, but he must be intelligent to run a college. I'm sure he'll back me up. Besides, I've made up my mind."

We say our good byes and I get on with my day, the thought that I'm going to be a grandmother repeating itself like a stuck CD.

At work Megan informs me that the dean has requested I change the grade. Pronto. No way.

After a few days to digest the news that we're going to be unexpected grandparents, I call our rabbi.

"Rabbi Turkeltaub," I begin to stammer. After all, this is the man who *bar mitzvahed* my son.

"Jean, you don't sound good. What's the matter?"

"Don't ask." I know I'm turning into my mother. She says that all the time.

I clear my throat and begin again. "I'll get to the point. My son, Michael, has gotten his Catholic girlfriend pregnant. What should we do?" I'm trying to be succinct and less dramatic.

He answers in the same vein. "Bring the couple in. Let me talk to them. Let's find out their feelings and attitudes first. Then we'll be able to make some decisions. Don't worry."

"Oh, Rabbi, Maury and I are so upset."

"Do you know the Hebrew phrase *Yie tov*?"

"No."

"It means everything will turn out all right."

"*Yie tov*," I mumble to myself. From his lips to God's ears. Now I really sound like my mother.

Next, I call my parents. After Lara's wedding they moved here from Florida to avoid hurricane season and be near us. My brief, shocking announcement causes a barrage of questions, as though I'm an accused embezzler explaining the money was for a good cause.

"Who is this girl? Is he going to marry her? Where is she from? Does she come from a good family?" My mother is on a roll and I haven't even gotten to the Catholic part yet.

My father is on another extension. "For cryin' out loud, didn't you tell him about birth control?" he demands.

"Of course we did," I say in a loud enough voice for them to hear me. "But in case you haven't noticed, kids don't always do what you tell them to do. Besides, he said it failed."

"What? He flunked out of law school, too? Jean, this child needs counseling. What happens to the semester of tuition?" asks my mother.

After I explain Michael is still in law school, I hang up, but not before I leave them with a bright spot of joy.

"By Passover you're going to meet your great-grandchild. How does that sound?"

Finally, I leave a message for Lara, my unconventional daughter, who resides in California with her husband, Gus. She responds with an email.

To: jeanrubin
From: lara
Subject: dumb brothers

Mom, you and dad are upset, but it'll be okay. I know you wanted both of us to marry double J's (Jewish with a job), but children can't live to please their parents. Tell him I'll call soon. We're swamped with work and school. Habla Espanol?

Love,
Lara

The next few weeks become a blurry montage of exhilaration about a new baby to fuss over and fear about my career crisis. I check the mail one afternoon and find an official letter from the university. I open it before I stroll back into the house. Megan informs me in one paragraph that my tenure is under review. Damn. I crumple it in my hand.

At dinner that night I hand Maury the letter, as I carefully smooth it out again. He sighs.

"It doesn't say you won't get tenure. You're just under review." Maury leans out of his chair to kiss my cheek, but I feel rotten anyway. Doesn't the dean have more important priorities than one Tiffany protesting a grade? All I know is that I need my Contemporary Women and Literature course right now. When I'm teaching I forget about everything in my life except the present. Even grading midterm essays I'm lost in the reverie of feminism, philosophy, and politics. I love to watch how these kids find their voice.

It isn't until the drive home that I indulge myself in *the what ifs*.

What if Michael and Rosa don't get married? What if she returns to Mexico with our grandchild? What if Michael doesn't finish law school? What if we can't support all these people? What if I don't get tenure after teaching for so many years? What if stress sends me over the edge?

After an intense conversation with Michael about finances, the consensus is he needs to save. Babies cost money. But the only expense he can cut is his apartment. He's on a month-to-month lease so next weekend he's moving into his old room. Maury and I aren't thrilled. It's not like we're Adam and Eve running around in fig leaves, but our privacy and solitude are something we enjoy, like an empty nest with two cactus wrens dancing around the top of a saguaro after the babies have taken flight.

After Michael abandons his studio and before he's unpacked the boxes from his truck, Rabbi Turkletaub sets up a meeting with the two lovers. I don't go, but the rabbi shares a few things afterward when I call him. He makes it clear he rarely marries a couple unless both partners are Jewish. Rosa says she's not ready to consider converting. It's a big step and Michael doesn't want to push her.

"He's very laconic for a *bar mitzvah* boy," says the rabbi. But I know he's laconic about everything. Even birth control. Even if she decided to convert tomorrow, it would have to be done in a shorter time than the usual nine months. What about emergencies?

Jews are strange. Our religion doesn't proselytize. Different sectors within it abide by different rules. Why do we make it so difficult to worship God and eat bagels?

A few evenings later Michael and Rosa come for dinner. She announces she's decided to drop all her classes but one. I ask, "Why? Aren't you doing well in school?"

"I'm doing fine, but I want all A's and I can't keep up right now." She helps clear the table. Her walk waddles sooner than necessary.

"Rosa, I'd like to call your parents so leave their number for me."

The next day I try to reach her family on the phone, but the connection is bad. I call again. They speak some English, but they're not accent-free so I have a few challenges. Of course, in some ways they're easier to understand than Lara's in-laws who are from Charleston. *Shalom y'all* has changed to *Shalom, Ustedes*.

Rosa's mother and father express concern. I assure them she is welcome into our family, avoiding the topic of religion. Elphidia, Rosa's mother, seems resigned that her daughter has changed the course of her life.

"I don't know why Rosa becomes pregnant. Our church believes in virgins." Only she pronounces it "weird-hin." Has she taken a look at this girl lately? She oozes sex. "When are they getting married?" her mother asks me.

"I don't know," I say. Is this the time to tell her we're Jewish?

"Elphidia, we're not Catholic."

"Sometimes when people are Protestant they don't mind a baby raised Catholic."

"Uh, we're not Protestant."

"Why not? Are you Godless? Ay, what did my daughter get mixed with?"

"We're Jewish."

She doesn't say anything for a while. Did she pass out? Are the ladies in black standing over her with fans?

"*Ay mi Dios*. Jewish? I'm in shocked. How did these two find each other?" This is not an enthusiastic response. I hear a noise. Is she slapping her head?

"We have to accept what is done," I tell her. The important thing is to get them married and have a healthy baby. We'll have to let them deal with religion." I sound more assured than I am.

"Jewish? Are you sure?" she asks.

"Yes, I'm sure."

4

"MEGAN, I'M NOT GOING TO SACRIFICE INTELLECTUAL freedom for academic pressure. I push forward in my chintz chair of interrogation. I don't have to change this grade and I'm not going to."

Megan looks at me as though I'm a six-year-old who wants to stay up until midnight. She slaps her reading glasses onto her cluttered desk. To avoid her murky eyes, my gaze shifts to the grazing sheep in a pastoral scene on the wall. Her chair rolls toward me, the arms of her gray sweater draped across the back drag on the floor. Our knees meet over the pink area rug. I smell the talcum powder mixed with sweet perfume. Her overflowing bosom is pushed into navy fabric covered in yellow daisies that rustles when she moves.

"It's apparent that you are not interested in tenure. If you were, you would change Tiffany's grade and drop the issue." Her voice grates with its faux-British accent.

"Are you saying my tenure is tied to this girl's grade? My understanding is that academic freedom applies equally to all professors, tenured or not. You're putting the intellectual integrity of this department on Death Row." I'm shocked, then relieved that this has come out of my mouth.

Megan rolls her chair away from me and stands up. "If you

persist in this rebellion, we will lose our funds for women's studies. Then both you and I will be without a job. Save the rest of us if you refuse to save yourself. Now make the correct decision and be done with it."

Her condescension aggravates me. I've done my best to get along with her over the years because she's bright and my boss, but I've always known she's a hand-puppet for the administration. She's never on the side of the teachers. I stand up, a bold move to give me the upper hand.

"I want to be clear about this, in case I have to explain this to the ACLU." I can't believe I've pulled out the big guns organization that terrorizes the right wing. "You're threatening my job if I don't change the grade of some air-head who didn't complete her class work?"

We're eye to eye, although Megan's shorter so it's more like belly to bosom. Megan moves into the beam of sunlight. It crosses her face to illuminate her bleached yellow mustache. Irrationally, I bless Glee, who taught me about waxing.

"I wasn't going to tell you this, but you are exasperating me." With a pause like a syncopated drum beat, she says, "Tiffany's mother is Flora Boudreaux."

The name stuns me. I drop back into the chair deflated. Flora Boudreaux, our legislative creationism expert. Flora Boudreaux, alien spotter. Flora Boudreaux, publicity hound. Maury and I joke about the in-breds living in her district who elect her each year.

Of course it would upset Ms. Boudreaux that her daughter might read about alternative lifestyles. She'd also be upset about war resisters, inter-racial marriage, non-church goers and gun control. I picked a doozy of an opponent this time. I steel myself, though I know I've made the right choice.

"Your decision not to change the grade is firm?" Megan asks. I nod, she sighs. "Then I shall have to inform Dean Gruber. I hope you know what you're unleashing. Legal bills can be quite devastating."

Suddenly, I'm not so confident. I feel my pits spout fountains, the aroma of nervousness floating upward. The warmth makes me prickly all over, even inside my ears. I flash forward on a tribunal court, a white-wigged judge who sits on high condemning me to a life of harridans berating me. Flora cackles from the side, her monkey hair flattened into a crushed cone. What if the legislature puts a sanction against me, banning me from living in Arizona because I'm a trouble-maker? I shift in the chair. The depressed cushion doesn't give me much wiggle room.

"I'm prepared to take this to the next level," I say, my voice and conviction stronger than the child inside of me.

Megan bites her bottom lip. "If I were you, I'd reconsider." She stares at me hard. Megan picks up her glasses with a shake of her head, the navy dress crackling as she rolls closer to her desk, probably for a quick pit re-powder.

Our session over, I gather up my books and briefcase, pull my shoulders back and exit with a grim nod.

I haven't spoken to Glee in ages. I call her on a Saturday morning as I peruse the newspaper for more Flora articles. After I fill her in on my current job crisis, we discuss the hideaway she and Ted are building in Sedona. He's starting another development in the rocky escape two hours from our valley after years of fighting the city's no-growth policies. Glee sounds elated because The Rock, her re-ignited spiritual center, has relocated to Red Rock Country to be closer to Sedona's vortexes. With the phone crooked into my neck I move into the family room, picking up after Michael and Rosa, my own resident alien slobs. The hamper in the downstairs bathroom resembles an exploded land mine.

"Darling, the vortexes give people more energy and increase intuition," Glee tells me.

"Are you trying to tell me you're psychic?" I ask.

"Let's put it this way. I think I could develop my intuitive abilities if I spent more time in meditation," she says.

I'd trust Glee's opinion if I decided to alter anything on my body because she's part of the suck-and-tuck crowd, but prescient abilities? I don't think so. As for the other, I'm not fixing anything unless it's hanging so low I can't see or walk. I've watched Glee go through weeks of hiding with droopy eyelids, mini-lifts on various areas of her face and body, a top-lip laser job that left her with oozing cold sores for weeks and the girdle she's currently encased in. No thank you. I'm going to get old and wrinkled and look my age, a unique concept among baby boomers. At least that's what I think now. I change the subject.

"How's your painting? Are you ready for the big show?"

"Almost. I moved some of the larger canvases over to The Art

Pod. Have a few smaller pieces for Monday. You and Maury will be there, won't you? Della, the gallery owner, expects a big crowd."

"We wouldn't miss it." Had her Delphi oracle of information predicted that, too?

"Met a fabulous couple on our Galapagos trip. They moved here recently so watch for a tall woman with red hair. You'll love her. They've got an interesting business happening, too. Anyway, gotta run. I need tile for the spa at Casa del Luna. Ted decided our new home needed a name. Later." Glee hangs up leaving me no opportunity to say good-bye. I wonder if the new couple will be another trophy to add to the usual crazies she collects.

Today Rabbi Turkletaub meets with Rosa. I want to see our two lovebirds married, especially with a baby on the way. I come from the generation who hid in their "aunt's house" when an unmarried woman became pregnant. Nowadays movie stars announce it. The rabbi's words, *Yie tov* bring little solace. Everything will turn out all right? I have my doubts.

Maury, still furious with Michael, practices the silent treatment. It's the longest I remember him angry and it takes its toll on me. I can't blame my husband, since Maury's plans for an early retirement have floated away, tumbleweeds in a desert wash. But I cringe over hearing his words in my head, "You're an idiot, Michael!"

I don't like family feuds even if Michael does have the common sense of a rutabaga. Once an adorable little boy with huge brown eyes, his level of common sense never developed past seventh grade. Many characteristics our children display are like ours, but there's a whole lot more that come from Mister Nobody, the mythical ghost of childhood blamed for spills and other accidents.

Rosa and I enter the Rabbi's office. Maury's trapped at his office with back-to-school immunizations and Michael can't miss class. Rabbi Turkletaub sits at his cherry wood desk, his shirt collar open in deference to the heat. Even with air conditioning our July triple-digit temperatures permeate every corner. His study, dark with bookcases on every wall, has windows perched high. A minimum of light spills across our laps when we sit before his desk.

"Do you have any questions, Rosa?" he asks, leaning back in his chair. Her hair, shiny and pulled into a ponytail with a red elastic band, accentuates her perfect profile.

"Yes." She shifts in the brown leather club chair, elbows pushing her forward. "I've studied other belief systems in my comparative religion course." Confident most of the time, she looks uncomfortable. Her voice, filled with hesitation asks, "If I change would I have to give up Christmas, the tree, everything?"

"Yes." The rabbi taps his fingers together, his facial expression patient. I don't know him well enough to guess what he might be thinking. All I know is he drives a Jeep Cherokee with the license plate PRAY emblazoned on the front.

"That's why I'm not sure, Father." She erupts in nervous laughter. "I mean, Rabbi."

"There would be no more confessions. In our faith we talk directly to God. How do you feel about that?"

"That part is okay with me. It's the shift in traditions that bothers me the most. I think I need more time." She pauses, a frown dancing between her brows. "It's important for me not to have dissension in the family for our child's sake. If we're all the same religion it makes everything easier, but Judaism is strange to me."

"Rosa, I don't want to push you, but you'd have to study intensively with me in private for two and half months. Our traditions and holidays can always be reinforced by your in-laws, but we have five thousand years of history, Old Testament, and the Torah to cover if you decide to do this before marriage."

Rosa presses her lips together. Her concerned expression, doesn't bleed into her body language. She sits in the chair, her spine straight, small belly invisible beneath her baggy blouse. Silent for a while, she stands up and shakes his hand.

"Thank you, Rabbi."

As we walk to the car I have no idea what she'll decide. I'm worried that if she does decide to embrace Judaism, I'll be responsible for getting all of our holiday traditions right. If she doesn't, I'll be in charge of coloring Easter eggs and dressing up as Santa.

Well, Maury's not going to do it. Oh dear. Red velvet and white fake fur make me look fat.

5

MAURY HAS TO STOP AT THE HOSPITAL TO CHECK on a patient. We arrive late at The Art Pod, a contemporary gallery of circular spaces in Scottsdale's art district, also called Old Town because it's the heart of the city. Set in an area of galleries and expensive shops, tourists are lured by savvy owners to purchase realistic bronze statues of cowboys wrestling calves to the ground and oil paintings with sad-eyed Native Americans. Its been a while since we've been to a Thursday night Art Walk where the galleries open their doors, serve cheap champagne, hire a few musicians and invite the public to browse.

It's a relaxing way to spend the evening if you don't want to see any art. Between the crowds and air kissing, the protocol for the artsy-fartsy crowd begins with the show business of marketing.

On the street in front of The Art Pod a small group of men and women are marching in a circle, thrusting hand-made signs into the air and chanting. As Maury and I cruise by searching for a parking space, I read the signs: NO MORE PORN, GOD IS ART, and BAN BODY PARTS. Their voices, raised in protest, yell, "Hey, hey, whaddaya say? Let's get rid of porn today!"

I hang my head out the window to grasp the scene in the evening lights. They're picketing Glee!

We park a few blocks away, behind a large van. Senior citizens climb down from it with the help of the driver, wire hanger bumps pushing out the shoulders of their jackets. Even Sun City retirees show up for Glee Barstow. As we approach some of the gallery crowd melts out to the sidewalk. Smokers share their camaraderie and watch the protest.

One of Glee's cohorts who attends all openings wearing a tie-dyed silk organza duster, waves at me. Her cigarillo almost ignites the iridescent feather boa around her neck. Another, an abstract artist rumored to pee on her collages, ignores me, although we've met numerous times. Still, a third dressed in cowboy gear, greets me wildly, although I can't remember her name. She hugs me with an unexpected hump to my pubic area. Maury suggests she has a crush on me. I don't care how old they get, men fantasize about two women naked. I'm convinced she has me mixed up with someone else but I engage her anyway, "What's going on here?" I point to the protesters.

She turns her head to take a deep drag of her cigarette, "Some crazies object to the art work inside."

I nod, anxious to get in there to see Glee's final product.

Maury and I break through the knot of smokers and jokers, and probably a few dopers, to the interior of the gallery, a large series of round spaces with white stucco walls and pin lighting. The paintings and a few sculptures swirl around us from the large central pod we've entered. They are a shocking arena of phallic wonderment.

In recent months I stopped by Glee's studio to view her

masterpieces of male envy, but now all those large, enflamed protrusions on six-foot canvases cause me to raise my eyebrows. Maury, on the other hand, had had no clue he's about to be bombarded with one part of the male anatomy.

"My God, where did she get the models?" Maury whispers as we pretend to eye the paintings. I'm consumed with people watching over Maury's shoulder. As I turn a gorgeous couple nods at me from across the room. She's a tall strawberry blonde and he's a matching Ken-doll with silver hair and a strong jaw line. A man with a shaved head in a black turtleneck and silver sequined shoes wanders by. One couple, dressed in black, wear silver concho belts double- wrapped around their waists. They stare back at me. I recognize an ancient society matron from her frequent appearances in *Fashionista*, our local society and gossip rag. She sports a cocktail hat with veil and carries a bald Chihuahua. The dog's wearing a tiny hat, too. Where do these people hide during the day?

"Glee's been going to life drawing classes, but I think this is a guy she saw in the baths at Esalen," I say in front of an engorged abstract penis painted in cerulean blue and violet on a stark white background. He's circumcised. The top looks like a shitake mushroom.

"How do you know?" Maury stands back to get the picture in perspective.

"Because Glee told me she watched a well-endowed gentleman when he got out of the tubs. Can't you see the big blue splotch near the bottom and the way it drifts to the left? It's the guy from Esalen."

A voice behind me with a crisp accent says, "Sorry to intrude, but that is definitely Ted."

Maury and I turn around. I know Glee likes to take her clothes off to show off her new anatomical enhancements, but I thought Ted kept some modicum of propriety.

"We got here early and Glee gave us a quick tour," says the stunning woman with a wild riot of strawberry hair. She extends her hand. "How do you do? I'm Tuni Sterling and this is my husband, Ellis."

Ellis looks like an Armani ad, all in black, even the Gucci loafers, their unmistakable saddle buckle on top. His silver hair combed straight back accents a sharp nose and wide blue eyes. Tall, too. Tuni, her high cheekbones and full melon lips, wears a copper-colored off-the-shoulder blouse and long skirt. A striking couple.

After introductions and a quick chat about the art, I ask, "What do you do?"

"Ellis and I own a manufacturing facility. We make gift items. I'm the creative muse and Ellis takes care of the business. You must come and see what we do some time. We're not as risqué as Glee, but I think you'd appreciate our line." Tuni smiles. Women always start the social contacts. Maury moves close to my side.

"What kinds of things do you make?" I ask.

"Upscale decorative items." When I look puzzled, she continues, "You remember the angel craze a few years ago? We started that with plaster sconces and it grew from there." I love her accent. It makes everything sound important.

"We ship all over the world. We're just looking for the next big opportunity and I think we may already be onto something," says

Ellis, his face enhanced by perfect white teeth that have never known a cup of coffee. "Business like ours is based on trends. There's emphasis on the spiritual. People are turning back to religion. It permeates the decorative home industry."

"So what's next?" I ask. My inquisitive nature drives me to pump for more information.

"Oh, we can't possibly say yet. Negotiations," Tuni gives Ellis a knowing look. She leans toward me. "I will tell you it's going to be the biggest commercial venture ever launched worldwide." She giggles a little and grabs Ellis' arm.

Okay, I'll change the subject. I'm trying to figure out their accents. I know it isn't British. Doesn't sound that elegant. Maybe South African. "Where are you from? I know it's not New York City."

"Tuni and I are from Melbourne. Ever visited Oz?" asks Ellis.

I've never trusted men this good looking.

"No, but I've always wanted to go there," says Maury, who is now alert. "Been reading quite a bit about the medical system in Australia. Even though you still have the Queen guiding you, your system is different than the English socialized. . ." Maury doesn't get to finish because Glee invades. Her beaming smile lets me know she's thrilled with the turn out. She always glows when she's the center of attention.

"I'm so glad you all met!" says Glee. She touches my back and Tuni's. Her dark curls have small---I call them rhinestones, but Glee corrects me---Austrian crystal butterflies throughout her mane. In a symphony of purple, this is her artist wardrobe instead of the

designer one. A dark slip with a sheer dress on top, it starts with
the palest lavender near her face and graduates to the deepest violet
at the hem. She looks lovely and very much the creator. She links
elbows with Ellis.

"Now why wouldn't I want to kiss this gorgeous hunk of a man
twice? Will you pose for me sometime?" asks Glee. Ellis shrugs,
a bit embarrassed by her forward approach. That's Glee though-
-a bit over the top, creative, and insecure enough that she can't
leave herself alone. I adore my friend, but it's a constant parade of
improvements: therapy, liposuction, even two nose jobs. "I had to
change mine because we all looked like Scottsdale cousins at the
charity luncheons," she told me.

Della, the gallery owner, a severe woman with Frida Kahlo
eyebrows, herds Glee away like a sheep dog, the theme of *Jaws*
behind her. A guy in studded leather pants wants to add a tumescent
Barstow to his collection. Glee floats off.

"Don't forget about my class to talk about freedom of expression,"
I call after her.

We return to Tuni and Ellis.

"Where do you live?" I ask.

Ellis answers, "We rent near Gainey Ranch. Construction,"
he sighs. "With all the building going on it takes forever to finish
a place."

My intellectual Maury hates small talk so he changes the subject
to the Aborigines.

Then April finds us. She's wearing a killer orange-knit-ace-
bandage of a dress, with her blond hair up, wispy tendrils over

her brows. April has the longest eyelashes on any human, almost cartoon-like, a live Jessica Rabbit.

"You look positively brilliant tonight!" says Tuni.

"So you've met?" I ask.

"Yes, we all sat at Glee and Ted's table at the psoriasis fund raiser," says Tuni.

Maury adores April because she's gorgeous and brainy, but tonight he's a bit burned-out on all the glitz and glamour. He presses his hand into the small of my back to let me know its time to exit. Maury's idea of a good time is arrive late and leave early. I'd rather delay our trip home because Michael moves back into his old room tonight. I'm in the sandwich generation with a boomerang kid and elderly parents. More like chopped liver. We excuse ourselves to finish our tour through the next pod, observing that a few of the signs next to the paintings have red dots next to them. Sold! Where does one hang a penis painting?

Maury's had enough. We wade through the crowd outside to see the group picketing has moved in front of the gallery. They're led by a tall woman in a blue suit with a ratty head of black hair piled high on her head, large bangs falling over her forehead, probably set with a beer can. She's followed by a half a dozen others, a motley group marching in a circle, some in shirts and jeans, another in a business suit, one an elderly man in a white T-shirt and vest, and a polygamist-following woman in a long paisley dress.

They hold their hand-lettered signs high over their heads. They've stopped their chanting because the woman with the wild black hair stands with her back to us in an aura of bright klieg lights.

An earnest reporter from a local television station interviews her, his cameraman over his shoulder.

I want to stay to see what's going on, but Maury looks at me, shrugs, and walks toward the car. I fall in next to him. When my man is tired, he wants to sleep. Not even picketing monkey heads can distract him.

6

THE WEEKS MOLD THEMSELVES AROUND MICHAEL, who is back in his old room, giving new meaning to the word slob. Law books, too heavy for the shelves Maury constructed for teenage soccer trophies, pile up on every available space. Clothes decorate the bed and the chair, a clown's handkerchief of riotous colors that never ends. Whenever he sits down he pushes the mess onto the floor. Taco Bell wrappers, cups of Diet Coke, and cellophane from CD's opened weeks ago clutter the little bit of counter space. The kid's never heard of a garbage can except once a week when he cleans. Then, for thirty minutes the room shines until the cycle begins again.

Rosa and Michael come to the astute conclusion they need money so they sell her car. After dinner one evening Michael brings up the subject that will change our lives. Rosa sits next to him in a demure dress.

"Mom, Dad, I know this is awkward, but I don't know how else to say this. Rosa needs to move in here." His expression has such hope, his eyebrows aim upward with expectation. I can't see her face because her lap fascinates her.

Maury looks at me across the table. I nod yes, go ahead. He says, "This is going to cause some inconvenience. Are you sure it's what you want?"

"Dad, Rosa and I have talked about it and we don't have the funds to survive on our own. Just let us stay here long enough to get our act together."

An awkward silence follows. "Michael, Rosa, welcome to our home," I say. Maybe it'll be fun. Or maybe it'll be a disaster.

By the end of the week, Rosa bids her roommates goodbye and invades our territory. She tries to set up housekeeping in Michael's old room, still decorated with pictures of racecars, but with hardly space for him, she can't find room to unpack. Finally, I help her move four suitcases filled with rocks. Boxes of books, hair dryers (why does she need three?), hangers of clothes, toiletries, and a plaster of Paris statue of the Virgin Mary with a miniature paper umbrella attached by a rubber band to her head land in our guest room. Mary, relegated to a spot on top of a basket of dirty clothes, stares up like an abandoned religious Barbie. Amid promises of "This is only temporary" and "We'll get jobs," life settles down in the cozy Rubin abode.

I'm not surprised Rosa doesn't want to share Michael's room. The familiar odor of old sweat socks reminds me he's here. After he first left I burned fragrant candles to exorcise his space after I found two bagels covered with mold under his bed. I shut the door when I walk by, unwilling to assault my eyes or nose.

Rosa's figure, enriched by her third month of pregnancy, drives Michael wild. When he's home, they're inseparable, twins with an insatiable desire to touch. If he's not pulling a strand of hair away from her face, then she's tickling his arm. Her voluptuous shape reminds me I'd like to transfer some of my bottom to the top. I remember when I was waiting for Lara and Michael to be born. If only I could have kept those breasts.

I watch them in wonderment. Maybe Rosa's not who I would have picked for Michael, but she makes him happy. My heart twitches when I see the way they look at each other, a ping of jealousy wafts over me. Little boys adore their mommies until they're replaced with lovers.

In the family room, Rosa, ensconced in Maury's favorite lounge chair, turns the gardening book she's reading face down across her small protruding stomach and dozes. Her delicate, long fingers, reminiscent of the ones growing inside of her, rest on her chest. They move up and down with her breath. Her dark eyelashes caress her cheekbones, a sleeping porcelain doll.

She runs to the bathroom with morning sickness, then complains about it afterward, surprised it occurs on a regular basis. Obviously, she's the first woman ever to be pregnant and carrying The Next Messiah, the one the Jews have been waiting for since the beginning of time.

A series of contradictions, Rosa grows purple iris' in pots on our patio and places them in an arrangement on my kitchen table, which I love. On the other hand, the concept of rinsing a glass is foreign to her so seven cobalt blue glasses sit next to the sink. It drives me crazy.

Rosa's decision whether to convert ricochets around them. I make a conscious effort not to influence her because I don't want her to blame me later if she's unhappy. It has to come from the heart, not a gesture for Michael. It can't be a temporary idea without commitment. I mean, is Elizabeth Taylor still Jewish? How many husbands ago was that? It's a shame there's not time to take the six-week seminar, "Tuna Fish and the Torah," at the Temple during lunchtime. She and Michael spend evenings whispering. Twice I see her crying.

One night, after I've finished grading midterms, my eyes bleary and my fingers stained with red ink, I stand in the doorway of Michael's room. Slumped over the books on his desk, his long legs cramped beneath the space made for a high school student, I ask, "Is everything okay with Rosa?" He looks up at me, questioningly, his eyes, sad. I try not to judge the mess and breathe through my mouth.

"Oh, Mom, she's torn. She loves me, but it's hard to give up Christmas." He opens a drawer to clear his countertop of food wrappers with a sweep of his hand. He's wrestling with the conflict, too. I sigh and head for bed, my briefcase in my hand. I have more papers to grade.

I'm relieved to be caught up in the mid-term rush because it seems Megan has forgotten about Tiffany. I wasn't ready for a fight anyway.

On the patio one morning a week after my talk with Michael, I enjoy the sounds of the cactus wrens chirping while they build their nest in a large saguaro near our property. I scan the newspaper for articles to tear out and save for Maury, an effort to wake him up from his HMO malaise. He's so unhappy with the medical system that has turned doctors into employees.

Rosa joins me and pulls out a chair. I put down a diatribe entitled, 'Mystery Group Finances Right Wing Candidates,' guaranteed to make Maury gnash his teeth.

The glow of pregnancy is in Rosa's face. Her flawless skin is a smoother mocha ice cream, the beauty mark near the edge of her mouth a tiny chocolate chip.

She places her unblemished hands flat on the table. "I've made a decision."

My mind comes to a full alert. Has she bought the bid for family unity? Will she remain true to her own traditions? I heard her speaking Spanish on the phone late last night, her voice emotional. Actually, she's on the phone daily. If there's a bump in the family dynamics, Maury and I give each other a look that says, two more hours to Guadalajara.

"I've decided not to decide."

I stare at her in silence. Her hand brushes her brow and the widow's peak at the top of her forehead. "I'm just not ready yet. Michael says I should take the pressure off myself. I'm open to learning more about your traditions so I'm going to study. Judaism is so pragmatic compared to the pageantry of my faith. It'd be a big shift for me. I think we should get married and I'll think about it later."

My heart, the one that resides in all parents for kids to stomp on, feels the heel of a cowboy boot, the spurring of another disappointment pang. "You have to do what makes you feel comfortable. If you're not ready, then don't do it."

Rosa moves to go inside and turns to look at me, a weak smile flashing across her face. I give her encouragement by smiling back. Inside, the cowboy with the two-step on my heart picks up speed. The nest harvester chirps with vigor, a prize twig to bring home. I return to my newspaper, reflecting on the excited bird sounds. I settle into my webbed chair to lament the fact that young people don't read the newspaper anymore.

"I get my sports scores on the net," Michael tells me when I push him on current events. Sports scores aren't news, but what's the point? My students are more aware because my courses are an elective, but they don't read or pursue an interest unless it's an assignment either. When Glee spoke to my class about art and self-expression, a few enamored young women said they wanted to see her show. None of them mentioned it since then. I'm more preoccupied with the quiet from Megan's office. Maybe the dean has forgotten about Tiffany and her balking grade.

I leave Lara a phone message. She responds with an email.

To: jeanrubin
From: lara
Subject: new sister

Hi Mom!

Sorry I have been incommunicado, but it's so hectic here. Spoke to Gus and he's jazzed about Rosa, too. How are you all getting along under one roof? I mean, we hardly made it with just us natural kids and no one ate tamales. Just kidding. If there's a wedding I don't think we can come. I've got exams and Gus has a new idea for a business on the net. Don't want to say what it is yet, but this is the big one. We're going to be rich!

Love,
Lara

The wedding, a small affair, takes place in Rabbi Turkletaub's study on a Sunday morning because he doesn't marry anyone on the Sabbath. Saturday nights are taken up with extravaganzas. Rosa's family from Guadalajara crowds into the room with us.

Her mother, Elphidia, a pretty woman with ebony hair in a chignon, wears a purple silk suit and gold jewelry. Her dad, Tomas, smiles with large piano-key teeth. His navy suit, red silk tie, and lapis cuff links add an expensive touch. His bushy eyebrows laced with silver dance when he speaks, a debonair Ricardo Montalban. He admonishes us to call him Tom. They're Rosa's height, which is tall for a woman, but short for a man. Hopefully, the kid is going to get their straight teeth. Ours required years of orthodontia. We still joke about the wing on Dr. Sherman's house.

Two of Rosa's married sisters, Tirza and Grazia, arrive without their husbands. They look at Rosa, the baby of the family, with devotion, their blue dresses stretched across broad rears. With perfect make-up, they wear killer shoes-- velvet mules with silk rosebuds, python sandals that wrap around the ankles, all with stilt-high heels. April would be impressed.

A few years ago we made elaborate preparations for Lara and Gus' wedding. This seems so simple. Perhaps after the baby arrives we can send them on a belated honeymoon.

My parent's faces are filled with emotion. They look small and fragile in their taupe jackets and navy slacks. My mother's added a straw hat for the occasion with a large dusty rose. My father leans over to her, an attempt to whisper, and says, "When do we eat?"

We stand solemnly among the glass cabinets of Judaica and

tomes of books. How foreign this must seem to Rosa's family. What is familiar to me--the *menorahs*, the elegant candelabra we use for Chanukah, the collection of *tzedakah* boxes, small metal receptacles placed in kitchens to collect change for charity, and *tefillin*, the square leather box with braided straps Orthodox men wrap around their head to help them focus on God—-must appear strange to them. I watch as their eyes eat everything in the room. Once in a while, they whisper to each other in Spanish.

The bride and groom look so young my heart almost breaks. Michael wears his graduation suit from college that barely fits his broad shoulders.

His unruly hair is slicked back instead of up. Rosa wears a serene expression, her prominent breasts anxious to burst through the front of the ivory lace dress her sisters brought from Mexico. She wears her hair up, baby's breath scattered through it. When she turns her head to look at Michael, I see her expression. She loves him.

As the rabbi repeats the service we've heard before, my mind wanders back to Michael as a child. A flash card presentation of him holding my hand as a little boy, skateboarding to elementary school, playing on a soccer team sponsored by *Dermatology Associates, Pimples Are Our Business,* emblazoned on his back, then going through his long-haired rocker phase in college. It went by so fast.

Maury almost disowned him during college that took a few extra semesters. With a used set of drums and not much rhythm, Michael shared a house in Tucson with his musician friends. We knew more than rock 'n roll was happening at that place. One night as the band members watched television, a rare, wet desert storm flooded through the flat roof. The chemically-enhanced group said, "Hey man, it's only a rental. Why get up to check it out?" The ceiling collapsed, painting them, their instruments and the TV with plaster, popcorn ceiling pieces and dry wall. No one was hurt so the newly crowned "white boys" dusted themselves off and went to bed.

I can still hear Maury ranting, "If there's a leak, there's a lake behind it. Why didn't one of you poke a hole in the ceiling?" The Stray Pussies disbanded when no one wanted to accept responsibility for the repairs. Guess who picked up the tab?

"And do you, Rosa, take Michael to be your lawful, wedded husband?" asks Rabbi Turkletaub in a resonant voice better suited for an entire congregation. A lawn blower drones in the distance.

"I do," says Rosa. The loose dress hides the next big event in her life. I can't help but think space between a wedding and a baby is more desirable.

"Then I pronounce you man and wife," the rabbi finishes.

Michael steps back. His heel makes contact with the wine glass wrapped in a white linen dishtowel that Maury, grim but supportive, has slipped behind him. As his stomp breaks the glass our side of the family yells, "*Mazel tov*" and Rosa's side says, "Congratulations, *buena suerte.*"

Michael pulls Rosa to him and kisses her with passion, her gazunta-sized breasts pressing into his chest. My last baby is married and going to be a father. Teary-eyed, I hug Maury and then my parents.

"Why does he step on a glass?" asks Elphidia.

Rabbi Turkletaub, figuring he might convert a whole family,

answers before I do. "It symbolizes the destruction of the Second Temple in Jerusalem in 70 CE, a small reminder that even in times of joy our people must reflect on our sorrows." In response to puzzled looks, he adds, "Instead of BC we say CE for before the Common Era."

Elphidia nods and then translates for her husband, who isn't as fluent in English. He nods, but the caterpillar eyebrows move upward in a question. I can imagine how it must sound to someone not familiar with the push/pull of our anguish. Be happy, but don't have too much fun. Leave room for a little guilt.

Afterwards, we gather for lunch at The Hyatt that overlooks rolling green lawns and pools of water dotted with gondolas. It's a strange, intriguing blend of families with a beautiful, pregnant bride and a shell-shocked groom as the centerpiece. Rosa's sisters sit across from my parents.

My mother asks Grazia, "How long will you be here?"

She turns to her sister for translation and then answers, "I'm living in Mexico all my life."

"No, I want to know how long you're staying in Scottsdale?" my mother asks, leaning forward.

I observe another conference between the sisters.

"I have a hair salon in Guadalajara."

My father gets up and heads for the buffet table, shuffling away shaking his head.

Our meal progresses as we have more in common than most outsiders would think: family, business, travel, and of course, the grandchild. It's our first and their sixth.

Elphidia, with Rosa's translation and some English, asks me, "What do the children need? Can we send a crib?"

I thank her and explain there's not too much space at the moment.

Rosa's parents stay a few more days and then return to Mexico. The newlyweds are in our hands. Since a honeymoon is impractical, Michael and Rosa lounge by our pool and go to the movies. I'd be devastated, but they seem to enjoy themselves, especially Michael. Anything to get a break from school. My underachiever's not a natural born student. Maury's fear is he'll take the easy way out when he graduates and join Steve Lefkowitz, April's husband, in his personal injury practice. What an anathema to be watching TV at night and see your own kid trying to drum up business to sue you.

We make an effort to stay out of their way so they feel as though they have some privacy. A week later, nuzzling in front of the stove, and unaware I'm there, Michael and Rosa, he, wearing jeans and she, poured into white pants, face one another, his hands on her waist.

"Ahem."

They separate, but not too fast, never breaking eye contact with each other.

"What are the plans for today?" I ask. "Could use some help with errands. Your dad's lab coats are ready at the cleaners and there's a prescription for my allergies that needs to be picked up."

Rosa puts her hands on Michael's waist. "We can't. We're going to the nursery to pick up some more iris and daffodil bulbs and then catch a movie."

I'm still on my best behavior. "What are you going to see?"

"The new Jennifer Lopez movie," says Rosa.

"I thought we're going to see Bruce Willis," says Michael. He pulls away in mock horror.

"No way. Violence is bad for the baby. *Mi alma* needs to be peaceful. I want to see a romantic comedy." She strokes his arms. I figure out *alma* means soul. "Miguel, *por favor?*"

Michael sighs and looks at me, smiling. "She's hard to resist, huh, Mom? Okay, Jennifer Lopez it is, but that's two chick-flicks for only one guy movie. I'm keeping track."

I watch them leave, hand in hand, she in her red-striped tank top, a horizontal peppermint stick, and white capri pants, the outer limits of decency, while I stew about the chores.

Later in bed Maury says, "Cut them some slack. They didn't have a honeymoon." He pulls a magazine out of my hand. "I'd like to have a honeymoon with you right now."

I giggle and reach to turn off my light as Maury's warm hand slips beneath the covers. I forget about our boarders downstairs as his adept fingers tweak the ripe spots of my body.

"Ah, you're always delicious," he says kissing me on my mouth.

"And you're always a great chef," I say as we begin our tryst.

7

"DEAN GRUBER WANTS TO SEE YOU IN HIS OFFICE AFTER your Tuesday class. I expect you to be there with a rationale for the delay in Tiffany's grade change." Click.

I replay Megan's Julia-Child voice on my message twice, convinced a puff of talc has risen through the phone. Uh oh. The administration means business. Rationale? How about it's flat out wrong? I try to set aside my thoughts, but it gnaws at me. Do I need another crisis in my life? So what if another Tiffany in the community college system gets an incomplete? Maybe I need to re-think this.

I wake up before the alarm goes off in a pool of menopausal sweat. I crave chocolate. No wonder I can't lose ten pounds. Glee says my seratonin levels are out of whack. She used to eat pieces of Godiva every day, but she tells me, "I've conquered chocolate. You need to elevate your mood by releasing endorphins through orgasms or shopping." She announced this during yoga. I was bent into a pretzel-shape called the wheel-barrow, on my back upside down peering through my legs. The women around me gasped.

Whatever she's doing, I doubt it can be duplicated. Would I want to? A few years ago Glee and Ted's exotic tricks got so wild on a winter evening, she fell out of their sleigh bed and broke her leg. Only Glee could injure herself during ski season and not be near the slopes. Our merciless teasing spawned many jokes. Glee said it was worth it as she hobbled around in a bejeweled cast for six weeks.

I step into the shower; the hard rain batters my plastic shower cap. Glee and Ted have attended some strange workshops to enhance their sexuality. Some people make their decisions with their head, others with their heart. For the Barstows it's the crotch. One workshop, Masturbation Mambo, given by the Rock group, had them sit in a circle with other naked people trying to get off. Maury says the thought of Ted and his millions from potato-chip condos staring at him would be enough to make him flaccid forever. Glee said the experience brought her to a rare state of bliss where she touched God.

I thought I had heard everything until the Organic Orgasms, a sex and food workshop that lasted an entire weekend, facilitated- -that's Glee's word--by a Cordon Bleu chef in a tall white hat and nothing else. It was supposed to teach them how to use the senses. The agenda included: a massage with corn starch; a nude blindfold game of identifying cinnamon, vanilla, and chocolate; body decorating with icing and sprinkles; and orgasms created with truffles. The sensual clean up ignited passions beyond the erotic menu. Two married participants formed an attachment that lasted past the weekend, a Scottsdale scandal.

I step from the shower and smile at her description of the banker in her navy pumps and the dog groomer who licked melted brie from her nipples. I confess, Maury and I tried the corn starch, a smooth treat, but we were a little sweaty and I turned into a plaster-of-Paris statue. So much for home-based erotica.

My temporary amusement overshadows the reality that today is the showdown with the dean. I've done some prep work, but Maury says to go and see what their intention is before I make a move. I dress in a blazer and skirt, my mind preoccupied with what's ahead.

It's still a surprise to come down from our second floor aerie in the morning and find Rosa at my kitchen table. Maybe I'll never get used to a new person in my space. Glee says it beats sitting with eight other bodies in a sweat lodge. Today my stark kitchen is unrecognizable; it's been turned into a cluttered room like an overloaded fruit bowl with dusty plastic grapes dripping off the side.

I pick up Maury's note next to an article he's left on my chili pepper placemat. *Pecker ngo sutz, I love you. Gd luck.* The first part makes no sense. I've never been able to read his hand writing. If I've been married to him all these years and can't read his indecipherable doctor scribbling, what do the pharmacists do? After a few tries I get it: pick up my pants. I remove my glasses and look at my refrigerator.

The blank white door lays testament to Rosa's large family. Her mother, father, five sisters, including Grazia and Tirza at a slimmer phase in their life, two brothers, elderly grandparents, married sisters' children, and probably a few neighbors and the OB-GYN who delivered everybody are plastered on the front. The curled edges of the snapshots are held in place by plastic fruit magnets.

Should I tell her I abhor people's lives on the front of their refrigerators? I have an acute aversion to apple, pear and banana magnets.

I glance at the usually clean white tile counters, a conviction of my minimalist cooking abilities. On display is every appliance I've ever hidden in a cabinet or drawer: the ugly yellow blender, a thirty-year-old wedding present; the can opener, crud jammed into the turning mechanism; the inherited toaster oven with a short given to us when an aunt passed away; bowls and mix master for the occasional cake when the kids were little; and a knife sharpener that I bought at a garage sale. The inanimate objects scream about years of disuse.

"Rosa, are you cooking today?" This past week she treated us to her enchiladas, a killer dish drowned in acres of cheese. At our horizontal bed meeting Maury and I decided she was planning our early demise.

"No, but I think it'll be easier to have everything out when I do."

"Ah, I know this sounds silly, but I kind of like the zen look of nothing on the counters. Do you mind putting these things back?"

I get The Look, the one that says you're a pain-in-the- ass. With drama she pulls herself up as though it's a struggle to move and goes over to the counters. She turns to me, small belly visible beneath Michael's white shirt, cleavage peeking from the top. I must remember to ask Maury when her breasts are going to stop growing.

"I was trying to make myself at home as you suggested."

"I do want you to make yourself part of our home," I hesitate, "but I'm used to having things in their place."

She doesn't move, her expression blank. "If it's going to cause a rift, leave everything," I say, even though I despise myself when I fall into the placater role.

"No *problema*. I'll put everything away." Her voice's agreeable but her body stiffens. I take my tea and retire to the patio, the only spot not invaded. I hear her bang my appliances back into their nesting places. Maybe the family collage left on the refrigerator will cure my munchies. I think about a Snickers I've hid behind the fajitas.

I scan the article Maury left me, "State Dumps HMO." He's torn it from the paper without a care as to whether I'd want to read what's on the other side. "About 75,000 Arizonans who are members of Sunshine Healthcare can expect to be transferred to other providers by next week. . .financial collapse. . . regulators haven't determined claims. . .$30 million dollar deficit owed to hospitals and providers." Sunshine Healthcare, a staple of Maury's practice, pays our bills. This is not a hiccup in our financial solvency. It's a major case of food poisoning.

The cell phone next to me interrupts my upset.

"Jean, dear, your father and I have a doctor appointment and it's so hot to go in the van from here. Besides, I don't want anyone to know where we're going. Could you pick us up?" My mother's slow speech drags out the words. Retirees have no reason to hurry.

"I'm free after my Women and Lit class." I head indoors and upstairs, phone in hand.

"What time? We don't want to miss lunch," she says, then continues not waiting for my answer. "My feet hurt. Do you think I should see the internist or make another appointment with a podiatrist? What if I have a pre-diabetic condition? Mrs. Haber two doors down says I need a family practice man. You think my circulation's been affected by the medication? Ask Maury what he knows about Epipradyl."

"Mom, I'll be there after I finish at the college and you can ask the doctor about it." I leave out my appointment with Dean Gruber. I move through my bedroom at record speed, grabbing driving shoes, purse, sunscreen to put on in the car. I drive in different shoes so the backs of my heels won't get scuffed since my mother notices everything. I sail downstairs, the phone still in my hand and grab my briefcase. The pile of graded papers sits on the kitchen table.

My cleaning compulsion appears at the strangest times. With the phone under my arm and the briefcase strap on my shoulder, I load twelve glasses from strategic positions scattered around the kitchen and family room into the dishwasher. Doesn't anyone know what a sink is for?

I'm out the door, throwing my load onto the Volvo's passenger seat. I don't notice the house phone until I'm a half-a-mile from the house at a red light. Too late now.

I enjoy teaching my classes with all those young minds to mess, suspended in time. I forget about everyone, except the feminist we're discussing. Today it's Joyce Carol Oates, a prolific author who takes random violent events and weaves narratives around them. However, the minute class ends I remember where I have to be.

Doris, my tattooed Texan, waits for me in the hall, the serpent on it's way up her leg ending who knows where. "Miz Rubin, can I talk to you?" Her expression is serious, the corners of her mouth turned down.

"Oh, Doris." I touch her arm. "Come back tomorrow during office hours. I have an appointment and daughter-duty today, unless it's something we can discuss while I walk over to the admin building."

"No, I'll wait."

I step back to get a better look at her. "Everything okay? You look upset."

"I'm okay." Her hair's disheveled.

I give her a concerned look, shaking my head. Something's wrong. Then, juggling my briefcase, purse, and papers into one arm, I hug her with the other, patting her on the back. "Whatever it is, it'll work out." I feel her sigh against me. I glance at my watch over her shoulder. I'm late. "I've got to run. Tomorrow." I watch her walk down the hall, her usual Texas saunter a sad slump.

Desert Brush Community College, founded in 1967, stretches across acres of desert land next to the Tonopah Indian reservation. When there's time I stroll, but today I rush past rows of acacia trees lining faux brick walkways, occasional patches of grass flooded with irrigation water and a rose garden dedicated to a former student who donated big bucks. Mounds of purple Trailing Lantana ground cover are meant to keep the dust down and an arid zone under the slat-covered entrance is filled with Totem Pole cactus, Prickly Pear and Desert Milkweed. I'm disheveled when I burst into the dean's office.

Megan waits in one of the anteroom chairs, feet apart and flat on the floor, another floral print stretched across her knees. Her mother must have forgotten to tell her to keep her legs together. She's gussied herself up for this meeting with a large amethyst brooch on her puffer pigeon-chest, lots of make-up and a cloying perfume that makes me choke. She greets me with a chilly nod.

I sit down, placing my purse and briefcase on the plastic chair between us.

"Sorry I'm late. I was teaching an Oates novel today and then a student stopped by and--" I begin to ramble at her profile, then scrunch into my chair to wait. My pounding heart slows to a steady pace.

"The dean will see you now," says Olive, the dean's efficient assistant. She holds open the door for us. I get a whiff of mothballs as we pass. Megan and I sit down on the burgundy leather chairs in front of him.

Dean Gruber, in a white short-sleeved shirt and regimental red-striped tie, leans back in his chair tapping a pencil on his desk, a sign he wants to take care of this pronto. His nod of acknowledgement means no small talk. I'm familiar with his bank-president-size office, a small sitting area with a black leather couch and chairs off to the side. A wilted philodendron sits in the window hungry for water. The white wall behind him is filled with official-looking diplomas and awards outlines his lanky basketball body.

"I'm going to get right to the point. We have a situation here that has the potential to blow up in our face." A small twitch starts in the middle of my thigh as he zeroes in on me and continues in his southwestern twang. "You're aware of Tiffany's mother, Flora Boudreaux?" I do my best to remain expressionless, but inside I'm saying, "Of course I'm aware of that idiot." He opens a folder and shuffles through the papers, holding up one with an embossed letterhead. "She has expressed deep concern over the subject matter being taught on this campus, particularly in your department. I think this is nonsense, but we depend on funding to pay salaries, give scholarships, and run the campus. You could save yourself and the college a ton of upset by changing the grade to an incomplete. Then we can all move on."

I feel the psychic pressure building in the room, the pulse in my leg dancing. Megan twists to speak to me. "It's almost time to assign courses for next year. I don't want you to think adjusting Tiffany's grade will influence us, but I know how delighted you'd be with a section of Women's Studies core curriculum. You think we could reach a compromise?"

She smiles sweetly at me, her blue-gray eyes glance at Dean Gruber. They want an answer and they want it now. I clear my throat to make sure I can talk, my twitching leg giving me rhythm. "Dean, Megan, I appreciate your concern over Tiffany's grade, but it would compromise my principles to alter it." Silence.

"You are treading in deep, dark waters. Did you not have an artist who paints parts of the male anatomy in your class?" asks Megan, her sweet voice replaced by grating saws.

"I did. My students enjoyed Glee Barstow's talk on creative expression very much." I raise my eyebrows when I ask, "Is there a problem with stimulating and engaging students?"

They are not swayed by my fake innocent question. The dean leans his long body across the desk. "Jean, we have consulted our legal counsel and academic freedom is an amorphous quasi-legal concept at best. Although we can't regulate how professors teach their classes, it is apparent the mind of a student is susceptible to instructor's ideas. This agenda of aberrant sexuality you're pushing is not part of our philosophy, nor is it in the best interest of the college."

I'm stunned. What has this escalated to? My brain races past the word *aberrant* to feel my heart flutter. Sitting up straighter, I speak with deliberation so I can remember every word to tell my champion, Maury.

"I'm not pushing any sexual agenda. Young people need to know that it's okay to be different. Tolerance of others through literature is my priority as well as creative expression. If I foster one student to be open-minded, I've done my job."

"That's all very noble, my dear, but Ms. Boudreaux is making serious threats. If this should be taken to the court of public opinion, we're all going to be embarrassed," says Megan. She moves forward on her chair, wagging her bosom with the amethyst brooch at the dean.

"If you're uncomfortable making a decision at this moment, why don't we set a deadline of next week to get the paperwork rolling?" He is not taking *no* for an answer.

I gather my purse and briefcase as I stand up. I want to quit and walk out on the spot, but the crashing HMO article from this morning floats by me.

"I need to think about this, but I don't see any reason to alter Tiffany's grade," I say, then add to make it more dramatic, "My ailing parents are waiting for me to take them to the doctor."

Dean Gruber stands up with his file folder. "You've been an excellent teacher, Jean, but this nonsensical stand is going to thwart all the good you've done. I don't have to remind you you're up for tenure at the end of next semester." He taps the edge of the folder on the desk. I've known him to be a good guy in the past, but his patriarchal patronage wounds me. I leave, but Megan stays glued to her chair.

After the disastrous meeting, which I decide not to mention to my parents, I drive into a murky haze. Although it's fall, it feels like summer with temperatures topping the 100's. According to the female meteorologist voted the sexist in the nation by *Playboy,* the brown cloud sits on our valley because we've got an inversion factor, which means warm air squishes everything. On bad days she gives us a breathless warning that old people, children and asthmatics shouldn't go outside.

My parents wait out front, *fapitzed*--my mother in light wool slacks and a blazer, a beret perched on her head, my father ready in a sports coat. The attendant on duty, a solicitous young woman dressed in a white uniform, opens the car door for them. They sit next to each other in the back seat holding hands, unwilling to be apart for a moment. Tandem parents.

My mother taps me on the shoulder. "How are you, darling? Is it always so hot here? We were never this warm in Florida."

"Mom, I warned you before you moved here, it would be hotter. Remember you said it was a dry heat?"

"I never said that. Herman, did I say that? I never said it was a dry heat. Look at me. I'm soaking wet."

"Turn up the air conditioner. We're *schvitzing* back here," adds my father.

"Mom, Dad, I have the AC on full blast. It's hot outside. Can't you remove your jackets?"

"What? And ruin the look of my outfit? I always dress up when I go to see the doctor. Young people today have no respect." My mother pulls herself taller and smoothes the front of her jacket.

I get ready for 'the' lecture. She doesn't approve of Birkenstocks or Jesus sandals as she calls them. She thinks people should wear hose and gloves when they travel. And she vigorously opposes VPL, Visible Panty Line. I wonder if she knows the thong is the trick.

I grade papers in the doctor's waiting room, thinking about my stress levels. And I thought it was bad when I was planning Lara's wedding! The baby has catapulted a whole new agenda to the forefront. Where are Michael and Rosa going to live? *How* are they going to live? Who's going to pay for the delivery? How many more hours can Maury work? What about the HMO that filed for bankruptcy? What impact does that have in our lives? How much longer can I survive my family home invasion? And what's going to happen with my job?

I glance at my watch. Why was this taking so long? I need to go home and drive Rosa to her OB appointment.

My parents come out smiling. "Except for my circulation, osteoporosis and the bunions on my feet, I'm in good shape," my mother says. "Although Dr. Farber said I have to go for another bone-scan."

My father thumps his chest with a fist. "I have a slight stomach condition, but it's not related to the headaches I've been getting. I'm solid as a rock."

"Herman, did you ask him about the gas?"

"Shhh, Florence. I don't want to discuss it now." My father, embarrassed, glances around at the other older people waiting. No one looks up. They can't hear either.

"Did the doctor give you new medication?" I ask.

My mother proudly opens a plastic shopping bag of samples. "I hope I remember when to take everything." She peers into it, her trifocal glasses pick up a glint of sunshine that streams through the window. Dust motes dance in the beam.

"Where are you going to keep all this, Mom?"

"Where I keep all the other medications. In the oven."

"But," I ask, as I open the heavy door from the office waiting room with two hands, "don't you use your oven to bake something once in a while?"

"Why should I cook? The meals at our place are perfectly adequate. Besides, we pay in advance. If I have to heat something up, I use the micro-range." She's always made up her own names for things. She turns in slow motion like The Tin Man who hasn't been oiled. "Herm, come on. Hurry up. We don't like to miss Thursday lunch. They have peach cobbler for dessert." She hooks her arm through mine.

I bring the subject up again in the car. "You have to keep your medications straight. Remember how you got so woozy in Florida you couldn't remember which frozen vegetable box had your jewelry? And the time you let the Jehovah's Witnesses in and they stayed for hours? That's why we moved you to independent living. We'll have to go over all this with Trudy." I regret I've said her name the moment it leaves my mouth.

"Trudy? Trudy? I can't stand Trudy. She flirts with your father. I don't want her in my apartment."

"Florence, she's not flirting. She's just being nice. What would she want with an old guy like me?" I can see my father smile in my rearview mirror, his hand touches the side of his gray temple, his fringe the only part of his hair that's left.

"Don't be silly, Herm. I read in the paper every day about young women going after older men. You're still a very attractive man. Look how that hussy from Guess Jeans went after that ninety-year-old guy and married him. You can't tell me *that* was love!" I check the rearview mirror again to see my mother's dour expression and crossed arms.

"Flo, even if someone was interested, I wouldn't look at them."

"What about if I'm gone? I bet you'd be a pushover for that Trudy."

"What would I want with Trudy? She's enormous. I like a woman with a slim figure." He fishes for his clip-on sunglasses in his front pocket.

"Listen, just don't let anyone get their hands on my jewelry. That's for the children."

You'd think she had the Tiffany collection squirreled away. We're talking about pearl earrings, a gold wedding band and a medium diamond. And, as for Trudy, she's a two-hundred-pound five-foot-four Filipino lady with a gold front tooth employed as a caretaker.

8

ON THE TWO HOUR DRIVE TO SEDONA, MAURY AND I decide not to discuss our expanding family situation, the failed HMO or my job in jeopardy. I lean my head back against the seat. What did Doris, my serpent-tattooed student, want and why hadn't she come back? The city fades away and the lower elevation of scrub brush evolves into high desert, lush with dense cacti. I marvel at the first sight of a saguaro in its natural habitat, its bent arms stretching toward the sky.

We listen to a Carl Hiassen mystery on tape peopled with characters from the underbelly of Miami, my former home. In the Sixties it was a sleepy place with wide, sandy beaches, palm trees dotting the shore and chubby tourists. Today, it's filled with radical Cubans pumped with Latin pride, chain wearing drug dealers and sexy-style. Anyway, listening to the tape enables us to mentally check out.

I close my eyes, exhausted. My insomnia's a chronic problem and exacerbated by night sweats. Once I'm awake Maury's nasal battles keep me up for hours. Dive bombing jets explode in a shower of thunder dying down to the lowest, loudest note played by a middle school tuba player. I've devised methods like slipping my arm under his pillow or pushing him a little to turn over, but nothing does the job. I leave ads from the paper on his placemat. *Cure Snoring Forever: One simple procedure and you'll never keep your loved ones awake again.*

"Sure," says Maury, "and I'll never breathe right or taste either. No way. I'm not letting some fruitcake hack-doctor experiment on me." Of course, if women emitted loud nasal noises equal to battling prehistoric mammoths, the men would ensure we had the surgery.

Now, my sleeplessness, fueled by an autocratic department head and a hormonal pregnant woman, fires up my stress levels. Rosa, whose erratic moods explode like flower seeds from the throat of a blossom, keeps us off balance. She bounces between mommy ecstasy and bulging evaporated-figure depression, baby paraphernalia excitement and familial longing. I'm a ping-pong ball suspended in air, never sure what will erupt.

It's funny how the little things annoy us when we're stressed. She never gets our garbage system straight. We recycle. She puts paper in the regular garbage can or forgets to place jars in the recycle one. I'm a teacher. I follow directions. I hiss to Maury that the garbage police are going to arrest us for violations. He says they're too busy to notice Rubin infractions. The city officials don't have the budget to hire people to analyze our refuse. Like most men he's oblivious to household details. Four people create a lot of debris. Am I the only person obsessing about garbage?

My mind wanders away from the taped story of fools, derelicts and alligators as we round Highway 89A's curve past the chain of outlet stores with their doubtful bargains. Then we see incredible rust-red rock formations, a confectioner's fancy. The shapes spread like squishy icing a playful Creator has tube-squeezed onto an earthly cake. Large purple-tinted boulders teeter to the edges of cliffs; others form Dairy Queen whipped tops. Bell Rock, a mesa of tiers, winds upward like a terra cotta bell.

No matter how many times I see the spectacular scenery of Sedona I'm always awestruck. Some people find it spiritual. It is other-worldly, a sweet God's dream. People from all over the planet relocate to this beautiful area, claiming they feel their energy shift. However, sky-rocketing real estate prices mean the fantasy may be evaporating.

We stop on the main street of Sedona, a wide band of black asphalt that stretches through a corridor of stores, the sidewalks jammed with gawkers in T-shirts and baseball caps that protect them from the high altitude sun. A pasty family of five in Iowa shirts, disembark from the minivan parked next to us, their white Elmer glue legs sticking out of Bermuda shorts. We're exactly halfway through the novel.

We wander past people, their mouths open at the incredible backdrop of red rocks named Cathedral and Snoopy. A group of weekend warriors pulls up on Harleys, love bugs smashed on the windshields, to strut around in macho garb.

A middle-aged woman in a oxford shirt, plaid skirt, and loafers in the New Age bookstore, Karmic Kandy, sidles up to us as we gaze at the titles: *Speaking to Your Inner Moon, The Sexy Saturn Return, Sedona for Dogs*. She peers at me with blue-gray eyes under her no-nonsense haircut with bangs. When she speaks her teeth are too large for her mouth, stretching over her lips, the kind of mouth that shows gums when it smiles. Her tongue laps out to lick them. "You're visitors, aren't you?" she asks.

I know Maury would prefer I ignore her, but she's harmless. "We're up for the weekend from the Valley."

"Yup. I could tell. I know most of the regulars. We have a lot of visitors here." She pauses as she drops her voice. "And they're not all from Earth." The blue-gray eyes give a furtive glance around the store.

I must have misunderstood. Maury gives me a look that says: "Don't get involved." He takes a step away to examine a copy of *The Complete Hiking Guide for Heterosexuals*.

"Have you had guests from someplace else?"

She moves in closer. "Norris, my divine guide, comes often. He does psychic readings and channels messages through me." Triumphant in her exclusive scoop, she flashes me a gummy smile. With the gray bangs she looks like a senior Buster Brown.

She's not a likely candidate to tell a strange tale, but her body, inhabited by an extra terrestrial, doesn't always belong to her. In a low tone, she takes weathered articles about herself and "Norris" from her burlap feedbag to show us, as though that's proof.

"They interviewed me for *The Sedona Sun* and *Extra Terrestrials Today*," she says with pride. "But Norris doesn't always come on demand."

"Yeah, and I bet she doesn't either," mumbles Maury. I ignore him.

"We have to have a lot of people meditating before he'll show up. Hey, what are you doing later? I could try to pull a group together."

Maury steps aside as she moves in closer, her large crowded

teeth chomping. Guiding my arm, he hustles me out of Karmic Kandy before I can buy a lollipop shaped like a flying saucer.

Maury knows me. I'd have asked a few more questions: How often does Norris visit? What does he say when he does? Do his psychic abilities dwell on domestic situations?

Maury makes a crack about Norris Neptune and his lascivious needs as we leave to look for low-fat yogurt. The young woman with long dark hair stationed behind the counter who never got off her cell phone yells, "Come back soon," as the door chimes tinkle on our departure.

"A direct line to Mars, no doubt," says Maury.

We spot an ice cream parlor. The Germans who run it moved here with twenty-eight members of their family to be part of the Gaia group, an enclave that believes in interdependence with the environment. We're not sure what that means, but the pistachio chocolate-chip tastes great. So much for low-fat yogurt. I take a seat near the window.

I grab Maury's arm. "OhmiGod, there's Megan Trumboldt!" Outside, on the sidewalk, Megan stands in pup tent-size shorts, a tank top and one of those strange hats with a beak in front and material in the back to cover her neck. She's surveying a map. I don't know whether to laugh or cry. I came up here to get away from everyone. She's the last person I want to see. On the other hand, Megan in shorts and a tank top is a revelation. Is she airing out the doughy bosom? I'm relieved when she heads down the street, the map folded under her arm.

Moments later, she's in the ice cream shop and there's no place to hide.

"I didn't expect to find you here." Megan hustles over to us, fanning herself with the map. "You must be Jean's husband." She holds out her hand as though Maury's supposed to kiss it. "I'm so pleased to meet you." I'm glum.

"Enjoying the scenery?" I ask in an attempt to be civil. She ignores me. Does she know how ridiculous she looks in that hat?

She gives me a hard stare. "If I wasn't so stressed with the dean's requests that are ignored, I wouldn't have to get away."

"I don't think I'm being treated fairly," I say.

"And I don't think you've treated this Boudreaux matter with the seriousness it deserves. You've opened up a can of worms that'll crawl all over us. Why don't you just change the grade and be done with it?"

"Tiffany does not deserve an incomplete. Academic freedom is my legal right according to the First Amendment."

"My dear, academic freedom does not give you intellectual autonomy. I refer to your subject matter." Her shrill voice attracts the attention of others. "This is hardly the appropriate place to discuss this." She turns to face the menu board with ice cream flavors. It gives us her best view of another map, her varicose veins. Megan orders a triple hot fudge sundae.

Maury holds up his hand for a hi-five and grins. "Come on, hon. Let's get out of here."

We check into the Inspiration Bed and Breakfast. After a quick change of clothes, me in an ethnic print and Maury in black, I pull out Glee's party invitation and map to Casa de Luna decorated with Native American petroglyphs. A dilettante student of our southwestern heritage, she's incorporated designs made by ancient peoples.

"They're rock art to mark the landscape," Glee shared with me. "The spirals represent the migration of a tribe or Europeans on horseback."

"How do you know that?" I asked.

"I have a subscription to *Arizona Highways*.

After a short ride to the Barstow's, Maury pulls our four-wheel drive vehicle close to the front door. The air smells clean, unencumbered by city life. Gingerly, I step over rocks, a small pile of bricks, two upended planters, a few uprooted small cacti, and avoid the hole of an animal's habitat in my stylish but sensible sandals. Glee's getaway, an adobe structure built into the red rocks, looks like an ancient ship floating in the landscape. Ever the creative force, she comes up with the ideas while Ted's job is to execute them. She's raved about the round living room and kiva fireplace for months.

The doorbell isn't connected so I knock a few times and then open the door. The smell of fresh cut wood, cold concrete, and recent grouting reminds me of the joys of new construction. My long, Indian print skirt swishes as we sail into a huge, empty room. "Yoo-hoo. Anyone home? Hello?"

The unfinished adobe mansion may not pass code, but the eight-foot windows are in, the toilets flush, and the doors lock. Saltillo tile floors stretch across the expanse minus baseboards. Without a proper inspection no one can stay here, but we can party. Glee dreams up any reason to have a good time.

Our hostess comes rushing out in a Pucci-looking patio dress, a headband tied hippie-style around her head, curls springing away from it, a Sixties throwback with designer flair. Her beaded sandals slap against the floor. She's the color in the room.

"Darlings, I'm so glad you've arrived. I can't wait 'til everyone else gets here! April called from the car and they're on their way. Tuni and Ellis will be here soon."

"Glee, this looks wonderful. When do you move in?" I ask.

"Whenever Ted gets the finishing subs up from his Phoenix project."

Maury wanders over to the wall of windows. "Wow."

"I'm going to do a tour when everyone arrives. Oh, this is going to be so much fun! Ted didn't want a big deal for his birthday, but I love to celebrate." Glee's carbonated personality bubbles to the top. She races toward an open kitchen that lacks appliances. A Coleman chest filled with beer and wine sits on the Brazilian soapstone counter.

"Corian is so over," she tells me. "We're going for an industrial look so the floors are stained concrete."

But won't that be over in six months, too? I say to myself.

I join Maury to look at the most incredible view I've seen from someone's home. Down below Ted moves large redwood pots with flowers near the lower patio and spa. The rocks, a sculpture painted gold, fuchsia and aubergine by the setting sun, meet stands of pine trees and aspens, a puzzle of jewels with the western sky ablaze as a backdrop. "Glee, look at your view! It takes my breath away!"

"Isn't it extraordinary? This is the dream house Ted and I have always wanted. It brings me closer to enlightenment. When I'm in the zone I can create." She pauses to push an errant curl out of her face.

I hug her, knowing these trappings make her feel secure.

"I'm so happy for you." Maury, although usually not demonstrative with anyone but me, hugs her, too. He appreciates where she comes from and where she wants to go: Maslow's model of self-actualization. Her childhood, a hodge-podge of too many step-fathers and financial disparity, flung her self esteem octaves apart. Once she told me, "One month I was a debutante-in-training and the next we inhabited a dive apartment with the Mercedes parked around the corner so the repo man wouldn't see it."

"How much time will you spend up here?" asks Maury. He drapes his arm around my shoulder to pull me closer.

"Oh, I don't know. Probably not too much at the beginning, but eventually, we'll be up here permanently. It enhances my spirituality, at least that's what my intuitive counselor told me." She blows the curl up again. "Ted's got some Valley projects he's working on and we're not totally set with our retirement yet."

Maury raises his bushy salt-and-pepper eyebrows. This time it's the we-aren't-set-with-our-retirement-either look.

But her expression gives no hint of worry. That's Glee. Let Ted take care of the finances. I'll roll along and make it fun. Maury gives me a small squeeze.

Her attention turns to the front door. Tuni and Ellis come in, their faces hidden behind three large white boxes.

"I'm so glad you could make it!" Glee squeals, hip-hopping over the slippery tile. The toe rings on each sandaled foot glitter as she dances to the door.

Tuni and Ellis, dressed in earth tones, pose for a moment in the doorway. We greet each other as they set their packages in the corner of the empty room. Tuni's gaze scans the expansive ceiling embedded with skeleton Ocotillo branches, a desert plant with Swiss cheese holes. "My, what is the ceiling made from?" she asks.

Glee says, "Ocotillo branches, a plant with long arms that sprouts tiny green leaves and torch-like blossoms. They look dead most of the year until we get our seven inches of rain. Lot of people up here plant them in a line to get a living fence."

"It's strange word," says Ellis. "What does it mean?"

Glee shrugs her shoulders.

Maury jumps in. "Ocotillo means coach whip in Spanish." Then he looks embarrassed that he's spouted obscure information.

"As soon as April and Steve get here we'll have some hors d'oeuvres, then go to Enchantment for dinner," says Glee. When she twirls around the bottom of her dress fans out.

The Lefkowitzes arrive in a flurry of air-kisses and back-slaps. April, breathtaking in a lipstick red sundress and heels looks like she's arrived from a *Vogue* shoot. Steve, ever cool, his streaked blonde hair combed back, sports a subdued Mafioso outfit: all black silk and panache with Italian sandals. Tuni moves the large boxes on the floor in front of us. "You must open these now," she insists.

"You don't mean me, do you?" I ask, placing my hand on my chest.

"Yes, sweet pea, I brought each of you a treat. Of course the largest one is Glee and Ted's house present." Her Aussie accent makes everything sound important.

April, Glee and I fall on the boxes like ten-year-olds opening FAO Schwartz boxes. Laughing, Glee keeps saying, "What is it? What is it?" The guys hang back amused at our excitement. Ever the klutz, I lose my balance and fall over from my crouched position. I sit on the tile floor rather than balance myself again.

"Ooooh. Look at this," says April. She lifts a candelabra with space for three fat candles. The base, supported by a bent wrought-iron man, holds the candles on his back.

"Oh, this is fabulous." Glee hugs the candelabra to her chest dramatically. "Thank you so much."

The ones for us are the same design only smaller. They're beautiful, but nothing I would have bought for myself. "It's lovely. It'll look wonderful on our dining room table," I offer.

"I'm so glad you like them," says Tuni. She grins at Ellis. "They're part of our Job line."

"Oh. Do you always do biblical themes?" I ask. I'm the female version of Job with my career crisis and insolent daughter-in-law.

"No, not really," Tuni says, as she examines one piece. Her finger runs over a rough edge on the bottom. "We must chat with them about a finer finish on these." Ellis nods in agreement.

We gather up the gifts, stuff them back into the boxes with their tissue paper crackling, and push them over the tile floor to the corner of the room. Glee passes crab and artichoke dip on fresh French bread while we finish our drinks. We all slide into a relaxed mode before we leave for dinner.

Enchantment, the premier resort in Sedona, represents high-end with its security guard, exquisite food and unparalleled views. The wrap-around geologic formations are stunning and the evening glows with ambiance.

We dine on the patio by candlelight as the sun sets transforming the reds rocks into shades of pink and purple. I space out, my shoulders warmed by heaters, my toes cool in the evening air. I sip a margarita, the salty rim of the hand-blown Mexican glass stinging my lips. I touch Maury's hand. He smiles back at me.

When Glee and April leave to fluff in the rest room, Steve dominates the conversation. "My client says the guy cut him off. Bullshit. I know damn well he's an inexperienced rider. I get a court injunction for the driver who skips, then my client, who claimed whiplash, takes a powder before I. . ."

My attention drifts away from his Harley mania. I shift in my chair. The stars shine brighter away from city lights, with the massive rocks as a curtain. Maybe I'm buying into all the spiritual myths about the vortexes, the swirling, sacred energy centers. Or maybe the surreal stories piqued my imagination—that this was a vestige of Atlantis, or that aliens landed here--or I'm simply more peaceful. All I know is I don't miss the Valley and all our tension. The turmoil melts away leaving me serene, a word I can't often use to describe my mood.

We wake early the next day. It's the first time I've slept through the night in weeks. Maury reaches for me across the soft sheets. Fresh air and pine trees make him horny.

"I feel Norris, the Alien cock about to spring from underneath the sheets." He nuzzles me. "Since Michael and Rosa moved in you've been so pre-occupied."

"Honey, we can't start. Glee has a jeep tour planned. We have to be there by nine." I stroke the space where his neck and chest meet.

"But, Norris has a message for you." He tries out one of his creepy voices, his hands in imitation Frankenstein claws about to pounce on me.

I roll out of the way to the edge of the bed, almost landing on the floor. "Tell Norris, the alien, I'll pick up his message during nap time this afternoon." I jump up and head for the bathroom. Maury falls back against the pillows.

"I bet Ted's getting laid this morning," he says in a loud voice.

"Don't count on it. When Glee's in charge of an event, she's focused," I garble back, my mouth filled with toothpaste.

"What about a quickie?" Maury yells out.

I return to his side of the bed, minty-breathed, and lean down to kiss him. "How quick?"

He pulls me on top of him rolling us across the sheets. I laugh in surprise. In moments he fills me with his love, his hand on my ass to keep the rhythm steady. "How 'bout this quick?" he says in a husky voice.

As we get dressed he comes up behind me and says, "This afternoon it's your turn."

A jeep tour isn't a novelty for us, but Tuni and Ellis are enthused, especially when they see our guide, Chip, in full cowboy regalia wearing a beige duster coat. His black cowboy hat, the brim circled with a leather band, appears to be a well-worn item covered with red dust. It shades his eyes. If he's not authentic, then he's got the right wardrobe for it.

He directs us to his red jeep, the sides etched by palo verde branches. We call them desert pinstripes. Laughing and holding onto our hats, we take off toward the promise of real petroglyphs ahead.

"How did you get the name Tuni?" April asks, her spandex halter giving Chip an eyeful. A gun in a holster sticks out underneath his coat. I abhor guns.

"It's just a pet name. When I first married I couldn't cook so I made tuna casseroles. My chums started calling me Tuni and it stuck." Tuni squeezes Ellis's arm and he looks at her with adoration. The last time Maury had that expression on his face was when his favorite golfer won The Masters on TV.

Our guide stops to give us a tour of Anasazi ruins from 1200-1500 AD. On a jutting ledge a series of ancient one-room homes appear, their front wall missing. A few, connected by a small interior doorway, have remains of a fire pit, the low rock ceiling smoke-stained. We take careful, small steps, trying not to disturb anything.

Of course I think about the ruins in my life. Did more than one generation live under one roof? And was one of them a Princess on the side of the Spanish Inquisition?

Chip says, "No one knows what happened to the civilization, but it's the cornerstone to the ancient peoples of the southwest." Pointing to primitive designs etched into the walls, his finger points to a rough cut in the rock. He traces the lines without touching it. "These petroglyphs are in the Anasazi-style and found all over the

Four Corners region. This is probably a bighorn sheep which might mean this was a good area to find them or it might have been placed to encourage fertility."

Maury moves behind me with his hands on my waist. "I'd like to encourage our fertility," he whispers in my ear and rubs up against me. I don't think anyone heard, but men get amorous at the oddest times. Besides, we've got enough fertility in our house with Rosa.

When Chip offers more detail, Ted whispers to Glee in a voice we can all hear, "With all this real estate, I would have built individual homes instead of these condos with common walls." April and Glee giggle, their hands cover their mouths like two geishas, their mammoth diamonds glinting in the sun.

We approach the end of the ridge and peer into each new abode until we all pile into the last one, the only structure with a front wall. "Look how small this place is. A family of ten probably lived here," says Glee, as we all turn our chins up and crane our necks toward the low ceiling. I'm claustrophobic in the tight space. The aroma of bodies makes me sneeze, a combination of perfume, after-shave, deodorant, shampoo, lotion, and old cowboy. Ted makes a joke and wipes his arm. I snuffle with no available tissue.

I glance at Maury's watch. I'm getting bored, wishing I was home taking care of the myriad of things on my To Do list. My impatience makes me think about a trip to the gynecologist. As a doc's wife there's all this chit-chat while someone is roto-rootering around in your private parts. *How are the kids? Taken any vacations lately?*

It gets very warm while Chip goes into detail about the Anasazi lifestyle. And smelly. Tuni asks more questions. Of course I have to pee. My membership in the TWBC, the Teeny Weeny Bladder Club, activates at the worst times.

Finally, we peel out of the tiny room and file single-file onto the path. Suddenly, Chip cries out, "Everyone stop. I hear a rattle." April squeals and hangs onto Steve, who puffs out his chest, macho-style. Tuni has her hand over her mouth as though screaming will cause the snake to rear up like a cobra.

Glee says, "Don't hurt it. It's one of God's living creatures."

All I can think about is the pressure on my bladder.

Chip pulls his gun. "Hold it, everyone." He stalks ahead of us on the trail, a modern day Wyatt Earp protecting us from mayhem.

Maury rolls his eyes.

"Okay, the coast is clear," says Chip, poking his gun back into his holster.

"How many times do they stage that excitement?" Maury whispers to me, ever the skeptic.

After the tour ends we head toward downtown. We stop at Tlaquepaque, a Mexican-style warren of art galleries, restaurants, and clothing stores around a series of courtyards enclosed by a high brick wall. The name is Spanish for the best of everything. Maury says it's a translation for, "Let's rip off the tourists." We fan out in different directions. Everyone's a shopper except my man who lounges on a tile bench among the marigolds and cobblestones to read the back of a menu.

An art glass gallery filled with bowls, vases and perfume bottles, their transparency greeting the natural light, splays a rainbow of colors and designs: cherry-red swirls, butter-yellow stripes and ice-blue polka dots. One huge periwinkle plate with curled Chihuly-like lettuce edges suspends from the ceiling. The two thousand dollar white sticker underneath the artist's etched name confirms how spectacular it is.

We meet at Maury's post to meander through the complex, then stop for lunch at an outdoor café under canvas umbrellas, shopping bags at our feet.

Before we leave, Tuni says to Ellis, "Don't forget. We have to go back to the glass gallery to pick up the periwinkle plate."

They bought it. Just like that.

Later, we retreat to our rooms for an afternoon nap before dinner. Maury snuggles next to me. I turn over on top of him. "Didn't you say it was my turn earlier?" I ask, slipping my hands under his back.

He begins to peel off my clothes, his adept fingers searching and stroking the spots that feed my passion. My breathing changes when my mind lets go of everything except my lover. In minutes a crashing wave sends me over a giant waterfall of no return.

When we're finished, before I attempt sleep, I scramble on top of him to yelp and bite his neck. He laughs. "Are you crazy? What's gotten into you?"

I respond in my deepest, scariest voice, and cross my eyes. "An alien has taken over my body. I've lost all control." Sedona inspires me.

9

BEFORE OUR RIDE BACK TO THE CITY WITH ITS TRAFFIC, khaki haze and our myriad of pregnant problems, we meet the other couples for a late breakfast at the Coffee Pot in downtown Sedona. We're relaxed and mellow. Our waitress, Beryl, in a uniform with an embroidered hankie that flowers out of her left breast pocket, wears her name emblazoned on a plastic tag. She takes our orders, which goes smoothly until Ted becomes testy about the lack of soy milk for his cereal. At least Maury doesn't embarrass me and order the colon-blow stuff he eats every morning. He gets an omelet instead.

"What a delightful weekend," says Tuni as she leans into the turquoise vinyl booth. "We enjoyed ourselves so much. Right, darling?" She turns to Ellis to touch his arm. Her creamy skin without make-up gives her the look of an ingénue.

"Very much so," Ellis answers.

"Thank you for the lovely gift," I say as I hold up the Job candelabra that Glee remembered to bring.

They grin. "You must come by the plant some time and see what we're doing. We're poised for a huge expansion, especially with our new project," he says pronouncing it pro-ject.

"What is it?" asks Steve, the consummate businessman.

"It's quite confidential," says Ellis. He leans in and glances around. "I'm not sure I should say anything yet, should I?" He looks at Tuni. She shrugs her shoulders.

"I suppose it's okay. But I must ask you to keep it in your confidence. We have so many details to work out, particularly with our creative sources and my family who's funding it," says Ellis.

If Glee's the celebrator and I'm the analyzer, then April's the detective. "What is it?" she blurts out. She adjusts herself on the sticky vinyl seat, seductive in a white shirt tied below her bosom that exposes her flat, tan stomach. I self-consciously touch my chubby, bloated one. I don't think it's a style that'll work for me.

We all lean in. "It's a multi-million dollar business so you can appreciate my reticence," says Ellis. "It involves an international conglomerate on the highest scale. I'm in negotiations with top government officials in Europe."

Even Maury's interest is piqued by this. He puts aside the front section of the newspaper to look at Ellis. I read the headline, "Legislature fights smut; Lawmakers visit topless clubs." I scan a few paragraphs while I pretend to listen.

A group of legislators, including my nemesis, Flora Boudreaux, went on a flesh-finding mission. Can you believe she wanted to see if lap dancing should be banned? The erotic routines performed in close proximity for fifty dollars sent them scurrying back to committee. Give me a break. Isn't anyone paying attention to our rotting educational system?

"I really shouldn't say any more. With worldwide rights it could easily reach a billion dollars," says Ellis. He stirs his coffee.

"What is it?" April asks again. The woman who's provocative can't stand being teased. "Is it going to be an IPO or is it already on the NASDAQ?"

Beryl interrupts with our food, a heavy tray on her arm. We figure out the orders, find catsup for the hash browns, move the Job statues again, knock over a water glass, and order refills for the regular, decafs, and herbal teas. No lattes available.

Although the subject of Tuni's pro-ject doesn't come up again during breakfast, I think about it. Some people know how to manufacture money instead of eking it out year by year. They learn from their families. Maury's parents were more concerned with union dues and mine aren't risk takers. We don't have any experience in amassing fortunes.

The table talk continues. Tuni and Ellis mention their house under construction and its problems. Ted commiserates with them. It sounds very palatial from their description of marble bathrooms, an elaborate bedroom suite, and a gourmet kitchen with appliances imported from Germany.

Beryl brings the check. Ellis snatches it before the other men can reach for their wallets. He pulls out a wad of bills.

"I've got it," says Ellis.

"Man, you carry a lot of cash," says Steve.

"Some of our small vendors who buy damaged or odd lots pay in cash. This is on me," Ellis says over protests.

"That's what I need," says Ted. "A cash business. Waiting for credit lines from the bank is the pits in the construction industry."

"Yeah, well, people aren't exactly anxious to pay their lawyers either," says Steve. He dusts crumbs from his jeans.

"Listen guys, if this is a contest, I win," adds Maury. "*Medical Economics* listed the twenty-five bills people pay. The car mechanic was first and the doctor was last."

With that we get up. I slide across the seat from my corner perch. Ellis throws two one hundred dollar bills on the table. Beryl's going to have a good day.

When we hug goodbye in the parking lot, I overhear Tuni say to Glee, "Darling, thank you so much for including us in such a glorious weekend. It's so difficult to make friends when you go someplace new. We appreciate you sharing yours."

Ted turns to get into his vintage black Porsche while Ellis stands near his blue Mercedes station wagon. Ted calls out, "Let me know if I can be any help with the house," and waves.

I settle into our car and reach for the knob to finish our novel on CD.

An aura of worry starts a climb up my spine: Megan, Rosa, Doris and Flora.

10

On Monday morning Rosa's spotting. I take her to the doctor after the guys leave. I have no way to change my appointment with Doris. I call Megan to cancel my class on Women and Their Poetry. No Adrienne Rich today.

"It upsets the students when professors don't show for a class. Can't you find a replacement?" Megan asks in her annoyed voice that sounds like Julia Child discovering someone has put margarine in her butter dish. Since Megan fired and rehired me a few years ago, I walk on eggs, hard-boiled ones.

"If this wasn't an emergency, I would be there. Please go to the room and put on the board the students should finish their reading assignment. Please." I know I'm begging, but I'm very anxious about Rosa and the baby. She's only five months.

"When will you be in to do the paperwork for the grade change? Dean Gruber wants to know." Her voice is low with annoyance. She's furious with me.

"I don't know. I have a family crisis right now. I have to go. Bye."

I try to distract Rosa in the car. I tell her about Marge Piercy, the object of my current curriculum affection. "You'd love her. She's a passionate poet who writes sweeping stories."

"We have a famous female poet who was the first feminist in Mexico." She pronounces Mexico without the "x".

"Who was that?" I didn't know feminists flourished in that machismo society.

"Her name was Sor Juana and she lived around the late 1600's." Rosa rubs a spot on the windshield, a frown on her brow.

"What do you know about her?" I'm more familiar with contemporary women who've made a stand like Benita Galeana.

"Sor Juana was our Shakespeare. She wrote sonnets, plays, and hymns. We had to memorize her most famous poem in school. *Hombres necios que acusias*." She sees my puzzled look. "That means, 'You foolish men who accuse women.' It's about the attitude of men toward women."

I'm impressed with her knowledge. "I thought Mexico glorified the male culture." I maneuver into the parking lot of the doctor's office.

"It does, but working women have fought for equality a long time, especially our *soldaderas* who fought in the trenches of the Mexican revolution in 1910. Pancho Villa and Zapata aren't the only heroes." She finishes as we approach the door to the office walking slowly.

I wait while she sees Stanley, our friend and my gynecologist, one of the few left who hasn't abandoned the obstetrics portion of his practice.

A short time later Rosa and Stanley come out to the waiting room, his hand on her shoulder. "She's going to be fine. I told her to take it easy. She needs to stay off her feet today. Just relax," he says to Rosa.

"Is everything okay with the baby?" I ask.

"Absolutely. I know this lovely young lady and Michael don't want me to say the sex yet, but rest assured you and Maury are going to be grandparents of a very healthy baby," my hero-doctor says.

"So, Rosa doesn't have to be bedridden?"

"Heaven's no. A bit of normal activity is fine. In fact, some mild exercise would be good for her. Just don't take up tennis. And stop worrying. Both of you." He smiles, the consummate professional, his stethoscope gleaming around his neck.

I guide Rosa to the car. "How do you feel? Would a little lunch help?" I ask.

"No, thanks anyway. I'm not hungry."

That's a first. She eats enough for me to be food shopping twice a week and then disappears after dinner with Michael for ice cream. A womb with teeth. Okay. Food as a bribe doesn't work. I'll go to a back-up plan. "What if we stop at the mall and get you another pair of maternity pants and a top?" Shopping always woos Lara.

Rosa likes that idea so after a brief stop at The Pregnant Pear, two pairs of pants and three tops later, we head for home. Four hundred dollars lighter. We'll recycle them.

Our relationship has been rockier than a hammock in a summer dust storm. I'm glad for the opportunity to mend our tarnished fence. Shopping is the great equalizer. We bonded.

After dinner and Rosa's feeble attempts to clean up, she models her new clothes. A few smiles and twirls. They've cheered her up. She puts her arms around me. "Thanks, Mom, for taking time off work and getting me new clothes. I really like them."

It's the first time she's called me Mom. I'm mushy inside.

When she and Michael leave for ice cream, Maury asks from his favorite lounge chair, medical journals stacked on his knees, "How much did that set me back?"

"You don't want to know."

11

"STEVE LEFKOWITZ CALLED ME AT THE OFFICE TODAY," says Maury as we lay in bed.

Amber crawls up the middle to be near us, a golden retriever Army recruit who elbows through a training jungle of orange-striped sheets.

"What did he want?" I put down the next subversive novel I hope to add to my Women and Literature list and pull off my reading glasses. The guys rarely call one another except for golf.

"He went over to see Ellis's business," says Maury, his voice soft and a bit hesitant.

"What for?"

"Remember? Ellis said he had a project. Steve's thinking of investing."

My brows rise. "Really?"

"Steve says Tuni and Ellis are heavy hitters. They've quite an operation going and they're expanding their gift line fast. He and April attended a charity event with them and Tuni bid on some crazy auction item. I think it was a slumber party with Morgan Fairchild or maybe it was Oprah. Anyway, they paid $20,000 for it."

"Wow." I'm impressed.

That's serious money. I know it's not nice to count other people's fortunes, but in private, we all do it. You have to have a lot of extra cash to spend it on staying up all night with either of those airheads. Maury's oblivious to details. He's the antithesis of star struck. I wonder who's on Tuni's invitation list.

"What's the deal?"

Maury wears a rumpled T-shirt emblazoned with *Melonheads,* the logo for kids who go through chemo. When he turns on his side to look at me, I face him, mashing my cheek into my arm. Amber's tail wags between us, a hairy dog fan.

"Steve's putting in a hundred thou. I'm short on details, but it seems Tuni and Ellis have negotiated the worldwide rights for gift items based on the Vatican's art treasures." His voice rises with enthusiasm.

Besides golf, medicine and me, Maury doesn't get intense about too many things. The idea that he could create income without looking into people's orifices has the compassionate curmudgeon awake.

"Really?" I never heard of such a thing. I knew the Vatican's art collection was vast, but I had no idea they were into marketing it.

"Steve wants us to put some money into the deal. He checked it out. His accountant went through their books and they're solid."

Is Maury's motivation coming from not wanting to face seventy-five sick people tomorrow? He complains about the evil HMO's and their reimbursements, but I didn't realize our economic situation was so precarious he'd consider selling religious items. I could perhaps make a dim case for yarmulkes and menorahs, but religious items that aren't even of our faith?

"Maury, you know we have a few cardinal rules, excuse the pun. Don't invest in crazy schemes. Never mix friends and money. Stay away from *mashuganas*." That's my mother's favorite word for crazy people. Or anyone she perceives to be unstable.

I roll onto my back to relieve pins and needles. Amber licks my face. I try to push her away, but she wins as I laugh and gag at the same time. Maury grabs the edge of the sheet to dabble at the slobber left on my chin.

"I know," he says. He holds his forearm up to discourage an Amber face bath, "I have a good feeling about this. First of all, Ted and Steve are money machines. They know a good business investment when they see it. Steve said he personally contacted the licensing agent at The Vatican in Rome and they said that TuniEl Company in Phoenix, Arizona had the rights to their stuff."

Steve and Ted have been business partners before. Those two are always cooking up a scheme. One year they invested in drive-through video stores. It wasn't a hit, but it made money. "I don't understand. What is it they're going to do with them? Put baby Jesus on plastic containers in the supermarket?"

Maury smiles at my irreverence. "Actually, it's not religious at all. They're using the secular items from paintings, sculpture, carvings and tapestries as inspiration for a gift line." Maury's information is more than I've gotten out of him in months. He's quiet unless it's politics. Or I'm sending him over the top.

"Oh. You mean like cherubs or lambs turned into something like the Job candelabra they gave us as gifts?"

"Exactly."

"How much do they want?" I'm worried, knowing Maury's pension plan is far from fully funded and we're still paying off Lara's wedding from a few years ago. Is Maury considering this?

"Steve and Ted are putting in between a hundred thou and two hundred and fifty." The numbers roll from his lips, like we're use to playing in that arena.

I whistle. "Whoa. That's steep. We don't have that kind of money."

"I know, Hon. I wasn't considering anything like that. It's divided into distributorships of $25,000 each." He pauses. "They're talking about these *tchotchkes* being in museum stores and gift shops all over the world, plus on the net. This could be big. With a baby coming and none of the kids working at real jobs, and my practice's erratic cash flow, I just thought--" His voice trails off, a vapor jet that fades into a sigh. He falls back, head hitting the pillow.

Ever since Maury's partner bailed and things had to be divided legally, we've been in monetary quicksand. First, the evil HMO dropped docs. Then they instituted new rules and hired twelve-year old bureaucrats. Our cash flow's capricious since Sunshine went under. Families Maury treated for years moved to other plans where he's not a provider. He's a hostage who sees twice as many patients and gets paid half the money. And that's not his biggest complaint. Some of the plans dock him when he refers to a specialist or sends a patient to the hospital. He fights with them all the time. When he calls from home, he raises his voice to argue with gum-chewing HMO peanut-brains entrenched in power. What's happening to his blood pressure?

I push Amber's big butt down to the end of the bed and turn over onto Maury's chest. I look into his sad, coffee eyes.

"Oh, honey. Don't worry so much. We'll be all right," I say to comfort him. I doubt my efforts to slay our financial burdens with verbal dragons works. I don't dare bring up my academic disaster that looms in the shadows. Megan's been skulking past my door when I teach, then avoiding me in the halls. Is she in cahoots with Flora and the elusive Tiffany to abandon me to the right-wing wolves?

"Let's think about it. We don't have to make any decisions for a few days. There's a meeting where we can get more information. I just know everything Ted touches turns to gold."

He puts his arms around me for a hug. We kiss. Our lips linger for a moment. I roll off and reach for my book. Maury sits up to pull off his T-shirt then falls backward into the nest of pillows and crashes into sleep faster than Amber, who sometimes collapses mid-bark.

I sleep in thirty-minute intervals, my mind racing past chubby babies, my course syllabus and a monkey-haired legislator who wants to kill me. What if I lose my job because I've taken an ethical stand? Will that comfort me if Michael and Rosa never move out? Maybe I've pushed Megan too far.

Maury sheet-wrestles most of the night. He destroys ninjas with his snores and an occasional moan.

Doctors are notoriously poor business people. All their years of training never include finance. I know he wants to get us out of our monetary crater, but is this it? I give up at four a.m. Sleeping is a waste of time. I can't wait to call April after ten. She'll know what's going on with TuniEl Productions.

I phone April while I open yesterday's mail. My leopard letter opener, a gift from Glee, slices through the bills. After we exhaust the subject of her daughter, Mia, whose engagement to a young man ended when she found out his hobby was cockfighting, I ask, "What do you know about this Vatican deal?"

"Steve researched it with his accountant and had a few attorneys at the firm examine it. Looks good. They're trying to raise capital from private investors so they can do massive manufacturing and save money on the molds."

"I thought Ellis said his family was putting up the money." I remember our Sedona conversation. I open an envelope with the IRS logo and peek inside. We're late. I set it aside for Maury.

"They've put in the seed money, but this is huge so they need more," says April.

April's savvy. I know she manages her own portfolio. "So you're investing?"

"Looks that way. Come to the informational meeting at The Ritz next week. Make your minds up after that."

"Good idea." I'm happy to delay the decision. I put the junk mail together for the recycle bag.

"How's Rosa?" she asks.

"She had a little spotting last week, but the doctor said she's fine. Oh, I can ask you." April was brought up Catholic. "Who's Saint Rita?"

"She sounds familiar. Hold on while I get my book about the saints." She returns and reads to me between slurps of espresso.

"Santa Rita is the saint for hopeless causes along with Saint Jude. Why do you want to know?"

"I heard Rosa tell her mother to light candles to her."

I hear another slurp. "It says here Santa Rita is the woman from Italy in the 1600's who was married at twelve to an abusive older man. They had two sons. Anyway, after twenty years, his gangster buddies killed him and dumped him on her doorstep."

"April, this sounds like Saturday night in the 'hood. They made her a saint because of that?" I stack the bills together.

"No, her sons became ill and died so she became a nun."

"I thought to be elevated in the church one had to be a virgin, which eliminates every one I know."

"Let's see. The convent rejected her, but then there was a miracle and they accepted her."

"Are you sure that's how she got to be a saint?" This is more complicated than some of the Old Testament stories where I have to suspend belief or accept burning bushes and avenging angels.

"While she was praying one night, Christ sent her one of his thorns. It festered in her forehead. Now I remember her. Sister Mary Margaret, my favorite nun, said it smelled putrid."

"How did Mary Margaret know?" I move toward the pantry to dump the empty envelopes and flyers into our re-cycle can, the phone crooked in my neck.

"Never mind. It says the holy mortification lasted fifteen years. When she died the smell became like roses."

"What do people pray to her for?" I'm hoping it isn't for pain-in-the-ass mothers-in-law.

"Santa Rita is for the impossible. We invoke her for infertility, loneliness, unhappy marriages or bleeding."

"The last one's my answer. Thanks. See you next week."

I call my parents, who continue their life long habit of talking on both extensions. I'm propped up in bed, student essays on my knees, Amber next to me. When she wags her tail, the papers fly.

"Mom, can you turn down the weather channel? That's better. How's the independent living place?"

"I don't know. Your father doesn't like it here. Herm? Are you there? Tell her what happened."

"We have no friends here," my father says.

"You had no friends in Florida. Didn't you tell me they all died?"

"Yes, but we liked them."

"Can't you make new friends?" I reach for a dog brush in the nightstand drawer. Amber rolls over to show me the inside of her legs and private parts. I begin to brush, hairballs taking flight with a few papers.

"Herm, tell her. We went out with another couple and we can't stand them."

"What did they do?" I ask. Stories have to be coaxed out of my parents. If I don't ask the right questions, they get annoyed.

"Don't ask. Herm, tell her."

"The van from our place dropped us off at a nice restaurant. We ordered. Everything was fine, until the food came," says my dad.

"Then what happened?"

"I ordered the grilled tuna and your mother had the brisket with vegetables. The couple asked us if we wanted to share. He ordered chicken with stuffed shrimp and she had the fillet."

"Herm, Gladys didn't have the filet. She had fish," my mother says correcting him.

"That's what I said." My father becomes impatient.

"I thought you meant a steak filet." Now my mother sounds contrite.

"Mom. Dad. I have to teach today. Tell me what happened." I abandon my dog chore and pile the essays on the nightstand. I head toward the walk-in closet Maury and I use, not equally, of course.

"We said we didn't like to share. They reached across the table and said they just wanted a little taste," says my father.

I pull out an old suit. If I wear it I'll have to put on hose. No way. I push it back into the line-up of hangers. The jeans skirt will work with a silky blouse. Casual but upscale. As if the kids will notice anyway. Except for a few most worry about how they're going to get laid on Saturday night and what their grade will be. Office hours are afterward. Hope Doris shows up so I can find out what the problem was.

"Did you ever hear of such a thing? Eating from our plate. Your father and I were appalled. You know your father doesn't like anyone touching his food. Right, Herm?" my mother asks. She demands corroboration.

"What? Who touched me?" asks my father.

"Mom. Dad. Avoid them. Make friends with other people. You're living in a large facility. What if I take you to lunch?" I stare at the mirror. Not bad. No prize but not bad.

"Okay. Call us tonight and we'll make plans," says my mother, her voice cheerier now that she's vented her upset.

After a morning of teaching and an afternoon of errands, I walk in the house loaded down with my briefcase, folders of papers, grocery bags and Maury's lab coats from the cleaners. It's quiet. Rosa's probably napping.

I turn on our ancient answering device to hear Megan's breathless voice leaving an ominous message. I can see the Dolly Parton breasts heaving. "Jean, Megan here. I entreat you to watch the news tonight on Channel Three. It has a direct bearing on the current situation." Click. No good-bye. Nothing.

I doubt she and the dean have gone to the press because of Tiffany's grade.

Maury and I go to a late afternoon movie because he can't stand when people talk in the theater. He says they're using their TV manners in public. Afterward, we meet a doctor from India for dinner.

When we return we stand in the doorway of the kitchen/family room. The odor of old food left on dirty dishes, the acrid smell of urine from our ancient Amber who hasn't been walked, and the smell of cooking oil distracts me. Apparently, Michael and Rosa partied while we were out. My mood sinks at the mess. I cleaned the kitchen before I left. Why are they such slobs?

The two of them, their bodies intertwined on one chair as she slouches back into his lap, face the TV to watch a basketball game. His hands rest on her belly. They're dressed alike in T-shirts, shorts and untied sneakers. Michael reaches his arm down the side of the chair to lift a Gatorade. I look back at the kitchen with the pots on the cook top, the bottle of oil, its contents dripping down the side, a sink filled with glasses, an opened bag of tortilla chips on the rug and my heart dives to a lower depth.

"Michael, Rosa, we have to talk. If you're going to live with us, we can't have this mess. Michael, did you clean the patio like dad asked?" My voice strains not to be as furious as I am. Rosa leans her head back to look at Michael.

I don't want the mother of my grandchild to hate me. On the other hand, I don't want to hate myself. Rosa struggles out of the chair. She lifts herself up with her arms and waddles to the kitchen table, her hand in the small of her back. With dramatic effort she pulls out a chair. Gheez! She's not that pregnant. I taught school until the week before I had Lara.

With a sigh Michael joins us. At our kitchen conference Maury and I reiterate the rules. Clean up after yourselves. Be considerate about the TV. Load the dishwasher. Use paper cups. Walk the dog. They're basics, but they're met with Michael's chagrined look and Rosa's stare.

"You asked to move home again and bring Rosa. We agreed so that you could finish law school. We need a bit more cooperation around here," says Maury.

"Rosa doesn't feel well and I'm in class or studying." Michael folds his hands on the table. "You know what a struggle this is for me with my learning disabilities."

"Michael, what your mother and I are saying is, pitch in a little. We work hard, too, and it's unsettling to come home to a mess. Don't forget it's been a long time since we had roommates." Maury smiles and reaches over to touch my hand.

Rosa's face turns cloudy, reminiscent of Hera, the vengeful goddess. "Honey, they don't want us here. Let's move out," she whines, her hand on his arm, her eyes never leaving mine.

"Mom, I can't take this anymore. I'm being pulled in too many directions. I'm getting a job so we can get our own place. Come on, Rosa." Michael's voice rises as he stands up.

"Calm down," says Maury, falling for the manipulation.

"No. I've had it. It's too much stress for Rosa and the baby. I can't concentrate on my studies with this conflict bubbling over all the time. We're moving out."

"Where would you go? Sit down," I say.

"No, I've made up my mind. I can work. I got myself into this and I can get myself out of it. I'll quit law school. I can always pick it up later."

"Michael!" says Maury as he slaps his hand on the table. "We've invested too much in your education to have you walk away. How do you think you're going to support a family? You have responsibilities now. You're going to need a house, baby stuff."

"I don't care. I'll get a job at a convenience store." Michael's defiant. It reminds me of his bedtime challenges when he was a kid. His chin juts forward and he folds his arms, a cartoon of anger. Rosa gets up to stand next to him. Her eyes send me lightning bolts, dark brows furrowing into the top of her nose.

I glare back. "Either abide by our rules or move out. If you're not going to finish law school, we'll withdraw our support." I can't believe I said that.

"Don't be ridiculous. You can't work in a convenience store. It's too dangerous," says Maury.

My face doesn't show it, but I'm thinking the same thing. The Jewish mother in me moves to the front of the battlefield, my emotional armor riddled with holes. For heaven's sake, I wouldn't let him play Pop Warner football. Hasn't some social psychologist wondered why all the Jewish kids join golf and tennis and hardly ever the football team? Convenience store represents linebacker to me. I'm sick over this conflict.

Rosa pipes up. "Michael, I'm leaving you and your crazy family. My parents would never treat me this way." She exits the room sure-footed. Does she wish she were Hera who could change me into a magpie or a boar? The door slams to her room.

I cave. I put my head down and start to sob. I can't hold back. As soon as Maury gets up to comfort me, Michael takes off. I hear arguing, and then silence. It's quiet for a few minutes. I calm myself, remembering Glee's warning. Wives are jealous of the way sons feel about their mothers. I'm not sure he loves me right now, but I know there is competition.

A diva-sized tantrum erupts from the room. Something gets thrown against the wall and breaks. I decide not to hang around waiting for them to emerge. I retreat upstairs to grade papers and eat an apple. I turn the TV on low and wait for the news. Maury joins me and props up his pillows. After a few local disaster stories about loose bear cubs desperate for water and an interview with a local podiatrist about why women shouldn't wear high heels, our television screen fills up with a mat of black hair and a wide mouth that looks familiar.

"Our young people are being unduly influenced by renegade teachers who promote alternative lifestyles. These unnatural behaviors are not in the Bible. I introduced a bill that eliminates programs not part of the core curriculum. Like Women's Studies. Let's get back to the basics." She looks triumphant with her head held high.

"Miss Boudreaux, what about your past legislation to eliminate evolution in the schools that failed by a narrow margin?" asks the young reporter with big earrings and blond streaks in her hair.

"I'm the education expert. My own daughter was subjected to subversive ideas and forced to go to a gay bookstore. It has to stop. Just like Black Studies years ago, Women's Studies is an idea whose time has come and gone."

"Thank you very much." The adorable reporter clutches her microphone and fills up our screen. "That was Flora Boudreaux from the steps of the capital and this is Brandi Smith signing off. Back to you, Ron."

Maury grabs the remote to mute the sound. We're stunned. Flora's on a rampage with her monkey hair and I'm the meat. Maury touches my arm.

"It'll be okay, honey. Remember the rabbi said, *yie tov*? It will turn out all right."

"The legislature is going to cancel my ticket." I'm devastated. It doesn't matter now whether I change Tiffany's grade or not. The phone rings at what is late for Arizona and mid-evening for the rest of the country.

"OhmiGod! Did you see Flora Boudreaux on the news?" April's squeal jolts me. "Does that mean you won't be teaching anymore? She's a wacko! Steve says you could sue. You might not win, but you'll get lots of publicity for the college. What's with her hair, anyway?"

"I'm shocked. I don't think publicity is what Dean Gruber is after, so it's good that at least she didn't mention the name of the college."

"What are you going to do?" asks April.

I watch Maury's chest moving up and down in rhythm. He's gone.

"I don't know."

12

THE ROOM AT THE RITZ FILLS WITH MEN IN DARK SUITS, their ties loosened from work, and women in St. John knits hiked above their knees. Some carry Coach or Vuitton briefcases, chat on cell phones or check the latest electronic devices. It looks like a business meeting of people who want to impress one another with how busy they are. I recognize a few of Phoenix's finest amidst the dark paneled walls, silk flower arrangements, and plush carpeting.

The Buddy MacKenzies arrive, newly remarried according to the *Fashionista* "Rumors and innuendos" column in the local society paper. The large bauble dangling from a gold chain around her neck lets everyone know he paid a price for leaving her the first time. A few enormous men strut by in tight, un-tucked silk shirts and flashy gold jewelry. Maury whispers they're sports heroes from our local teams. A society doyenne, her blue-rinsed hair piled high, swishes by in a leopard print swing coat, white satin cuffs rolled to her elbows.

I recognize Slim Dudberry and his wife, Margarita, from their weight loss center advertising on TV. *Try our guaranteed weight loss program and they'll be callin' you Slim, too.* Their commercials annoy me almost as much as the chubby guy with the mortgage business who calls himself the loan arranger. The abomination of his wife standing there as Tonto in drag must offend most of our citizens. An outcry from Native Americans changed the name of our freeway called the Squaw Peak to Piestewa Parkway. (Squaw being slang for slut, someone in the legislature brought up the issue to honor the first woman killed in the Iraq War. People still call it the Squaw Peak, an insulting monument to our forebears' heritage.) From where Maury and I sit in the back of the room I can make out Glee, April, their husbands, and Tuni. No Ellis yet.

The people-watching ends with the entrance of officials who remind me of the Price Waterhouse accountants at the Miss America Pageant. Navy suits march in, hair slicked back, documents under their arms, and take over the front row. Tuni approaches the podium in a body-conscious rust silk suit, her wild red hair tamed into a ponytail with a demure bow. She taps the microphone with a finger.

"I want to welcome you all here tonight." Her accent captivates the crowd. "So many of you have expressed interest in our pro-ject that we decided to disseminate the information to you in the most professional way possible. As you know this is an exciting time for TuniEl. We're thrilled to have such wonderful support. At this time I'd like to bring up the partner in all aspects of my life, Ellis Sterling."

Ellis, in a navy blazer, white silk shirt open at the neck and gray pants, runs up the aisle from the back like a movie star being called to accept an award. A bit too theatrical I think for a business presentation, but I've never been to one of these. His silver hair and impeccable grooming make him the center of attention as he leans into the wood podium with the Ritz's logo on the front.

"Thank you, Tuni. Isn't she lovely?" He waits for applause. "Welcome. Welcome to all of you who have been so supportive through the stops and starts of this pro-ject. I know some of you are new so allow me to review a brief history of our exclusive Vatican-inspired gift line, which we call, The Ecclesiastes Pro-ject."

After his explanation of how they generated the idea and arranged licensing through the Vatican, he asks for the lights to be lowered. A PowerPoint slide show with Ellis' red laser beam guides us through charts and graphs and an array of magnificent artwork. The crowd oohs and aahs at paintings, friezes, tapestries, sculptures and icons from the centuries. When he's finished and the lights return, Ellis calls up two accountants who explain the investment and how the money will be used. They lose my left brain after they pass out packages filled with numbers. I glance through to see columns down the left side with headings of assets, liabilities, stockholder's equity and down the right side of the page, numbers. Lots of large numbers. Maury fidgets a little, but with the rest of the audience, he's consumed with this worldwide adventure that's going to see angel cornices sold in the jungles of the Amazon. Actually, a report on CNN said even Avon is being sold there so what do I know? My mini-movie camera trips out on two Masai women in Kenya, their heads wrapped in red turbans, comparing their cherub doorknockers stuck in the mud of their cow dung *manyattas*.

"Our special treat tonight is ten slides from our new line. Lights, please," says Ellis.

The room darkens once again for a presentation of gift

prototypes. First, we view a slide of the actual art piece and then we see a decorator item no one really needs created from it. The audience makes sounds of approval as close-ups of a rococo shape of a frieze or an icon evolves into a vase or wall sconce. A museum-class show captivates even the most plebian. When the lights come on, the audience applauds. Ellis thanks everyone and repeats the deadline for participation in two weeks.

"Our accountants will be in contact with you and we look forward to having you on board. This is a most unique opportunity. Your participation may insure your family's solvency for decades to come. Thank you for attending. Good night," says Ellis. He removes the tiny microphone from his blazer's lapel.

The room empties, people filing out with their white packets, the TuniEl logo emblazoned on the outside in gold letters.
Glee spots me and steps up her pace. Her tomato-red sarong, drapes across the front revealing a hint of bosom, her curls pulled into a bunch in top of her head.

"What did you think?" she asks with enthusiasm. April joins us, oblivious to the stares of the gigantic sports figures surveying her body packed into a bright pink mini-dress. Her backless heels are the same color and make her three inches taller. I pull myself out of my frumpy posture.

"Interesting," I offer. Maury stands next to me, his hands in his pockets, silent.

Steve, April's husband, looks like he came from court in a navy pin-striped suit, white shirt, its collar unbuttoned, and a multi-colored silk tie around his neck. He sidles over to Maury, a look of knowing on his face. "Maury, say something. Does this look like a hot deal or what?"

"I don't know," says Maury, a bit glum. "Jean and I have to talk about it."

"Maury-man, this is the big one we've all been waiting for. Once they fill the spots, you won't be able to get in. They'll raise, oh, probably ten mil by the end of this week and by closing they'll have twenty-five million. Don't miss this." Steve's motorcycle tan shines bronze in the lights. A strand of sun-bleached hair falls onto his forehead.

Steve pulls Maury aside, his arm around his shoulder. I hear him say, "Look, if you want me or Ted to front you the money, just say so."

Oh God. How humiliating. I freeze. A sudden surge of foul taste erupts in my mouth. Maury will be furious. He has so many things to be angry about he'll be silent for days. Everyone knows they changed the rules on docs in the middle of the game then took away the rulebook. They're even talking about cutting Medicare reimbursements.

Glee offers that investors get some of their money back early. But I wonder how much. Maybe this is what we've been looking for, a rescue to catapult us toward retirement. And parlay Michael and Rosa into a place of their own. And start a college fund for the grandbaby.

We move through the foyer. I notice clumps of people discussing the presentation, including Tonto and her Loan Arranger. Outside we hug good-bye. While we wait for valet to bring our cars, Tuni and Ellis come out beaming, arms filled with extra folders and boxes of slides.

"Thank you for coming tonight. Big success, don't you think?" asks Tuni. "Darling, you were brilliant," she says to Ellis. She leans over to kiss him on the cheek.

April says, "I can see it as an IPO. Look what Starbucks and Krispy Krème have done. Very entrepreneurial. I'm just wondering about the secular market in eastern Europe and--." Our sporty Le Baron convertible comes, not too flashy among the Mercedes and other fancy cars, before we hear all of April's answer.

Maury hunches forward in worry on the drive home. "I can't believe Steve said such a thing to me. Does he want the whole world to know we're in a cash flow crunch? Jean, did you tell your friends anything?" He sounds angry.

"No. I never said anything to Glee or April."

"I need to think about this," he says after a long period of silence. That means staring at the golf channel for a few hours.

13

AFTER A BORING DEPARTMENT MEETING where Megan ignored me on a cool Friday I grade papers in my teacher's cubicle. The assignment was to write about personal freedom in Margaret Atwood's *The Handmaiden's Tale*, a ponderous topic for undergraduates. I like them to reach. Also, they can't buy this kind of essay on the internet. I change the topics every semester.

"May I come in?" asks a small voice beyond my semi-soundproof cave.

"Yes?"

A petite, sparrow of a student with hair parted on the side gelled to smooth it back steps through the door in baggy jeans and a faded rock T-shirt. "Miss Rubin, I'm Callie, Doris' friend."

"Have a seat, Callie." I wave her to the one regulation chair in my pocket of space. She sits down and puts her beat-up backpack on the floor. I search her face, but don't remember her from any of my classes.

"I came because of Doris."

"What's the matter?" When she doesn't respond, just stares at me through her dark lashes, I say, "She was supposed to come by and then she never showed up. I missed the last appointment because of a family emergency. Is she okay?"

"Not exactly." She pauses, her doe eyes wide with fear. "She tried to kill herself though she didn't do a very good job of it swallowing a bunch of pills and Ex-Lax. Sure made her sick." Callie's eyes brim with tears.

"I'm shocked. How awful," I exclaim, stabbed by guilt. Could I have stopped her? Why would Doris, who's always so cheerful, try to kill herself? "When did this happen? Is she in the hospital?" My barrage of questions shoots arrows of agony through me. Doris, one of the brightest students I've taught, came to see me and I didn't have time for her. On our previous visit she seemed excited about finishing college and exploring law school.

"She's in Safford now and had to drop her classes for this semester. She just wanted me to come by and tell you she's okay in case you heard about it from someone else. I've gotta go now." Callie stands up, backpack over her shoulder.

"Wait a minute. How can I contact her? Why did she do it?" I feel terrible, so preoccupied with my hormonal daughter-in-law, menacing Megan and financial worries.

"She doesn't want me to say. She's staying with her brother cause her family's in Texas. I'll see her when I go home for Thanksgiving. I'll ask her if it's okay to give out her number. Bye." Callie lifts her hand in a child-like wave and leaves.

I sit for a few minutes to reflect on Doris and why she would do such a thing. I don't know her well, but she seemed well-adjusted. I close up my papers. I'm no longer in the mood to correct spelling errors. Perhaps I can track her down through the dean's office.

Olive is not thrilled to see me since I've interrupted her Slim Fast lunch. She says the files are all on disk. I'll have to come back next week because the person in charge of that area is out with the flu.

"Should I tell the dean you were here?" she asks, her pinched face anxious for scoop.

"You can tell Dean Gruber I stopped by and my decision is the same."

Olive smirks at me with the straw in her mouth.

I leave, troubled about Doris. As I drive home a ferris wheel spins my head around conversations I've had with her and I can't find any clues. Nothing. She's an intelligent girl looking for her purpose. Maybe the reality of coming from a small town and moving to the sixth largest city was too much for her. I don't know much about her family. They must be so upset. Problems with your children are the worst. Was there anything I could have done?

I walk into my house, preoccupied. Maury makes an effort to comfort me when I tell him about Doris, but I'm feeling awful. Then I look outside through our glass doors. Toilet paper and dog turds grace the patio. The downstairs commode is stopped up. Am I the only one who notices? The back yard decoration requires a call to a plumber, who, Maury points out to me, makes more per hour than he does. Of course no one can come until tomorrow and it's double because it's Saturday.

"Lady, if you're the ones with the oleander trees eating your pipes, we're not coming out," a gruff voice tells me.

I hang up and ask Maury, "Is there any way to disguise our ten-foot oleander hedge?"

He peers at me over the top of his reading glasses, "Unless these guys are sub-normal, and I don't think they are because they figured out how to make a six-figure income without going to med school, they'll notice all the pink and white flowers littering our driveway."

"Oh." After I call a different plumber, the phone rings and Maury returns to his paper.

"Jean?" Glee cries out with enthusiasm. "We're having the most amazing speaker over at Church of Joy. You've got to come."

"Glee, I have a plumbing crisis on top of a few other stressful situations. Thanks anyway. I think I'll pass." I move around the kitchen table to gather newspapers and half-filled coffee cups, the phone in the crook of my neck. The sink's full. Rosa sits at one end of the table in a white chenille bathrobe that barely closes, reading a letter from her mother. She hasn't combed her hair today. My ever-distracted Maury kisses my forehead as he leaves for the hospital after a search for his glasses, keys and phone. I'm invisible.

Glee goes on. "I'm concerned about your mental health. Come and listen. April and Tuni have already said yes. Ted's out of town at a building supply trade show. Come on. It'll be a girl's night out. We'll go to T.Cook's."

I sigh. I don't want to go. I look at the mess outside and Rosa in her bathrobe. What the hell. I deserve a break. T. Cook's is one of my favorite restaurants with a two-week reservation waiting list. I'm abandoning ship. Let my Mexican Princess wait for Roto Rooter. I put all the glasses on the counter next to the sink.

"Okay. I'll go. But if it's really bad, can we leave?" I change the position of the phone while I count out my herbal supplements.

"Just wait and see. It's going to be fabulous." Glee knows I'll dismiss any of the hype surrounding this latest enlightened individual so she skips the embellishments. I suppose I'm lucky. Only your dearest friends worry about your soul.

"Okay. What should I wear?" I ask.

"Scottsdale casual," Glee says and hangs up.

What does that mean? Probably something in silk or linen. In my bedroom I begin the great closet stare. Black is always safe.

That evening Glee greets me at the entrance of the restaurant in a khaki safari suit with a myriad of pockets, a leopard purse on her shoulder and zebra sling-backs. A costume for eating meat. Her hair flies wildly in an aura around her head. Gold bangle bracelets wind around her wrists like a kid's fourteen-karat-gold slinky.

April arrives in her going-to-a-seminar outfit, a fitted purple suit with a jeweled rose pin that nestles in her plunging neckline. Our air kisses suspend mid-flight so no one smears any make-up.

Tuni, in a pumpkin cashmere dress, sweeps into the loggia area, breathless from rushing.

"What's wrong, honey?" asks Glee, touching Tuni's arm.

"We're swamped with our pro-ject." She relaxes and smiles at us. "I'm ready for a toddy." A statuesque blonde shows us to our seats. We all order white wine except for Tuni who drinks Dewar's.

"What's happening with you?" Glee asks me across the table.

I place my wine in front of me, twirling the glass' stem. When I look up my eyes meet Glee's. "My department head is furious with me, the dean thinks I'm a recalcitrant fool, Flora, the legislative pariah, wants to cancel my ticket, one of my favorite students tried to commit suicide with Ex-Lax. I have a plumbing crisis and my home has been invaded by alien slobs, one of whom prays to saints in Spanish. Other than that, everything's fine."

"Oh, Jean. I'm so sorry," says Glee. She reaches for my hand.

"What's the biggest problem? Home or work?" asks April, her luscious mouth outlined with two different colored pencils.

I think for a minute. "Work. I'm getting used to sharing our space and I am going to get a grandkid out of the deal, although I think about what our relationship will be like if his mother hates me." I smile. I don't want to be a downer for the group. "Maury says it'll all work out."

Tuni raises her glass for a toast. "To success in all endeavors," she says clunking her glass against ours.

We're interrupted by the waiter. "I'm Stefan and I'll be your server tonight. What would you charming ladies like to order?" Our Adonis poises his pen over a pad of paper. After he takes our selections but not before he is grilled on what's in the sauces (he's instructed to leave them off), what's in the house salad dressing (he's instructed to bring it on the side), and to save something chocolate on the dessert tray, he slides away.

Glee says to me, "I can't believe you're going to be the first one in our group to be a grandmother." She looks at me misty-eyed.

"Neither can I." I put a bite of warm roll smothered in butter in my mouth, not as enamored by the idea as Glee.

"Are the kids all set for the baby? Do they need stuff? I'd be happy to have a shower for them," offers Glee.

"Thanks, you're a sweetheart, but no. We don't have room for one more thing and as of yet, there's no baby's room. His mama needs a job so they can move out after the baby arrives. How is it that none of my kids has a real job?"

"What do you mean?" asks Tuni.

"My daughter's finishing her masters degree, her husband, Gus, invents a new business every three months, Michael's in law school and Rosa's incubating a baby."

"We need some help at the plant. Can your daughter-in-law do data entry?" asks Tuni.

"I don't know, but I can assure you I'll find out." The   w i n e relaxes my shoulders.

Then April shares some Scottsdale gossip. "Remember Maggie?" Glee raises her eyebrows at the mention of a woman who made a play for Ted a few years ago. "She's still in-between husbands, so she borrowed money from three different people to have her boobs done!"

We bombard her with questions like why did she have to go to three different people and how does she look now, but Glee admonishes us to finish eating so we can leave for the Church of Eternal Joy.

After a ride past estates semi-hidden by hedges, we arrive at the church, a converted bank from the savings and loan debacle of the Eighties. Glee, our impresario, guides us inside, smiling and nodding to other people. She moves us from the somber lobby down a hallway. April trails behind to view children's crayon drawings from Sunday school while Glee, in full animation, hands waving with excitement, bangle bracelets tinkling, hustles us toward the lecture hall.

It's a cavernous room painted hospital mint-green. Except for the chairs, a podium and a table, it's bare. I'm surprised at the absence of religious items. The beige vinyl floor shows scuff marks. Glee insists we sit on the metal chairs toward the front. I protest and let Glee know I prefer the back. I don't like to sit so close. It's not a good vantage point for people watching.

Glee says, hands on hips, "How can you become fully engaged if you're not where the action is?"

Glumly, I move into the spot she indicates and try to look beyond the tall man with a comb-over blocking my view. Glee settles next to me while Tuni sits next to her. April minces in last on her beaded Blahniks, squeezing down the row to sit next to me, her ostrich bag held high.

People file in. An overweight man with suspenders takes up two chairs. An ant of a woman with frosted hair in a turquoise shantung suit and skinny heels clip-clops by us. Young lovers with matching two-tone crew cuts hold hands and slither into the front row, jeans hung low on their hips. Tattoos of barbed wire double-wrap around their upper arms.

In the front a pious young man in a plain white shirt and brown tie, his face clear as a baby's, wears a lavalier microphone on his collar. He tells us how honored The Church of Eternal Joy is to have Dr. Phillipa Blackhead as their speaker. When he reads her credentials and publications, I don't recognize any of them. "But, first, let's have a testimonial about Dr. Blackhead's marvelous intuitive work. I'd like you to meet Grace Feebus, a long-standing member of our church. In fact, Grace was with us when we still called ourselves The Eternal Ecstasy. Isn't that right, Grace?"

A "Yes, Brother" comes from behind me. I'm wedged in my chair and can't turn, but I hear chairs scrape as a woman makes her way to the front.

The young man continues, "She has the unique situation of having her husband live in Alaska for salmon fishing season while she keeps house for her ex-husband here. Isn't that a wonderful example of getting along? Grace?" Scattered applause breaks out.

I expect a hussy in red to slink to the front, competition for April. Instead, I get a short, middle-aged lady without undergarments under an Apache-inspired print dress, sporting a gray bowl haircut. Her unsupported breasts sway as her short legs carry her to the center. Barely able to see over the podium, Grace grabs its edges with pudgy fingers.

"I want to tell you how much Dr. Blackhead's workshop enhanced my life." Her voice is scratchy, as though she ate sandpaper for dinner. "Before I took it I was filled with penis envy." A few women in front gasp, including the turquoise suit, her blonde head shaking no.

"That's right, honey," Grace says directing her comments to a lady in a Hawaiian muu-muu. "Our world is all screwed up and I was, too, until Phillipa showed me solid techniques to relieve stress."

Glee elbows me at the word stress. I purse my lips together turning my mouth downward. She whispers, "If you don't release your stress, you're going to crack up."

Our podium Pocahantas continues, "I envied my ex because he could have any job he wanted. I drove him away with my resentment and nagging. After we divorced I met Dennis and we took Phillipa's workshop to ensure that our relationship would endure. Besides, I didn't want that penis envy to sneak back."

A titter erupts from the listeners. Her smile becomes a smirk. I can see she relishes using the word penis for shock value. "It may seem like a strange living arrangement to you, but in salmon season Dennis's happy fishing and I'm happy cooking for my ex."

The audience applauds as Grace moves back to her seat, her tummy and bosom jiggling together like a jellied parfait on a kid's school lunch tray. An angular design of arrows that stretches across her rear reminds me of a cartoon war with the Indians winning.

Mr. Straight Guy comes back to center stage. "It's my pleasure to introduce an extraordinary psychologist, author, speaker and dear friend, one of the greatest minds of the twenty-first century. The author of, *Change Your Underwear, Change Your Life,* the book that's one of the most significant treasures of personal growth, the inventor of Neuro-psychological Escapes, a revolutionary program to empower you. Let's give a warm welcome to Dr. Phillipa Blackhead."

The audience applauds wildly after the hype. Glee's face is filled with rapture. Tuni and April look more skeptical, but applaud anyway.

A very tall woman with broad shoulders wearing a knee- length flowered dress and a black blazer takes two strides into the middle of the floor. She waves her arms in a victory greeting. Her hands are huge.

Dr. Blackhead has us breathe with our eyes closed. "The breath is the center of all life." I almost fall asleep after the big meal. "This is the LAB technique I invented. That's right. L-A-B. Loose. Now take a deep breath. Act. Imagine yourself taking action and destroying all that ails you. Breathe. Let a big sigh out and blow away your troubles."

Unfortunately, the man in front of me misinterprets what to let out. His loud noise from the wrong end makes me giggle. Glee pokes me and gives me her shush look.

"Don't you all feel more relaxed?" our speaker demands.

A murmur breaks out in the audience. I glance at Glee. Her eyes are closed, posture erect and chin jutted out in defiance, dark curls *boinging* from her head. Relaxed? I'm almost comatose from the food, wine and the deep breathing. I wouldn't know a stress neuron from a marauding elephant right now.

April's chin falls forward as though she's hypnotized. I tap her exposed thigh and she opens her eyes in confusion. "Oh, thanks. I played tennis today and walked the dogs. I'm wiped." She sits up straight, her feet next to one another, expensive shoes in alignment.

Tuni whispers across all of us to April, "Love your suit."

"Thanks. It's Escada." April smiles then turns to pay attention. Tuni's arms remain folded across her chest. To my surprise her face hardens as our speaker commands the room. Dr. Blackhead's style, one where she takes giant steps across the floor, includes expansive hand gestures and bending forward from the waist to shout into the faces of the people in the front row. I think I can see a few drops of spittle eject from her mouth. Thank goodness Glee didn't make us sit there.

Phillipa's feet look enormous, pushed into black leather pumps. I
wear a nine so hers must be size thirteen boats as she clomps around,
jabbing her finger into the air and crouching forward for the first
row victims. Then she pulls herself up to her full height and barrels
up the aisle toward the back of the room. Boy, someone must have
fed her mega-vitamins. And her voice. It's louder than any football
coach's yelling at a kid who ran the wrong way down the field.

"We have a film of our lives in our minds, a constant reminder
of our pain, playing a double feature over and over again. We take
the es-cu-lator upstairs to the balcony every day."

Wait a minute! Did she just mispronounce escalator? Now I'm
paying attention.

"But we can break the cycle of torture."

The female part of the crew-cut team in the front row begins to
sob. Come on. She can't be that into this. I look around. People are
captivated by the horse-woman of the apocalypse, including April
and Glee.

Except Tuni. I watch her eyes graze the room. I wonder what
she's thinking.

"You heard what Grace said about how her life has improved?
You can do the same. Maybe you don't have the time for hours of
therapy, but I bet you've got the money for my twenty CD series for
$495. It's the e-pit-tomb of neuro-psychology research."

"She mispronounced epitome," I whisper to Glee as I speak out
of the side of my mouth.

"Don't be so critical. She's a marvelous teacher. You need this,"
she hisses at me, then turns her face back to the front, her face beatific.

Glee gravitates to these people because she looks for the missing pieces from her childhood. She believes the right combination of workshops or gurus will have the answer. What a sweet, naïve soul. We tease her, but she doesn't care. She's convinced there is a Holy Grail in Scottsdale somewhere.

"Reinvent yourself! Script your life into the film you want," Dr. Blackhead implores. "The world is changing every day and you can, too. Recent scientific findings show that our universe is not shaped like a potato chip or curled like a ball. That it is, indeed, flat. Cosmetologists around the world affirm what we already know."

Wait a minute. She means cosmologists, scientists who study the earth, not cosmetologists who dye people's hair. This woman is a fraud. She doesn't know anything. I start to rise to share my outrage when Glee pulls my arm back into the hard seat.

The Amazon woman continues, ignoring my potential outburst. "Breathe. Just breathe. Your life is a movie and you control the script. When you get to the parts of your life you don't want, just erase!" She thrusts a finger into the air for punctuation.

She drones on about the director of our life (us) and the producers (our parents) and the cast (the other family members) until I can't stand it. If my life's a movie, it must be a low-budget, Ed Wood special.

"My extensive research has been done on prisoners because, unlike my parents who deserted me, they couldn't leave. I encourage you to take the challenge and buy my CDs. I'm offering them at a discount. They'd be $1000 if you bought them at a bookstore or online, but today, one time only, they're $495. A bargain at any price.

How can you not want to improve the film of your life, change the credits, cast new talent? Let's all breathe together. Remember LAB. Loose. Act. Breathe."

Applause breaks out from the converts in the front row. Wait 'til I tell Maury about this.

"Didn't you love it?" Glee turns to me in excitement, her hands clasped to her enhanced bosom. She pats my arm, not waiting for an answer. "I'm getting the CDs and you can listen to them after I do." She hustles off to join the crowd surrounding Dr. Blackhead, who waves her arms and then emits a loud whistle, two fingers in her mouth, to get everyone's attention.

Breathless from her performance, she says, arms over her head, surrounded by the crowd that only comes up to her chest, "I forgot. Ten percent of all proceeds from sales go to the church, so make sure you get yours now." The crowd surges forward again.

I sit there dumbfounded, April staring straight ahead, as the room erupts in confusion. Tuni stands up to follow the Hawaiian muumuu lady who elbows her way into the knit of devotees around Phillipa. "Tuni, are you buying the CDs?" I ask. I thought she was smart.

"Yes. I think Ellis will find them quite interesting." Tuni's hand touches her throat in a wistful way. "We're always receptive to information for our growth." She moves off to follow the path of the muumuu lady.

Glee returns to us beaming, hugging a boxed set with Phillipa's headshot photo encased in plastic. Tuni comes back a few minutes later holding two sets of CDs. That's a thousand dollars down the drain. Uh oh. Drains. I hope our toilets are fixed.

As we walk to the car, Glee says, "Wasn't that wonderful?"

April murmurs something about not needing any help. "Frankly, a massage at Camelback Spa would be better," she says with mincing mini-steps. "But, thanks for inviting me. I'll call you tomorrow after my trainer leaves."

Tuni responds to Glee's comment, her voice awed. "What I can't get over is how many people bought CDs. I figured out she made about sixty thousand dollars. That's not all that much money, but it's impressive for a few hours work." Her accent sounds clipped and business-like. She hugs us good-bye, waving as she moves toward her car. "Enjoy your Thanksgiving. Ellis and I are off to Saint Barts."

Glee and I trek across the parking lot, the cool November air giving me a chill. She asks, "What did you think?"

I don't want to hurt her feelings. She's a generous friend who means well, but I doubt Dr. Blackhead will solve my problems. Judging from the enthusiasm in the room, a lot of people think she will. "Not my style. I couldn't handle the mispronounced words."

"You're too critical. Forget you're a teacher. Be open to solutions."

April and Tuni wave to us as they pull out of the parking lot in their Mercedes.

We approach Glee's car. "Glee, Doctor Blackhead's very tall. Probably six foot two. I wonder why she wore heels."

"Well, if you must know. Phillipa used to be Phillip."

I'm incredulous. "Are you kidding me? She used to be a he?" A transsexual psychologist?

Glee looks at me across the hood of her car, keys in hand, "It's not so odd. She says it gives her better insight because she's experienced both." In the car she finds the ignition in the darkness on the first try. "That way she understands her clients male and female sides, penis envy and vagina longing." She says the last part smiling at me as the Mercedes engine leaps to a roar.

14

"Is this Tiffany girl so important you're willing to sacrifice your job?" Maury asks, looking at me over the top of his glasses.

I feel my stomach tighten. Is Maury doubting me? "Are you challenging my decision not to change her grade?" I'm defensive. I've had tinges of insecurity buried in my bravado before, but if my champion deserts me, will I abandon ship?

"I'm saying you're going against the current." He pauses because I give him my annoyed look, one of pressed lips and extra wrinkles. "I just want to find out what's driving you."

My face burns. "She didn't do the work. She never even came to see me. Why should I be manipulated to do something against my principles?"

He pulls off his glasses. "If you get fired you won't get hired anywhere. And for what? Some twit with the I.Q. of a pea."

He doesn't say it, but the word salary looms. It's true. There aren't tons of jobs for Women's Studies instructors steeped in Gender Equity. "What are my choices? Give in? Megan's been looking for an excuse to get rid of me. But I can't give in now that I've made such a strong stand." With angry drama I announce, "I'm going to bed."

I grab a *Newsweek* out of the bowl in the center of the kitchen table and retreat upstairs. I can't concentrate on the political cartoons. I slap the magazine onto the bed as Maury comes into the room. He stretches out on top of the duvet and takes my hand. My anger begins to retreat. We can't go to sleep not speaking to each other.

"I wasn't challenging you. I was just trying to get to the depth of your convictions," says Maury.

"You know how committed I am. The stress is killing me. I wouldn't do it if I didn't believe it was the right thing to do." My voice changes. "I hoped that at least you'd be behind me no matter what."

He scoots across the bed gently pushing Amber out of the way to hold me.

"I am with you no matter what. If you've thought it through and believe you're doing the right thing, go for it. Don't change anyone's grade. Ever. Especially if their mother wants to cancel your ticket. Even if their mother says you're the cause of moral decay."

I laugh as he kisses me. My waves of anger subside.

The next morning before class I return to the dean's to find a number for Doris. No luck. I'll have to wait until she contacts me. I teach with a dark cloud over my head.

When I return home the lack of joy makes me feel like a stranded armadillo on a steamy Texas blacktop. Maury and I retreat to our bedroom like mischievous teenagers. We even smuggle snacks. I haven't hidden Mallomars under my bed since I was a teenager.

Michael and Rosa stay to themselves for a few days, emerging to join us for dinner one evening and propose a truce. She cooks Mexican food and something from my old cookbook, a combination of tortilla chicken soup with taco matzo balls. It's awful. She's still sensuous looking but resembles an errant ballet dancer with turned out feet balancing a balloon-belly.

I'm a lifeless zombie who stumbles through my day, especially with the late night watch I'm keeping on our local cable channel where Ms. Boudreaux appears with frequency banging her conservative drum. So far her bill has only been introduced in committee. The legislature is obsessed with an alternative fuel bill that's going to clean up our environment. Maury says someone's going to get their pockets lined and it'll cost the taxpayers millions.

One afternoon Rosa joins me at the patio table. I put down the papers I've been grading. She looks down with a serious expression before she says, "You know I've been wrestling with religion. I loved my Catholic upbringing, but I'm in a different situation now. Michael and I need to be of one mind."

I take a deep breath. Does she want the baby baptized?

"I've been studying and I want something larger than myself." She pauses to take a breath. Her eyes, intense, widen. "I'm ready to be a Jew."

For a moment I'm wary. Is this a trick? Don't tell me. It's a ploy for more maternity clothes. But her open face, shows a sign of relief and expectation. She's sincere. She's made a decision. Now I'd be lying if I didn't confess my body and soul didn't leap out of my chair with a hooray. "Oh, honey, are you sure this is what you want?"

"Yes, I discussed it with my momma and poppa and my grandmother. In the beginning they were against it, but now that I'm sure, they support me. I kept worrying about burning in hell, but then I thought about Jesus and I don't think he'd do that. It's taken me a while to become comfortable with the idea. I want our family to be the same faith. My mother said they love me for who I am. Besides, I don't think Jesus will miss one more Catholic."

I push back the heavy patio chair with a scraping sound and move around the table to hug her. Rosa stands up. We embrace each other, her head resting on my shoulder. I can't get too close because of her basketball belly, so I stroke her hair, highlights gleaming in the sun.

When we break apart her dark eyes stare into mine. I can barely breathe.

"I'm going inside for a nap." Her bedroom slippers shuffle toward the open family room door. I grab the phone to call Maury.

Lara and Gus arrive early in the week for Thanksgiving. With Rosa in the guest room and Michael camped out everywhere, I put them in our cozy home office with its Murphy bed. The top of my desk becomes their dresser.

"Rosa, I'm so happy to finally have a sister," says Lara, sitting next to her on the family room sofa. I chop celery for the stuffing at the kitchen table. I'd rather have them establish a relationship than help me at the moment.

"I come from a big family, but I have room in my heart for another sister," says Rosa.

"How does it feel to be carrying another life inside you?" Lara sounds younger than she really is.

"It's awesome. Quick, put your hand here. The baby's moving."

Lara moves closer to place her hand on Rosa's stomach. "Wow. I can't believe it. When do you go for your ultrasound so I know if I have a niece or a nephew?"

"Soon," answers Rosa. "But I have an important announcement to make at dinner." She gets up and disappears into her room, her hair swinging down her back. Amber's my only kitchen company since Maury, Michael and Gus have been missing for hours scouting stereo equipment at the only open store in Phoenix. Before they left Maury helped me get the enormous pink-pimpled turkey into the oven. I've been basting it with onion soup all day. The aroma permeates the house. Since I skipped lunch, I keep salivating. If we don't eat soon, I'll need a bib. Amber's already left a slobber spot at my feet.

My parents arrive with Maury, Michael, Gus and a bag of pills. "Grandma!" yells Lara, jumping up. The prospect of becoming great-grandparents thrills them. They've been goading Lara about Michael being first.

"Okay, everyone wash up. I'm going to carve the turkey," says Maury. We take off in different directions, some to wash hands, others to finish setting the table. I leave to freshen my lipstick and change blouses, stuffing my old one with the gravy stains into the hamper. Once downstairs I direct traffic from the kitchen into the dining room. After two days of cooking and shopping, there's a feast on the table. We join hands, eyes closed, while Maury leads a prayer of thanks that we're all together and healthy.

"Let's eat," says Michael. The first few minutes there's silence with an occasional *mmmm* or *this is so good*. Then conversation starts again.

"Rosa, what's your big announcement?" I ask.

She puts down her fork, looking straight at me. "I feel an affinity for the Jewish people, their customs and history so," she takes a breath, "I've decided to change my name."

"What are you changing it to?" I ask, my fork and knife suspended. My hungry family continues to eat.

"Why didn't you discuss this with me?" asks Michael, his mouth full of turkey, eyebrows arched in surprise.

"Whose name does she want? She can have mine. I'm tired of Florence," says my mother, sawing at her turkey slice with a butter knife.

"Sssh. Let her talk," says Maury. "What's it going to be?"

I think maybe she's going to get rid of Rubin and add all her Spanish names.

With a satisfied grin, she announces, "I've decided to use a Hebrew name. Rivka." She's triumphant.

Rivka? It sounds like she's living on a kibbutz in Israel. Jews have two names from birth, an American one with at least the first initial of the name after a relative who has passed on, and a Hebrew one that corresponds to that. It ensures that the deceased relative will always be remembered. Few Americans use their Hebrew name.

"Have you considered using Rose?" I ask. I've stopped eating.

"No, because I want it to be more ethnic. I like the sound of Rivka Rubin." Her clear, lovely face is confident. "The baby will be here in less than four months. As of today I'm Rivka. I would appreciate all of you calling me by my new name."

"Where's Rivka? Did she call? We haven't heard from her in years," says my father. He's remembering a Hermione Gingold neighbor from long ago named Rivka, her bejeweled harlequin glasses hanging from a rhinestone chain. I explain in his good ear that Rosa is changing her name.

Lara breaks the silence. "Well, Gus and I were going to wait until Sunday, but now seems like a good time, especially since my grandma and grandpa are here." She beams at them.

Uh oh. It couldn't be. Maury and I look at each other.

"What is it?" I anticipate another surprise as a bite of cranberry sauce slides down my throat.

Lara, forever the drama queen, pauses to grab Gus' hand, punching them into the air as a victory symbol, "We're pregnant too!"

A missed drumbeat of silence reverberates around the table. "OhmiGod! That's wonderful!" I scream, pushing out my chair to run around and hug each of them. "Isn't that exciting? Maury, we're going to be grandparents again!"

Maury, stuptified, says nothing. I give him my *say_something* look. "Congratulations. That's wonderful." His voice lacks energy.

I repeat to my parents. "Mom and Dad, Lara's pregnant. You're going to be great-grandparents twice." They look at me bewildered.

"*Mazel tov*, darlings," my mother says. "You're both going to have gorgeous babies."

My father pipes in, "Another baby? Why?" My sentiments exactly.

"We're manufacturing cousins for you," Gus says to Michael

and the newly-crowned Rivka.

"Congratulations, sis. That's awesome!" says Michael, reaching for a hi-five. Rivka beams. I repeat to my parents. "We're getting another soccer player for our team."

When Maury carries in his super-duper secret-spices pumpkin pie, he whispers to me, "How many more HMO's am I going to have to join to support all these grandkids?" Lara and Gus' financial position barely keeps them in rent and food without a baby. She's still in grad school and Gus, ever the entrepreneur, started a remodeling business with a friend's father recently.

Later, during clean up, which takes hours longer than the eating and the preparation, I carry the turkey carcass into the kitchen. Gus shouts at my father who semi-dozes on the sofa, "I've got a great idea. I want to sell organic vegetables on the internet. I can get all the little farmers into a co-op--."

When my kitchen counters reflect nothingness again at one AM, I head upstairs. Maury and I pat Amber, overweight with years of table scraps. She stretches out between us in bed. I let the warm glow of Thanksgiving wash over me. We're going to be grandparents twice in one year. Lara's baby is going to arrive seven months after Rosa's. Rivka's. Where is everyone going to live? The glow shifts to a bright burn. Who is going to pay for all this?

I call Glee and April in the morning to tell them the news. "Don't worry about it," says Glee. "I remember when I was in Taos for a workshop and we meditated near the base of the mountains. The Santa Clara tribe has several generations sharing their pueblos. They manage quite well." She hangs up to attend her Pilates class, a mind-body technique executed on a moving sled. "It's torture, but it makes my abs look like a taut dancers."

I know she's trying to cheer me up, but it doesn't help.

April's words are less encouraging. "If you're going the bubbe route, wear a babushka. Just make it an Hermes or a Chanel."

15

LARA WAKES ME ON THE CELL PHONE Maury purchased for me after Rivka's bleeding scare. "Hi Mom! Guess what? I've made a decision not to use the general hospital. It's too sterile. We've booked the Alternative Holistic Womyn's Clinic so we can use a midwife."

Groggy from a nap, student papers strewn over the bed, I mumble through dry mouth, the miniature phone to my ear. I can't stand the tiny device. Either I forget to turn it on or it rings at the most inopportune times playing the William Tell Overture. Yesterday it rang while I was in the faculty bathroom. I lunged for it in my zippered bag and almost fell off the toilet. I didn't break a leg or drown, but I'll probably be constipated for weeks.

"Mom, are you listening? I can use a birthing ball that gives me a bouncy seat to rock on while I'm in labor. They even have a birthing tub. Gus and I feel it's very important to have the baby come into the world in water with candlelight and Mozart."

"Lara, can I call you back later? I'm not awake yet."

"Sure, Mom. Bye." I roll over into the fetal position crushing some of the papers, collapsing the phone.

The pressure of a financial decision, my job in limbo, my Jennifer Lopez with attitude downstairs, and now Lara's latest scheme for delivery has me spinning. Worse, the end of the semester keeps me late at school with panicky students and papers to grade. I'm a sucker for extra credit.

In recent weeks we observe changes in our household. Rivka gets the house ready for dinner on Friday nights. Neither Maury nor I have been brought up religiously, but if that's what she and Michael want, it's okay with us. She cuts flowers from the garden out back, wraps *challah* bread in a cloth, gets the candles ready, and pulls out *yarmulkas*. We have a multi-colored collection from our time on the bar mitzvah circuit, imprinted with the name and date of the honoree: Ethan Gordon Labovitz, June 14, 1986 or Everett Todd Schmellstein, November 9, 1990. She leads the prayer in halting Hebrew, covering her eyes at the end and motioning her arms inward to welcome the sacred evening.

Sabbath dinner is subdued. Maury rents a movie that we watch after Michael and Rivka leave for temple. It isn't until Saturday morning that we find out *which* temple.

"What's the agenda?" Maury asks, our bodies wrapped spoon-style around one another. The affectionate warmth feels like melted chocolate.

"You've got to fix the sprinklers in the yard. Two trees are dying. The area rugs from the family room and living room need to be dragged outside. They smell of Amber." Amber, curled at the end of the bed, reacts to hearing her name by thumping her tail and crawling to lick us. And I thought our morning breath was bad? "The pool needs work. The tile looks like there's a nest of scummy-slime breeding life from another planet."

"Must you be so descriptive?" Maury turns to face me. "What are you doing today?"

"Don't worry. I've got plenty to keep me busy. Besides trips to Costco, Trader Joe's and the vet to pick up Amber's diet food, I've got to clean out a few drawers in the kitchen and then we both have to tackle the office. We're drowning in papers and--."

"STOP! Tell me one pro-ject at a time," says Maury, mimicking Tuni, pulling the covers over his head.

"Okay. Let's get started." I jump from the bed with unusual enthusiasm.

Rivka, stretched out on what used to be Maury's favorite chair, makes camp reading a book on nursing from the La Leche League. Magazines, coffee, hair accessories and the accoutrements for a pedicure clutter the area. Her toes, splayed with pink foam pieces, shine with brown polish. What contortionist pose did she do to reach them over her sixth month belly?

"Good morning, Rivka," I offer.

"*Buenas dias*," she says, with a rare smile, her mouth and teeth perfection.

In the kitchen I slice grapefruits from our tree, the pink, juicy insides releasing a fresh, citrus smell. Is this what she's going to do all day? Michael left for the law library at the crack of dawn. Her eyes return to her book. I love being ignored.

After breakfast Maury and I launch into our work list. His gardening outfit consists of a Dirtbags T-shirt from Michael's favorite Tucson bar, a water bottle hanging from his baggy shorts, wrap-around sunglasses and a shocking pink baseball cap that says, "Happy

Birthday, I'm 30", a leftover from April's birthday years ago. He forges outside, a bizarre gardening Martian. The neighbors must think he's another strange minority in the diversified city of Tempe.

In my angst to complete everything, I ask Rivka if she'd like to help me with an easy job: cleaning out the kitchen drawers. After all, she's rearranged my kitchen before.

"No, I don't do any work on the Sabbath."

"Since when?" My voice screeches, owl-like. A ball of acid begins to circulate in my stomach.

"Since now." I hear the resolve in her voice. "I decided after services last night I want to switch temples. The reformed one is like church with its guitar music. I've decided to become Orthodox."

Now she's religious? How convenient. I bite my tongue not to ask her motivation. I doubt it's a spiritual calling. "What does Michael say?"

"Michael says he can't be observant with me right now because of his study schedule, but I should do what makes me happy." She bends forward with a groan to pull the pink squishy things from her toes.

I'm acutely aware that now God is focused inside my house and I'm a sinner. Before, I was anonymous. I'm also suspicious. "What changes are you contemplating?"

"Let's bring in the dishes you don't use from the garage. We're not supposed to mix meat and milk on the same shelf in the refrigerator. And we can't put butter on the table at dinner."

She's kosher? Does she have a clue to the inconvenience? My stomach clutches into a medieval spiked ball that rolls toward my chest. The next step is I'll have to be her *shabbos* goy, a person employed to turn on the lights and appliances for observant Jews before crock pots and timers. Elvis was a *shabbos* goy as a young teenager in Memphis. Why do I think of Elvis at the most inappropriate times?

"Rivka, we've never followed the *kashrut* laws. Do you realize it's not just separating the food? You have to shop at special stores to get meat that's been blessed by a rabbi. I don't have time for that."

"You're out anyway so what's one more stop?"

The phone rings next to Rivka. I look at her with expectation. If I reach across her to get it, I'll knock over the brown nail polish. The spiked torture ball rolls upward toward my frontal lobe.

"I don't answer the phone or use any writing utensils on the Sabbath," she says as the phone switches over to voice mail. "God doesn't want me taking any messages except from Him."

Is it too early to have a glass of wine? The spiked instrument sails around my head screaming, "Divine justice." I can hear my ancestors from the ghetto in heaven laughing.

The Monday after Rivka's religious announcement, Maury finds out two more HMO's have dropped him. He comes home for dinner defeated.

"I don't know what I'm going to do. Maybe I should go to work for the enemy." Maury sits at our kitchen table, his head falls forward into his hands. "Jean, I don't know if I can be in the system anymore. If they squeeze me out, and I can't pay my staff, then we're finished."

I've never seen Maury so disconsolate. I leave the spaghetti sauce I've been stirring to comfort him. His practice has been sinking, but I figured we'd stay afloat. "Honey, isn't there something we can do? Another alternative?" I touch his head.

"I don't have many options. One is to let staff go and have you fill in at the office part-time." He picks up his head to look at me with Amber-hopeful eyes.

Me? In a medical office? I can't stand to see anyone in pain or look at anything gushy. If there's one thing I'm not interested in, it's other people's body parts and their fluids. What about my career? How am I going to fit in one more thing? I have enough to do. I don't say all that, although I'm screaming it inside. I want to comfort him.

"What did you have in mind?" The bubbling, spitting tomato sauce decorates my pristine white counters.

"Maybe you could come over in the afternoons and help in the back office, go into the patient rooms with me and free up Mary to go after collections."

I turn to face him, wooden spoon in my hand. "You know I adore you and I'd do anything in his world for you, but do you really want me in the office? I have an aversion to anything that even slightly resembles pus." Maury gives me an I-need-your-help look. I feel selfish and rotten.

"I wouldn't ask you if I didn't think it would make a difference. You could come over after your morning classes. Mary will train you. Just three days a week," says Maury.

I shiver with Willie chills even though I'm warm all over. The steam from the sauce rises and clouds my glasses.

"I'm not suited for this."

"Jean, you're not that big of a wuss. You changed diapers, for Chrissakes!" says Maury. Anger creeps into his voice.

Uh oh. I'd better find a solution fast. Maury gets upset more often lately, especially with all the financial pressure. I don't want it to be with me. "What about her?" I offer. I point my thumb to the dozing Rivka, the same brown polish next to her from days before.

"She's pregnant. She can't be exposed to sick people. Besides, she's got a part-time job with Tuni."

"Oh. And I can?" I ask, my eyebrows arching upward. Damn. I thought that was a good idea. "There must be something else besides drafting me into a short white uniform."

"Unless we find a solution, the Rubin household is going to be taking on water very soon." He pauses. "And, they wear scrub suits in the office, not white uniforms."

Damn again. I pictured myself at least looking sexy as we saved lives together. "I'll cut expenses. We'll eat less. I won't drive as much. I'll ride my bicycle to the college, schlepping my papers in a backpack. I can't work at the office."

"It was only an idea. I'm exploring all options. Maybe I should dump the HMO's in this crazy two-tier system." His eyebrows create a vertical crease.

I perk up. An alternative to smell disgusting things and watch blood ooze? "What is it?" I ask, hopeful for my rescue. Though I know that I'll do whatever it takes to help my prince of a guy. Even if I have to wear a mask and shut my eyes.

"Some of the docs are resigning from the plans, notifying their patients they no longer accept payment from Medicare, HMO's or insurance companies. They're cash only."

"What happens to the patients who can't pay? What's a two-tiered system?" I ask.

"That's the problem. You lose the ones who can't pay out of their own pocket. Nah. I don't think it'll work. The HMO's have made the patients so miserable that people who can afford to, leave the system. The wealthy have one system and the middle class and the poor get another, one where the doctor is rewarded to give them fewer tests and medication. And less time." He sighs. His head falls forward into his hands again.

"Why do people put up with it?" I stir my spaghetti sauce sans meatballs. I didn't have time to buy kosher hamburger so I added mushrooms instead.

"They have no choice."

Rivka wakes up with an exaggerated yawn and stretch. I ask her to set the table, a reluctant participant. I clear papers and glance at *The Arizona Republic*. Our esteemed legislature has focused on an important issue: transportation bill #236 allows us to purchase Ronald Reagan license plates. I can't wait to order one for my car.

The deadline arrives for us to invest in The Ecclesiastices Project. Maury and I have endless discussions as to whether it's a good idea or not. Should we let it pass? What if we regret our decision later? If we do it, should we take money from his pension plan and five thousand I have squirreled away for a vacation, or sell some stocks? Finally, after Steve calls us twice in one night to read us what the numbers look like on our ROI, which I learn means return-on-investment, we say, "Okay. Let's do it."

Even though I know we'll be in big trouble if this doesn't work out, I'm relieved. At least we made a decision. We're going to pull the money together and plunge in with our eyes shut. For the first time in a long time, Maury feels hopeful about our future, a vision of golf and no telephones. I hope I'm in the background with my laptop.

Lara whips up the wind in the hurricane of my life when the phone rings early in the morning.

"Mom? Hi. Is Dad there?"

"He's at the office. What's up?"

"I want to discuss *doulas* with him."

"*Doulas*? What's that?"

"Everyone in Mendicino has one."

Mendicino is the hip art community in northern California I dream of as my refuge. "What's a *doula*? Another birthing device?"

"Mom. No. *Doulas* are guardians of the birth experience."

"What does that mean? They stand over you and wave feathers? *Doula* is Greek for female servant," I add.

"No," says Lara, exasperated with me. "It's a woman who coaches you during the birth experience."

"I thought the husband was supposed to do that."

"Mom, Gus is going to be dealing with a lot of anxiety. A *doula* soothes the mother, using massage and acupressure points. Gus makes me nervous. Athena, who's in great demand, uses aromatherapy."

"How much?"

"That's why I want to talk to daddy." She waits a beat. "I also want to ask him about the placenta."

"What about the placenta?"

"My friend, Mavis, is burying hers."

"What for?" I swing my legs over the edge of the bed.

"Don't get excited, Mom. You dig a hole for the placenta and then plant a fruit tree over it." Her response to my silence is, "It's symbolic. Anyway, tell Dad to call me. I love you. Bye."

A message of *doulas* and placentas will send Maury reeling, especially since he's not enthusiastic about Lara refusing to use a hospital.

An uneasy peace settles over the Rubin household during the holidays. Maury grumbles about American consumerism. We don't celebrate much except for the minor holiday of Chanukah, one that's turned into a major one because of its proximity to Christmas. We keep it simple with candle lighting for eight nights to celebrate the destroyed temple and small gifts.

Rivka gives us plastic placemats with photos of Masada in Israel, a symbol of heroic martyrdom when the Jews chose death over enslavement by the Romans in 70 AD. How can I use them? If Maury looks down at breakfast and sees the ancient fortress after he reads about another sinking HMO, I don't know what he might consider.

16

GLEE HAS US OVER FOR CHRISTMAS EVE DINNER, an opulent affair where we're greeted with Wassail punch and carolers in turn-of-the-century costumes. I watch Rivka's face and our eyes catch. There's no sign of the nostalgia I thought she might feel without her first Christmas since childhood.

She moves next to me. "In Mexico Christmas is different. It's about family being together rather than show." She slips her arm around my waist, the affection a welcome surprise. Maybe I'm not a monster-in-law.

The Barstow home reflects Glee's penchant for over-the-top taste, a Scottsdale Martha Stewart. Beside the eighteen-foot Douglas fir decorated with gold bows and giant balls in her living room, two smaller trees grace the family room and patio. Blinking lights from the other trees twinkle. The fireplace mantle, blanketed with pine boughs, sends a wonderful aroma throughout the room. There are so many candles it looks like she's trying to heat the house. If there's anyone who knows how to create ambiance, it's Glee.

In the dining room a single painting decorates the textured charcoal walls. Large and colorful against a white background, pin lights illuminate the subject from the top. I squint, get closer, and recognize it as a male appendage. Is this one Ted's?

"These place cards are exquisite," I say as I pick up a hand-blown glass star. My first name, scripted in calligraphy on gold-edged paper, is stuck into a slot.

"They were a gift from Tuni," says Glee, pouring water into crystal glasses from a pitcher. Giant kerosene lamps with silver bases line the table in between poinsettia arrangements. The smell of apple pie wafts from the kitchen.

"How did you find the time to do all this?" I wave my arm at the decorations.

She smiles and lowers her voice. "I didn't. I hired people from The Rock."

"You mean the trees and decorations aren't yours?"

"No, I rented them for tonight. They'll be here on December twenty-sixth to dismantle everything." Then, leaning closer, she adds, "I think they borrowed everything from one of the department stores. One of them works in display."

When we're all seated, Della, the owner of the gallery who represents Glee, sits next to me. "Glee says you know the woman who picketed the night of her show." She gazes at the painting.

"I haven't met Flora Boudreaux." I'm not happy about bringing up her name before I have to eat and I mumble under my breath, "But it looks like all that is going to change soon."

Two days earlier a letter arrived from the Dean informing me that a hearing had been set in January for a review of Tiffany's appeal for a grade change. I can't wait. Maury said I should push it aside until after New Year's and not let it ruin the holidays, but it gnaws at me like a rat in garbage.

"An insane woman, but great for publicity," says Della as she dips into her consommé.

After appetizer and salad dishes are cleared, a white-coated chef, sweat beads on his brow, rolls a crispy goose and a slab of roast beef in a cart next to the table. With a deft movement of knives, our plates are filled with pink meat, roasted potatoes, string beans almondine and mango chutney.

During dinner Ellis discusses The Ecclesiastices Project. "We've raised the funds to start production on three gift lines. The molds will be made here, but the items are constructed in the Philippines. Labor there saves us millions."

"When will items reach the stores?" asks Maury, sipping a glass of merlot.

"Our up-market items are in route now. For the lower price point lines, production, completion, shipping and packaging will be about six months. Right, darling?" he asks Tuni.

"What? Oh yes, dear," says Tuni. She turns from her conversation with Rivka.

Ellis says, "You'll be amazed at the ROI on your money in the next few months. We'll hit the retail shows next summer for the holiday season. Retailers make fifty percent of their entire year's revenues in December. We're also posting a catalogue on the internet."

"Think we'll see any money before that?" Maury asks.

Ellis nods. He places his silverware on the plate. "Absolutely. My accountants and solicitors, I mean attorneys, tell me the investors who came in for the full Monty will receive some money because we won't need everything for collateral. With this kind of progress we'll have substantial contracts next year, a dozen more lines, and then an IPO." He loses me. I have a literature brain not a business one.

"What's with Sunshine HMO going under?" Ted asks Maury as he leans back in his chair, his burgundy velvet jacket signaling he's the lord of the manor.

"We've found another plan to replace it, but medicine is in a terrible state." Maury pushes his meat around the gold-edged plate. "Hey, it's a holiday. I don't want to bring everyone down."

"Listen, you'll never have to think about an HMO again after this deal goes through," says Ted, pointing toward Ellis with his thumb.

"I hope you're right," says Maury, looking into his glass.

"How 'bout some golf next week while things are slow? We'll get a couple of rounds in and smoke a few cigars." Ted leans back in his chair and pats his belly. "Great meal."

"You've got it," says my man, pointing his finger at Ted.

I'm glad Maury has Ted and even Steve. Without them he'd be friendless. He tells me I'm his best friend, that he doesn't need anyone else. I love him dearly, but I need Glee and April too because he never wants to discuss diets and bras. I turn to eavesdrop on Tuni and my blossoming daughter-in-law, her skin aglow in the soft lighting.

"I bet you can't wait to see what the baby looks like. Are you keen on the idea of being a mother?" Tuni asks.

"It was a surprise at first, but now I look forward to it. I've been reading about primitive cultures and how they raise their babies. Pygmy babies are in physical contact with an adult fifty percent of the time." She pauses to look down and straighten her silverware. "I like the idea of attachment parenting. Nowadays they swaddle them like a burrito. It's supposed to make them more secure."

"How does the father feel about that?" asks Tuni.

Rivka leans into Michael and smiles. "Michael will adjust. I'm going to keep the baby in a sling with me all day and have him sleep with us at night."

"What?" says Michael, alert for the first time. "A baby in our bed? Do I have a say in this?"

"It's only 'til I stop nursing."

"When is that?" he asks.

"In Mexico we nurse 'til the baby is three," says Rivka with a self-satisfied smile. Michael begins a prolonged cough. He puts his utensils on the plate while Rivka slaps his back. When he recovers he dabs his eyes with his napkin.

Michael gives me a *Mom, do-something* look. I shrug my shoulders. He leans over to Rivka, "Can we negotiate this later?" She smiles. He saws into his second helping of roast, head down in concentration.

A baby in their bed all the time? No, I can't see my hormone-ravaged son going for that idea. I think the honeymoon's over.

"Tuni, have you spent much time around children?" I pull at my tight waistband and slip off my shoes.

"Heavens, no. I'm an orphan with no brothers or sisters. My mum slid down the pole into dementia before I popped off to America and then passed on. But I'm keen on babies. Haven't you seen all the cherubs in our gift line?"

I've noticed all the babies but I thought it was just bad taste.

Tuni shifts her body back to Rivka. "I want to thank you for pitching in at TuniEl. I know it can be a bore sitting at a computer. Your help is very appreciated." Her smile reflects the gratitude in her voice.

"It's fun. At home I use Jean's computer for e-mail," says Rivka. She asks Tuni, "Can I ask you a question? You're so busy at the office."

"Of course."

"When do we see something? Like the cherub door-knockers or angel vases?"

"Any time now from the Philippines. The lines coming from Indonesia take longer. Then we'll bring on more staff to get everything out to the wholesalers. Anyway, that's all Ellis' job." Tuni waves toward him. "I'm responsible for marketing." Tuni pauses to take a bite. "After the baby arrives, would you still come in a few times a week?

Rivka shrugs her shoulders. I get an instant hot flash at the thought of her being productive. A dribble of perspiration winds its way between my breasts. Am I flushed from the wine?

"You can bring the baby with you and we'll triple your wages," says Tuni as she fluffs her hair. Her fingers sport French-manicured nails and a swimming pool-size diamond ring. "We'll be in major distribution and we need someone capable."

Rivka remains non-committal, playing with her mashed potatoes. She looks at Michael. "We'll see. We want a place of our own by then." He kisses her forehead.

That's good news. At least a separate home is in their game plan. I change the subject. "How's the house you're building coming along?" I ask.

"It's so frustrating. I've been like a chook with its head cut off. The builder can't find the type of wood we want for the vaulted ceilings."

"A chook?" I ask.

"Oh," Tuni laughs. "A chook's Aussie-speak for a chicken."

"Why don't you ask Ted? He might be able to help you."

"I couldn't possibly bother him. We'll muddle through."

"I'm sure he won't mind. He's good-natured. Let's ask him. Ted? Excuse me. Tuni's having a problem with their home and I thought maybe you could intervene..."

"What? Sure, doll. All the builders are buddies. Tell me what you need." Ted's relaxed. I glance at Maury. He looks like he's having a good time, too.

"I hate to be a bother," says Tuni.

"No trouble at all."

"It's not a big deal," says Tuni backtracking.

"Why don't you call me at the office and give me the details next week." Ted returns to his conversation with a guest whose name I forgot. Must be Lungs considering the amount of cleavage that spills onto the table. A diamond dog collar circles her neck. Her escort, a gentleman with winged gray temples, slips his arm around her to pull her closer, jiggling The Lungs.

The evening concludes after dessert, when Maury receives a call from a patient, a sometime golf partner.

"Anything serious?" I inquire.

"Naw. People eat too much this time of year. I told him I'd meet him at the emergency room. Sounds like a gall bladder. I'll drop you at home first."

We drive toward Tempe in our satiated state on the 101 Freeway that cuts through the Indian reservation. On our left are fields with stacks of hay and a giant white tent for gambling. The parking lot is full. On our right is Big Surf, Arizona's manufactured beach. It's really a giant toilet bowl that flushes to make waves.

When I glance in the back, Michael dozes, his head on Rivka's shoulder, just like when he was a kid.

17

To: jeanrubin
From: lara47
Subject: babies

Hi Mom!

I'm green as my houseplants. When does it end? I'm not only losing my cookies in the morning but it hits in the evening, too. Gus is very sweet and brings me crackers in bed. None of my pants button anymore. It's strange to look at myself in the mirror and see how my body is changing. My waist looks like a tree trunk. What happens to my belly button ring when it's all sticking out?

Did you ask dad about the *doula*?

Love,
Lara

To: lara47
From: jeanrubin

Subject: reply

Dear Lara,

Hang in there. You'll feel better in the second trimester. Daddy says *doulas* are a gimmick and he's sure your school health insurance won't cover one.

Rivka is getting larger by the minute. The ultrasound says it's a boy! We're so excited! Her family is going to come from Mexico for the *bris* even though she confessed her mother thinks it's barbaric. I explained that the tradition is five thousand years old and circumcision is *de riguer* for Jewish men.

Love,
Mom

Days slide by. On New Year's Eve our bedroom becomes an illicit dining room where we eat in bed. Maury smuggles in ribs smothered in bar-b-q sauce from Don and Charlie's so Rivka won't see. Amber likes this almost as much as when someone in the family has a cold.

New Year's Day April and Steve invite us for brunch on their patio. They greet us with mimosas, a combination of fresh orange juice from their tree and champagne. It makes me giddy on an empty stomach.

The crisp air smells fresh. Phoenicians live for this kind of weather after our ungodly summers. The guys practice at the miniature putting green while her shih tzus scurry after golf balls looking like tandem dust mops. I smell hickory from a neighbor's barbeque. A mockingbird chirps from a giant palo verde and picks at the desert mistletoe colonized near the top. It flies back and forth across the yard, red berries in its beak.

April looks luscious in Capri pants and a cerise turtleneck. "How's school?" she asks.

I set my mimosa on the table. "I've painted myself into a corner and I'll probably lose my job over it. But damn it, I'm not going to be intimidated into changing a grade because the administration is worried about donations and publicity."

"I've never heard you so angry. You're passionate about this, aren't you?"

I nod. "There's a review this month. I can't wait to hear what, Tiffany, the little twit and her manic mother say. I'm going to fight this to the end."

April pats me on the knee. "Maybe you better think about a good lawyer," she says as she glances at Steve.

I've upset myself. Maybe something good is on the horizon.

"What's happening with TuniEl?" The noon sun warms my back.

"I think we're all going to make a ton of money. I saw the prototypes of chubby babies with lyres, flutes and mandolins. Ellis told Steve we might have to put in a bit more because raw materials have gone up," says April with authority.

"Are you concerned about the money?" I ask, watching a hummingbird dip down to drink nectar from a trumpet flower.

"No, not at all. We checked it out. Wait 'til you see how much we're going to make," she says with a smile. "The large investors got their first check. Wasn't huge, but it's a start. We put a deposit on a condo in La Jolla and we're going to Australia this summer. It's winter there. Tuni and Ellis will meet us for a dive at the Great Barrier Reef." I admire her indefatigable enthusiasm. Maury and I haven't played in high stakes games before.

Days float by with our unit of four in a routine. Maury arrives home from the office too tired talk. He gets used to no mayonnaise or butter on the table. I accept the fact that when the phone rings on Saturday, Rivka won't pick it up. Michael appears and retreats to his room. I start the new semester next week on shaky ground. Megan hasn't returned my calls so I don't know if my classes are filled.
My brother, Richard, and his pseudo-intellectual wife, Asia, invite my parents for my nephew's graduation.
"Your father and I don't like to travel, especially if I have to stay with Asia," my mother tells me in one of our daily phone calls.

My myopic stare in the make-up mirror inspires me to seek improvement. "Mom, don't worry about it. It's only a weekend. Everything will be fine." It's hard to talk and not move my lips. I roll on the gooey stuff April gave me to keep my lipstick from bleeding.

"Last time Asia gave me a used present."

I don't remember a used present. I observe my handiwork. It must be the wrong color because I have a dark purple decoration around my lips, a tattoo of pomegranate.

"It was perfume, but I could tell it had been opened. The bottom said not for resale and it smelled awful. Like that smelly cheese she cooks with." My mother pauses. I frown, waiting.

"Can you take me shopping? You made me throw out such good clothes before I moved and now I have nothing to wear. I need shoes." Good clothes constitutes anything bought after 1950.

I rub off my purple moustache with a cotton ball and cleanser. "No problem." My Saturday is shot. My mother makes decisions as easily as a cowboy picking which pony to ride. "I'll pick you and Dad up at ten."

The next day at the mall I'm in new sneakers made from one piece of molded plastic. It feels like I'm walking in soup cans. My mother doesn't approve of my casual outfit. She dresses up in case she sees someone she knows.

We navigate the stores, lions in search of wildebeest flesh. My father brings his newspaper. In every store he seeks out a comfy spot, a domestic pet circling to make a nest. The shoe departments look the same. I stalk the aisles to harass sales people as I hope for a purchase that will release me.

"Mom, what about these black ones?" I don't remember what store we're in. "They're on sale."

"I don't know. They're not too stylish." Mom prances over to my father, his head buried in the editorial page. He's a man who can't discern high heels from orthopedic space shoes.

"Herm, what do you think?" she asks the top of his head. "These people are idiots. This guy wants the city to fund another sports stadium and raise our taxes," he says, talking to the paper.

"Herman, look at my feet. What do you think?" My mother

demands his attention in her spiffy attire. I pray he likes them.

"They look like shoes." He notices my mother's needle brow and adds, "If they're comfortable, buy them."

"But do they look good?" That's like asking Amber if she's a Democrat or a Republican. My father, whose idea of dressed-up consists of old pants and a Cubavera, is not a style maven. My mother's job is to make sure he matches when he leaves the house.

"Yeah. Sure. They look fine. Let's go," says my father. He folds the paper, places it under his arm and heads for the exit.

"Wait a minute." My mother stomps her foot. "Are they stylish?"

"How should I know? Florence, just pay and let's go. It's almost time for my nap."

"Mom, what about the shoes? Why don't you take them?"

"I don't know. Maybe we should have lunch first and I'll think about it." She searches another display, picks up a shoe, then returns it to its plexi-glass stand when she sees the price on the sole.

"There's nothing to think about. Besides, it's a long walk through the mall. Why don't we get them now? They fit. They're on sale. Let's just do it," I say mimicking the Nike ad.

"No, I have to think about it." She slides them off her feet and puts them in the red box on a bench. I trail after her as she follows my father into the herds of people in the mall. April calls this tantric shopping--you go for hours and buy nothing.

We pass by the food court, a circus of moms, screaming babies, teens with clown hair, and other tired retirees, all accompanied by rap music. We move to an enclosed cafe nearby.

"Herm, watch your cholesterol."

"I'm out for the afternoon. I'll eat whatever I want."

I glance at my watch. One thirty and no shoes.

Mom says, "Asia's so difficult. She plays tapes of Lillan Hellman's books to analyze her relationship with Dashiell Hammett, that drunken smoke-fiend." My mother slaps her hand against the table.

"Tell her not to play the tapes when you're there," I say. This coming trip is a bright spot for me.

When the waitress arrives to take our order, my parents interrogate her with the enthusiasm of a military tribunal. "Is the hamburger made with egg? Can we substitute a different bun? How much mayonnaise is in the coleslaw? Herm, you can't eat that apple wedge, it'll break your bridge. Can we get cottage cheese instead of chips?" We send her away twice. I'm sure she's in the back offering the cook tip money to kill her with a sharp knife.

We abandon the shoe search. I drop them off at their place where a smiling Trudy waits to open the car door for them.

There's no point hurrying home to a Maury engaged in the golf channel and a Rivka who complains about her swollen ankles. I decide to go to the flea market. Haven't been in years. The thought of wandering around in anonymity appeals to me.

The deteriorated neighborhoods I pass are a sharp contrast to Scottsdale. Van Buren, one of the oldest streets in Phoenix, is an amalgam of tacky stores and tawdry women. Clusters of boarded-up stores, a check-cashing place with neon letters in English and Spanish, and a market with bars on the windows bake in eerie emptiness. Neglected tract houses, their yards filled with weeds and junked cars on concrete blocks, cry for a can of paint. Young men in muscle T-shirts, their gang bandannas wrapped around their heads, lean against a fence. They glare at me through my tinted windows. I like young people, but this is not the place to get a flat tire. Do they know a few miles away there's plenty of everything?

The Phoenix flea market, held on weekends at the Greyhound Racing Park, has aisles of every unwanted item you can imagine. They're displayed on tables, crates, and toilet seats. Serious people show up before seven AM to pick through stuff and re-sell it for double the price so things are sparse by the end of the day. The afternoon sun beats down as I wander past collections of forty-five records, used water filters, hand-painted ceramics, crotch-less underwear, Amway cleaning products in their original boxes and hundreds of other items like the ones I discarded from my parent's house.

A glimmer of lusterware catches my eye on a table with pastel depression glass, sugar bowls, and an Aunt Jemima cookie jar. Assorted bottles add to the clutter. I've collected the pre-World War Two china from Japan for twenty years. My cabinets overflow with mismatched tea sets, salt and peppershakers and orphaned plates. I've convinced myself the assorted pieces match because most are finished in an iridescent blue or peach. I hear Maury's voice say, "You hardly ever use it." I just love the hunt.

A blue teapot captivates me, a treasure with a delicate painting of a teahouse on the side. "That there's a real beauty," says the overweight woman in a ladybug-print housedress behind the table where she and her man perch on the open end of a truck.

"How much?" I pick it up and hold it to the light to see its translucence.

"A hunnert dollars, but I'll take a little less." She's chewing something.

I don't need it. There's no place to put it, but I want it. The shopper's mantra. "Will you take eighty?" I put it back on the card table, the surface stained from rain or maybe a spilled soft drink.

She glances at the man next to her, an older version of her in suspenders. A jellyfish belly sinks from the front of his chest. His jowls shake when he moves his head.

"Nope. We dragged that near a thousand miles from up in the mountains. I'll take a hunnert," he says.

I could walk away or stay and deal. My eyes wander to the next stall. Another bargain hunter picks through the junk.

"Tuni, what are you doing here?" I walk toward her.

"Oh, gracious. I'm a sight," she says, adjusting her red hair in the ponytail and visor. "I didn't think I'd see a soul. Do you come here often?" She looks chic in white shorts and a green Polo. My mother would say crisp.

"No. It was an impulse. What are you doing here?" Shopping bags surround her feet. I can never get a handle on this woman. No kids. No parents. An adoring husband. Lots of money. It sounds so uncomplicated. How can everything be so wonderful all the time? Am I the only one with problems? How did my life get so messy? I'm not a jealous person, but Tuni represents a slice of simplicity I've never seen.

"Nothing really. In Melbourne we have fairy shops where I can find incense, tarot cards, and metaphysical books. I'm looking for inspiration. My next item for the Vatican line will be a series of small fountains with some animals on top, a tribute to Saint Francis."

"How are things going?" I ask, frumpy in my soup can sneakers.

"Quite well. Ellis left town Wednesday for Rome to show the Vatican prototypes of the musical cherub line. It was very well received."

"Have you raised all the money you need?" I move closer to her and the stall she's perusing.

"Almost. We're a bit short, but I leave all that up to Ellis. He's an astute entrepreneur. He was a millionaire at twenty-two." She turns back to the table and picks up an old *Life* magazine.

My antennae roll up. "Why did you come to the States?"

"Tall Poppy Syndrome."

"What's that?"

"Women can only advance so far before other women become threatened and cut them down. In Melbourne I had an awful female boss. Ellis said she was jealous of me."

"I've never heard of that. How does it happen?"

She returns the magazine and picks up an antique hatpin. "Back stabbing. Gossip. Fraudulent business deals. Anything to make you look bad and cut down the one tall poppy that sticks up above the rest." She thrusts the pin back into a velvet pillow.

"Is that what happened to you?"

"The climate's better here for my creativity with Ellis handling finances." She glances at her watch. "I'm late." She adds, "I've got an appointment to get my fringe trimmed." I'm puzzled. "Bangs," she says, making a scissor motion across her forehead. She picks up the bags near her feet. "With Ellis gone a few ladies are coming over for wine next week. April and Glee, too. A fun girls evening.

Love to have you."

"Thanks. I'll be there." Any chance to find out more about this enigma of a woman intrigues me.

I abandon the teapot even though the woman yells after me, spitting onto the ground, "Okay, lady, we'll take ninety 'cause it's the end of the day."

18

To: jeanrubin
From: lara47
Subject: cast

Dear Mom,

I'M REALLY HAVING A TANGERINE!!! The ultrasound has no stem on the apple! We'll have four generations of Rubin women. Gus is thrilled, too, even though he wanted a boy for his soccer team. I reminded him girl's play, too.

Tell Daddy *doulas* are not a fad. Athena's a necessity. She and the midwife do lots of deliveries together. We're using the birthing room at the Womyn's Center so we can get in more people.

I want a plaster of Paris belly cast. Can you ask Glee if she'd do one for me when I come in for Passover? Everyone at the birth ritual can sign it and then we can hang it on the wall. Tangerine will love it when she's older and I show her that's where she came from.

Love,

Lara

Maury and I are excited Lara and Gus are having a girl since Rivka and Michael are having a boy, but does Lara *have* to name the baby after a fruit? Maury threatens to tell Lara the psychological damage a strange name can do to a child. I convince him to hold back because she might change it to a vegetable and we'll end up with a Rutabega.

Glee agrees to set aside her current art project to cast Lara's belly. "I'll cancel the strippers I'm using for the life-size resin vaginas."

"What?" I must not have a pulse on the local avant-garde.
"I call the smaller versions vag badges. People can wear them on their lapels."

"Vag badges?"

"They're wonderful with metallic paint." It's a good thing she can't see my clamped lips and rolling eyes. "Lara's request has inspired me. I want to decorate the elliptical stages of pregnancy with natural materials like twigs, leaves, and animal bones. Wild turkey feathers will work for the pubic area."

Time to change the subject. "Will I see you at Tuni's?"

"No, Ted and I are attending a seminar on how to dispose of our remains. Cremation and our ashes scattered on a beach sounded like a good idea. I want something more long lasting. With an Eternal Reef our ashes are mixed with concrete and dropped into the ocean to create a new ecosystem. Ted says it's our way to give back for the desert land he destroyed in the name of progress."

April and I drive to Tuni's guesthouse that's tucked behind a two-story stucco adobe on a quiet Scottsdale street. It's reminiscent of the witch's cottage in *Hansel and Gretel*, covered with cat's claw, a hearty vine that not only survives our torrid heat, it eats caulking to grow through windows. The foliage around the hideaway, lush with fuchsia and red bougainvillea, scatters petals on to the driveway.

"I wonder if we'll know anyone here," says April. She holds my elbow on the pebble walk, teetering on her Blahniks.

"I don't know," I answer as I move along a path lit by luminaria in my shoes with crepe soles.

Tuni comes to the security screen door. "Come in." She holds it open for us. "So glad you could make it." A purple-draped dress accents her body and wild hair. She touches my arm. "I have something for you."

We step inside. A floral gift bag appears with colored tissue paper.

"For me?" I can't imagine what it is. I set my purse on the floor to take it.

"Go ahead, but be careful," says Tuni. "It's fragile."
I look at April, a bit bewildered. It's not my birthday. "What is it?" I ask, as I pull the riot of tissue out.

"Something you wanted," says Tuni. She grins in excitement. "It's the teapot! Tuni, you shouldn't have." I'm surprised she's given me another gift. I hold the treasure to my chest. "But I'm so glad you did. Thank you." The iridescent blue gleams in the candlelight. I hug her, then turn to April to explain about the flea market. I touch the teahouse design, then nestle it into the tissue paper.

"I knew you wanted it." Tuni guides us toward the living room. "Let me introduce you to the girls. Put your purses under there." She points to an antique table.

I run my hand over it. "This is beautiful."

"I brought it back from Morocco P.E., Pre-Ellis." She hands us a glass of chardonnay as my eyes adjust to a candlelit room. The inside fulfills the outside's promise: a cozy place where angels hang in profusion from beams as divine cave bats and gilded mirrors cover an entire wall. Gothic Renaissance gone awry.

Is it all from the TuniEl collection? "Of course this is temporary until we move into our home," Tuni says as she waves her hand around the room.

"Hello, I'm Kat," says a tall, bony woman with a hard handshake and no-nonsense hair. "This is my partner, Angela." Angela, also of Amazon-size with a face devoid of make-up, smiles. Her midnight-blue silk jacket drapes across her broad shoulders. She's so tall I look down at her feet. Of course. Killer shoes. Leather ankle boots with spike heels, *fuck-me* shoes according to April.

"What kind of business partners are you?" I ask them.

Kat laughs. She places her arm around Angela's waist and pulls her into her side. "We're everything but business partners," she says with a grin. "Need a refill anyone?" Her hand jabs the empty glass into the air as she peels off. Angela eases herself away.

April stands so close to me I can feel her breath on my neck. "Ohmigod," April whispers in my ear. "I think they're gay."

I know I have to be the mature one. April becomes a hysteric in strange situations. "Why do you say that? Just because--." Tuni interrupts as April, about to climb into my armpit, digs her French-manicured nails into my palm.

"Let me introduce you to some cohorts we met cruising San Carlos Bay. Trina, I want you to meet these darling friends of mine, Jean and April." Do they think we're a couple, too? With April's shoes, I'm the butch.

Trina, a stunning, deep-voiced woman dressed in an expensive sweater, wool slacks and a multitude of necklaces, locks her gaze into mine. She's interested in what I'm teaching and whether the young women in class are receptive to it.

"The students take the advancements made in their behalf for granted. I bring in novels from other cultures like the Indian writers who wrote *Mistress of Spices* and *God of Small Things*. They see the significance of dealing with a caste system on top of sexism."

"Do you use Bonheim's book, *Aphrodite's Daughters: Women's Sexual Stories*?" asks Trina. We're losing April. Her body language drifts into what experts call the leaky foot, a half turn of her body away from us, pedicured toes facing the door. April slips away to examine a series of black and white sailing photographs on the wall.

"I have that in the course syllabus. What do you do?" I pick up an artichoke canapé from a table.

"I own a southwestern craft gallery in Tucson. Came up for the party and to see my niece who lives here. Isn't the Ecclesiastices Project exciting?" She sips from her drink.

Oh, she's invested, too. "Yes, I can't wait to see the prototypes when Ellis returns from the Vatican. When did you meet Tuni?" I ask. April returns to my side.

"Come with me to the bathroom." She does a little dance. "That woman likes me." April's eyes motion toward a guest on a suede sofa.

"In a minute." I turn my attention back to Trina.

"I met them a few years ago in Mexico. They rented a boat for a month and had great parties. She's quite a gal, isn't she?" says Trina. She looks in Tuni's direction to make eye contact.

I escort April to the bathroom. "Jean, they're all lezzies!" she hisses at me.

"Don't be absurd." I pause, look around. "Maybe, but so what?" April becomes conspiratorial. "I've never had a woman flirt with me before. It's a revelation." She glances at her Rolex encrusted with pave diamonds. "Let's make our exit before they all want me." She smiles before we check our teeth for lipstick in the mirror.

"Okay. Ten more minutes and we're outta here."

We float around to say our goodbyes. I'm trapped in a conversation with a long-winded chiropractor who expounds on the virtues of homeopathic remedies. When I can't find Tuni, I open the patio door. Two cigarettes glow in the darkness. Have I interrupted an intimate moment? April, a few steps behind me because of her shoes, says, "They're busy," and hightails it back inside.

Tuni waves her arm for me to join her. "It's perfectly all right. Trina and I are old friends. Hmm, darling?" They smile at each other, arms draped around shoulders.

After air kissing, I gather my shopping bag holding the teapot. I have to drag April away from Angela and a serious discussion about her boots. She moves with speed over the pebbled-driveway into the headlights of a car that pulls up, gets in my Volvo and locks the door. The engine dies behind me and a car door slams. As I place the gift in the trunk, I hear crunching gravel behind me.

"Miz Rubin?"

I recognize the Texas drawl at once. "Doris! What are you doing here?" I turn to put my hands on her arms. "Are you all right?" Her hair is clipped short.

"I am now." She looks down toward her feet.

"What happened to you?" My voice fills with concern.

"I hope this won't shock you." She pauses and moves a step closer in the darkness. "I had a crush on one of the girls in your class and she didn't feel the same way." Her clear blue eyes stare into mine. "I'd been wrestling with my sexual identity and there didn't seem to be a way--"

"Doris, attempting to take your life is no solution. Are you seeing a professional?"

"Oh yes. My aunt owns a gallery in Tucson. She wants me to see her shrink, Doctor Blackhead."

April taps a fingernail on the rolled-up window.

"Trina?" I ask, my thumb gesturing toward the cottage. Doris nods. Oh no. "Listen, Doris, we have to talk. Can you call me tomorrow? I'll be at my office. Better yet, give me your number." I search for a pen in my miniscule purse. No luck.

"I'll call you, Miz Rubin. Nice to see you." She looks sad as she slumps away, the Texan saunter gone, the snake tattoo covered by pants. Blackhead? I've got to save Doris. What if the LAB method dumps her back into a depression?

On the way home April has fifteen minutes of ohmiGods alternated with "They're lipstick lesbians!" We finally agree that yes, indeed, Tuni might swing both ways, but we weren't going to talk about it anymore.

My parents return from my nephew Andrew's graduation. It's a convoluted story with my sister-in-law, Asia as the villain.

On the phone the litany starts with, "I asked her to buy prunes for your father's breakfast. You know what he gets like. She forgot so I asked Andrew to drive me to the store. That's when he told me what they do on vacation."

"What?" I push Amber's fat dog ass toward the door to go out, the phone locked into my neck. I have the downstairs to myself because Rivka's working at Tuni's.

"Your brother never had weird ideas." She pauses. "They take old clothes with them, the kind that have a stain or need a button, and they wear them. Then they leave them for the maids so they can come home with an empty suitcase." My mother ends in a triumphant tone, proof that they are indeed, insane. But I think the idea has merit. I'm always running out of suitcase space to bring home treasures. Maybe next time I can convince Maury to dump the T-shirts with the leftist logos and buy more folk art.

My mother's on a roll. "That name, Asia, like she's some exotic creature instead of Linda from Miami Beach." The best news is my mother's feet didn't hurt because she wore her old shoes.

Time to wrap it up. Besides recalcitrant Amber, I have work

to do. The college hearing about Tiffany is this week. I don't have anything to prepare. I'll just tell my story, but I have a feeling of dread that weighs down my soul. I camp out at the kitchen table with the semester's reading list but can't concentrate. Our mailperson's truck chugs down the street.

The invitation for Glee's fiftieth birthday party arrives in a black envelope with studs glued to the outside. It's a Harley Hawg party where we're instructed to wear motorcycle duds. I call to RSVP before anyone else.

"Of course we'll be there. What are you planning?"
"It's going to be a blast. I've hired a band called The Fat Boys from a biker bar. They're coming on their Harleys except for the keyboard guy."

"Wasn't your fiftieth a few years ago? You said you weren't going to celebrate because everyone would remember and know how old you were."

"I'm really fifty-five, but no one knows except you and April. I don't think I look it, do you? Anyway, I wasn't ready for a party then. Ted and I went to Macchu Picchu to meditate. It was either this or getting my face lasered." The phone is quiet. "Don't tell anyone, okay?"

No one except Maury.

I arrive early at the designated conference room. Olive, the dean's assistant in her prim dress, ignores me. Her gum cracks as she places name cards where people are supposed to sit--Dean

Gruber, Megan Trumboldt, Sarah Geiser, Faculty Liason, Sean Smith, Student Liason, and a bunch of names I don't recognize of student government leaders and a few other department heads. She's probably done many faculty/student hearings, but it's my first. I take a seat at a place without a name. The paneled conference room smells of Pine-Sol, the ministrations of a zealous janitor. The silence is torture. I clear my throat, tap my fingers on my knees.

"So, Olive, uh, what does the Dean think is going to happen with this case?" Like Miss Pimento is going to give me some scoop. "You know I can't comment on internal affairs," she says as she straightens the cardboard names, which must have taken hours on the computer. She puts a pitcher of water on a paper towel near the Dean's place card, the plastic cups to the side.

"What time do you have? My watch must be fast." I look up at the large clock on the wall when it clicks another minute. Olive busies herself with her laptop setting up the secretarial minutes.
The Dean and Megan arrive together, he in a brown rumpled suit and she in a dress that's a departure from her floral motif, her purse with the two straps on her arm, a briefcase in her hand. Bees. Yellow ones buzzing on a navy background. Who makes textiles like this for adult clothing?

The room fills and about twenty people take their places. No one says much other than a grumbled hello, but the sound of over-stuffed roller chairs being squeezed into tight spaces with a few crunched fingers creates a distraction. They don't move very well on the ancient industrial carpeting. The agenda sits in front of each spot set by the ever-efficient Olive.

The Dean admonishes Olive to close the door. He directs his gaze toward me at the farthest end. "Jean, you're the first on our docket today. We're going to bring the offended party in shortly. The way it works is you will both state your case and then the Advisory Board votes. You will have to abide by our decision." He looks around at the group. Not a smile anywhere. Megan sits with hands folded in front of her. He slaps the table and says, "Olive, bring in Tiffany Gordon."

Olive pushes back her chair and heads for the door. In moments it flings open. Instead of a blonde sorority-Suzie, a sun-damaged face with midnight, egg-beater hair steps into the room wearing a black suit. Flora herself. Up close and personal.

"Good morning, Dean." She acknowledges the rest of us with a nod but addresses him. "My daughter, Tiffany, couldn't be here today. She is so overwrought with the trauma of failure, especially in a course that promotes lesbianism, a crime against nature and the church, I might add, that she can hardly get out of bed. She felt justified in not doing the assignments because the material was offensive. Even pornographic." Her hand flies to her chest for drama. Oh no. Red Lee Press-on Nails.

"Now I believe in freedom of speech, but the good Lord knows this class is a travesty and that woman--" Her eyes search for who is responsible. I sit taller in my chair, my hands flat on the table in front of me, looking alert. Might as well make a good showing. "She should be fired," she says. She pulls out an empty chair near the door and sits down.

"Miss Boudreaux, I understand your upset, but we cannot hear this case if Tiffany is not present. I explained to you on the phone she had to be in attendance." The Dean's voice sounds patient but tired.

"What?" Flora screeches. "You mean to tell me I can't plead Tiffany's case and the grade won't be changed because she's not here?"

"I'm sorry. It's policy. Both parties must be present for us to take action. College rules. He turns to Olive. "What page is it in our student handbook?"

"Forty-three," Olive answers, her fingers dancing across the computer keyboard.

Flora stands pointing an accusing finger with a fake red nail. "Which one of you is responsible for Tiffany's grade? I want to hear the incompetent Communist femi-Nazi defend her position." Some spittle lands on the table when she spits out *Communist*. Most eyes look down.

Megan's eyes bulge like a praying mantis. Then she raises her eyebrows at me with a *get-up* look. The room gasps in silence. Someone shuffles their feet.

I stand after a brief struggle with the chair that seems to be stuck, a nerve pulsating in my thigh. No point giving her the advantage of height. I gather my inner calmness which almost always escapes into panic. "Miss Boudreaux, I'm Jean Rubin, Tiffany's instructor." Her mouth scrolls down into a scowl.

"At the beginning of the semester I state the course requirements. They are also in the syllabus. Your daughter had the opportunity to drop and receive an incomplete before mid-term, but she chose not to do that. She could have asked for an addition of her choice to the reading list and she didn't do that either. She simply refused to make any attempt to do the assignment. She received the grade she deserved, an "F"." I begin to sit down and then pull myself up to speak in a calm, confident voice. "By the way, my political affiliations are of no bearing on this case, but I can tell you I am not a Communist nor am I incompetent. My student evaluations prove the latter. I'm a progressive feminist who encourages self-expression." With my chin held high I sit down and paddle my feet to move in toward the table.

Flora rushes around the conference table toward me screaming, "You've ruined my Tiffany's life. Our family is humiliated. You liberal mongrel."

Bony hands, stretched out in front of her, reach toward my throat as she comes to my end in swooping pterodactyl steps. She is so close I feel her breath, eyes huge with rage. I struggle to stand up in defense. The chair doesn't budge. I'm trapped. Frozen. I start to hyperventilate. Is this my end? My karma? A monkey-haired wench at the other end of the political spectrum is going to squeeze the life force out of me? Poor Maury and the babies. For a split second in my mental drama I feel good being eulogized as a martyr.
An inch before her talons encircle my neck, the Dean and Sean grab her arms. I see her feet scrambling like a bicycle rider trying to win a race as they escort her out of the room, their arms placed with firmness under hers. She flings parting words, "You're going to pay for this!"

I'm stunned. I've never been so eloquent and elicited such a reaction. My chest pounds like a tympani. Then I realize I'm wet everywhere--my pits, my neck, the side of my face, even my crotch. This is way too much pressure.

The Dean re-enters the room pushing the back of his shirt into his pants. He swipes his hand across his forehead to replace hair that has fallen. "Sean, take Ms. Boudreaux her purse. She's waiting in my office. Jean, the case is dismissed because Tiffany didn't show. You're free to go. Grade stands."

"Olive, who's next?"

I lift my head with pride as a young man saunters through the door in a Coors beer shirt. Olive's voice states, "Jason Plotz was found smoking marijuana in the cafeteria bathroom."

In the hall I lean back against the wall, close my eyes and take a deep breath. Then I dig into my purse for the nine-hundred pound phone.

"Maury?"

19

"I FEEL LIKE A FOOL IN THESE FAKE LEATHER PANTS," says Maury as we walk up the street toward Glee's birthday party, parading past haciendas with Totem Pole cactus, Mexican honeysuckle and dense lantana for landscaping. The plants grow among gray river rock and pastel gravel with washes and arroyos that create lumps like a topography map I made out of clay in elementary school. The end of a warm February day turns into a cool evening. How could I forget that the temperature drops thirty degrees in the desert?

"Honey, it's not fake, it's Pleather. We're doing it for Glee." I'm sweaty from sitting in the car.

Glee Barstow's lawn is a desert Zen garden with a fat Buddha nestled on a rocky mound. A trio of Saguaro cactus reaches with majesty toward a fading pink-orange sun. The daddy of the group stretches above the two-story roof.

Maury nudges me with his elbow. "Saguaros take thirty-five years to get nine feet tall. Those must be over a hundred by now and at eight thousand dollars a pop, I'd say Ted's got one expensive front lawn." Big bucks for a plant that'll outlive us.

And we look ridiculous. I'm in a black leather vest sans shirt, while Maury's in a biker hat with silver chains and Doc Martens we found at a garage sale. The persona of doctor has disappeared under the salt and pepper hairy tufts that poke out of his Harley vest. If he crossed my path, I'd be frantic with fear. My teddy bear's a motorcycle maniac. That is, until he trips on the steel toe of his bargain shoes as we schlep up the circular driveway.

I stroke the red place on my chest where I reapplied my dagger tattoo. The skull and crossbones on Maury's biceps look authentic. "Welcome to Glee's Biker Bar," says a sexy, young blonde, her voice sugary-sweet. A black leather contraption covers her nipples with spider pieces extending from it, barely covering her. I don't know what's on the bottom half of her body except fringe. "Food's in the area to your right and drinks are on the patio," she says, motioning toward the back yard, her wrist encased in leather.

We head for the patio. "Maury, did you see what she was wearing?"

"I wouldn't recommend it. Not much support," he says, his expression droll.

I choke in laughter.

Outside we find a crowd of suburbanites in various stages of undress, trying to look tough. I don't recognize anyone. Maury and I have wandered into a kinky S-and-M club.

"How 'bout a drink?" he asks me, moving toward the bar. This will be a scotch night for him. Costumes require fortitude.

My white wine in hand, we introduce ourselves to a couple who look sillier than we do. He has a fake ponytail attached to the back of his bald pate and she, a bit hefty for black leather shorts, wears a dark wig that sheds into her drink.

"We're the Barstow's next door neighbors," she says, picking a hair from the rim of her glass. I try not to stare at the roll of white flesh above the sea of black leather. "Isn't Glee a hoot to invite the entire neighborhood?"

"You mean those people are from your block, too?" I ask.

"Glee invited everyone because we're going to be making a lot of noise."

"We are?" My black-penciled eyebrows shoot up. Maury snorts and chokes on a mouthful of scotch.

April and Steve arrive, looking more authentic than the rest of us. After all, motorcycle mayhem is Steve's business. He represents boomers who need speed in their mid-life crises. With his slicked blonde hair, wrap-around sunglasses and black muscle T-shirt he reminds me of the fast boys in high school my mother warned me to stay away from that she called sharpies.

After I introduce everyone to April in her cleavage-defying halter and painted-on black pants, Mr. Fake Ponytail motions with his drink, "That's some outfit you've got there, young lady." April smiles.

A deafening noise whips our attention to the back fence, past an elaborate waterfall, a lagoon and grape arbor. Our obscene greeter and the macho bartender open a wooden gate that leads to an alley. With a cloud of dust, Glee and Ted make an entrance on his Harley. As she squeals and waves Ted brings the machine to a halt, its kickstand in the shape of an eagle's talon digging up a small chunk of green lawn. Glee slides off the back, a tattoo on her liposuctioned globes visible through fishnet stockings.

The sexy greeter closes the gate and rushes over to help Glee remove her jacket, revealing a black, skimpy outfit. Outrageous screams to a new octave.

"Thank you all for coming. Let's party!" Glee yells, her dark curls hidden under a black cap. Most of the men wander over to look at the gleaming machine, pure artistry in chrome and red enamel. Glee plays hostess and greets people. The biker band at the other end of the yard plays "Happy Birthday" before it launches into rock. Drinks have loosened up any self-conscious guest. The party has begun.

"Darling, you look smashing," I hear behind me. I turn to see Tuni and Ellis, their biker outfits un-costume-like.

"Is that your stuff or did you borrow?" I ask, my vest sticking to my back.

"This is ours. Ellis has ridden for years. His leather chaps are well broken in." She pats his leg.

We chat for a few minutes before I bring up business. "How was your trip to the Vatican?"

Ellis sips his drink first. "Excellent. They loved Tuni's porcelain figurines. We presented glass paperweights, globes with angels circling the equator, dessert plates and window ornaments. We'll outsell Lladro's limited editions."

"How is the investment part coming?" I ask. Is our retirement money working for us while we party? Is what I really want to know. Tuni jumps in. "Fabulous. Ellis is brilliant. More investors joined the last few weeks. Our accountants tell us some people will get back eighty per cent of their initial investment in the first six months.

We had a meeting for Glee's neighbors last week. See Malcolm Burgess and his wife over there? The tall gentleman with biceps. She's petite." Tuni's ice-rink diamond ring glimmers in the fading light. Maury and I glance to the end of the patio. "Malcolm Burgess is the owner of *The Phoenix Courier*. They've invested."

Now I know why they look familiar. *Fashionista* features them often in tuxedo, ball gown and jewels at the charity events.

That fellow over there," Tuni says, pointing to an older man, his belly peeking from under his Harley T-shirt, "owns a private bank in Scottsdale. He's promised us all the financing we need."

"Really?"

"Oh, yes," says Ellis. "We'll be marketing all over the world. These gifts will rival anything Lucas and Spielberg have ever introduced for a movie. Some items are available now through internet malls."

"Wow." Their enthusiasm drowns me.

Our conversation ends when six scary men with greasy hair roar into the backyard on huge machines. The one who hasn't shaved in a week says, "We're here from the Hell's Angels to give everyone a ride. Who's first?"

"OhmiGod, Maury, his tattoos aren't fake." I dig my black biker-chick fingernails into his semi-flabby bicep.

He looks down at me grinning. "You look really hot in that outfit. Maybe you could put it on for me again on Sunday morning."

"You can't be serious." My mind floats to last Sunday when we stayed in bed as long as possible to avoid the terrorist daughter-in-law. Maury rubs the tattoo on my arm with the back of two fingers.

Maybe I don't look as ridiculous as I thought. I stand a bit straighter. For the next hour the Angels give people whose asses sit on leather luxury seats the thrill of their lives. No wonder Glee invited the neighbors. We're making enough noise to have everyone arrested.

Later, Glee drags me into a corner behind the acacia bushes that hide the pool pump. "Tell me the truth. How do I look?" She takes a step back so I can see her full length, the bottom of her costume barely covering her pubic area. The Brazilian wax job must have been a killer.

"You look fine. Little over the top maybe."

"Do I look silly?" She turns around, her tush hanging in the breeze. "Whaddaya think? Did Doctor Reingler do a good job?" I squint closer at her ass. It's a little lumpy with a few cellulite bumps, but basically it's okay. "It looks fine."

"Are you sure?"

"Yes. Why?"

Her face is worried, her face devoid of the party mask. "As a kid I was a mess--glasses, braces, overweight, pimples. I just want to know I look okay for fifty."

"Fifty-five," I correct her. "And you look great for any age." I hug her before we step back into the party. I see my husband, his hand on his hat, streaming away on the ride of his life.

20

SITTING AT MY DESK LIKE A WORN-OUT OLD DOG I sip another Diet Coke, piles of essays balanced on the corners. It's hard to concentrate on bad writing if you haven't slept the night before. Between Maury's snoring and Amber and I both getting up to go to the bathroom, I'm Godzilla without the roar. Once I'm awake my problems file across my head. By four o'clock I was up for the day.

"Busy, Miz Rubin?" Doris peeks her head around the corner of my cubicle. I'm in the midst of slicing up a semi-illiterate's essay with my red pen.

"No," I push aside my papers. "Please come in. I'm so glad to see you." I motion to the empty plastic chair.

"I just wanted to come by and say I was okay." She looks at me, her face subdued.

"Can you tell me what happened?"

"I got overwhelmed with the idea of being gay and telling my family. When that Tiffany girl I met in your class rejected me, I just collapsed. I know it was stupid to swallow pills, but I just didn't know what to do."

"Wait a minute. Tiffany? Which Tiffany? Gorden?" My heart beats faster. No wonder Flora's been on a rampage.

Doris nods her head. "We were seeing each other for a short while and I thought we were a couple. One day in class she was real pale so I took her back to her apartment. Turns out she had an abortion and didn't want me to find out."

"Tiffany? An abortion?" I repeat. I'm too astounded to do more than blink.

"Yup. She was ticked at me, but I stayed overnight anyway to help her out. She claimed it was date rape but I had my doubts. Anyways, she was real weak and didn't want to go back to the doctor or nothing so I sat with her. Brought her soup. Ignored the phone. Smoked a little pot." She giggles a little. "Just hung out watching old movies with some broad named Barbara Stanwyk."

Doris stops to take a breath. Her head lowers, eyes filling with grief. "Tiffany was so sweet with that pretty blond hair. I was giving her a back rub in her bedroom. It got so hot we took our shirts off." Doris' voice chokes up. "Before ya know it, this crazy woman with rat's nest hair comes in and starts screaming at me like a wild banshee. Couldn't get out of there fast enough. When Tiffany didn't come back to class, I went to look for her and she was gone." She shakes her head in sorrow. "I got depressed thinking that maybe my affection for her made her run. I guess I got involved with a straight girl." She sighs, her shoulders slump forward.

A pang of guilt spears me. "Oh, Doris, I wish you had come to talk to me." I pat her arm instead of her leg. The snake tattoo crawling out of her skirt gives me the willies.

She brightens. "I've learned my lesson. Doctor Blackhead says I need to find out if someone is gay before I put my energy into them.

I'm going ahead with my plans to finish college. Who knows? Once I finish law school maybe I'll run for office or somethin'." She looks at me with confidence, then nods. "Gay people need a voice, too."

"Sounds like your therapist gave you good advice," I say, thinking, that nut? I encourage Doris to come back and talk to me anytime. The revelation about a rebellious Tiffany as a pot-smoking renegade is a wow. No wonder Flora flipped. When it comes to kids, they do the opposite of what you expect. Flora and I have some things in common.

With a clear no gook-in-the-air day I can see the Superstition Mountains. It's not one of those days. As I hustle outside to bring in the mail I glance at the return addresses. The TuniEl logo embossed in gold decorates a large manila envelope. It's an official looking packet. I pause to rip it open, anticipating a check. Instead, it's a formal letter. My eyes cruise the ivory paper. Production has begun on holiday and window ornaments with a four-color reproduction brochure. The gist is that they want more money. We put in one unit of $25,000. Then, Steve and Ted urged us to pony up two more units. Maury did some fancy juggling with our finances and his pension fund to reach that level. That's our limit. We haven't received any return on our money yet, but April and Glee got checks the last two months for five thousand dollars each. Smaller investors don't recoup anything for six months.

I don't want to give them any more money. The stock market corrections, as the experts call them, send us into a spiral of anxiety.

It reminds me of the clown in the circus who spins the plates. Only ours crash. One day Maury's up. The next, he's morose.

I do something uncharacteristic of me. I tear the letter into strips and then into smaller pieces and drop it in the can. They drift down to the bottom. Even if the garbage analyzers come, they won't be able to put it together. I feel terrible about concealing something from Maury but it's too late. Should I have hidden the letter for a day? Then it would be premeditated. Now it's a crime of passion. The guilt hammers in my chest.

It reminds me of one of the few negative stories Maury ever told me about his parents. They didn't want Maury to go away to medical school, expressing that he stay in New York near them. Of course, Maury, who spent his college years living at home and studying in the basement, was anxious to escape. He applied to one medical school nearby and others far away. His only acceptance came from the med school close by. During Maury's senior year, after his dad died, his mom became ill. She confessed to him that he had been accepted to every medical school he applied to, including Johns Hopkins and UCLA, but she destroyed the letters so he wouldn't leave home. What do you do with that kind of resentment?

This wasn't as bad. Was it? No, I rationalize. We've already invested. Our accountant said we need to diversify. Why should we take our retirement fund and put it all in one place? The resolve genie gives me confidence. Maury's got a lot on his mind. Then the little guilty creature with fangs who resides on the spineless part of my back croaks, "You should give him the option of saying yea or nay. It's not right to withhold information from your partner."

If Maury read Ellis's convincing rhetoric, he might be tempted to invest more money. The unhappier he gets with medicine, the more he looks for an escape. I press my lips together.

"He doesn't need to know about this," I say aloud as I slam the top of the can down.

Babies are the main issue now. Maury says he's done crying infants twice with our own and he's not up for it again. The kids have to get a place of their own. We'll have to subsidize them for a while. One neighbor commented that they're adults and I should kick them out. It's easy to say and hard to do. Besides, the baby's an innocent. Yet I'm ready for Michael and Rivka to be their own family unit. I want my house back.

That night Michael and Rivka leave for Cold Stone Creamery to get their chocolate ice cream with Snickers after dinner.

Maury says, "At least it got her out of my chair." He grabs the remote control and aims it toward the TV. His voice sounds tired after seeing fifty patients, many who coughed in his face from our worst flu epidemic in years. "What does she do all day?" He mangles the buttons to search for golf. He's found a repeat of a Senior Tournament one of his heroes played years ago. I'm losing him.

"Honey, she works in the mornings, comes home, reads pregnancy books, talks to her hypno-birthing specialist, watches Spanish soap operas, emails her family, gardens a little. She's nesting."

"Can't she nest by putting up fruit or something useful?" His voice sounds irritated. He's miffed because the hospital removed the china from the doctor's dining room and replaced it with Styrofoam, another sign that doctors rank low on the respect scale. He sinks farther into his chair, belly pooching over his belt. Should I suggest participating in exercise instead of watching it?

"What about if Rivka cans crab apples?" I offer.

21

THE BACK OF MY LEGS STICK TO THE LEATHER CHAIR. I've never been alone with the Dean before. Did he exclude Megan because of our animosity? I cross and uncross my ankles in the stifling office. Muffled music from Olive's radio fills up the silence.

"This law suit compromises the college. Let alone what it'll do to us financially. Do you understand the position you've put us in?" Dean Gruber shakes a copy of the same piece of paper I have in my hands. "Flora Boudreaux decides we've damaged her child's morals by teaching subversive literature, so our legal department has to scurry around to examine our options for a settlement. We're obligated to defend you and the college, but I suggest you engage your own attorney on the corrupting morals charge. If this thing goes to court, we'll all be unemployed. Forever."

"Wait a minute. This Flora person sues me, you, Megan, the college and can get away with it? All because I failed her daughter? Where's the justice?"

Dean Gruber adjusts a paperweight on his desk avoiding my eyes. "You've unleashed a hurricane and now we have to waste our time and resources to defend it. You may think Flora Boudreaux is a joke, but I can assure you she commands power in the legislature and is elected every year in a landslide." I notice sweat stains creeping into the underarms of his blue shirt.

"Giving students choices is not corrupting their morals. My reading list has selections . . ." I fade. The air conditioner hums like a fly trapped between a window and a screen. I've lost my resolve.

He sighs, looking at me as though I belong in the Special Olympics. "Number one--you didn't follow the syllabus or heed the suggestions of your department head. Number two--your selections were controversial because they advocated alternative lifestyles in our conservative community and number three. . ." He searches through his stack of papers. "You invited in a guest lecturer, a Glee Barstow, who is a known pornographer."

Glee? A pornographer? If Maury heard that, he'd croak.
"Hold it. Glee Barstow is a well-respected artist. She spoke to my class on artistic expression."

The Dean stands up, slapping his hands on his desk. "I urge you to seek legal counsel. Don't you dare speak to the press. We could all sink on this one." I am dismissed.

As I drive I slump lower in the seat of the Volvo. I'm in a giant cauldron of trouble. An attorney? Just what Maury and I need. Another expense. I'd better wait until he's in a good mood to tell him this.

At home I sneak past a very pregnant Rivka asleep in Maury's favorite chair. I squirrel myself upstairs on my lap top searching the yellow pages. A nasal voice says, "Harding, Collier, Smith and Lefkowitz. How can I help you?"

"Steve Lefkowitz, please."

Maury takes the news better than I expect. My fight appeals to his liberal sensibilities, especially the part about the corruption of morals. He gets excited for an hour, then fights off the day's exhaustion by nodding in front of the History Channel. The Allies are bombing the Nazis at Ploieste in Romania, one of his favorite battles. I disappear into the bathroom where, instead of our usual *National Geographics*, I find reading material on the development of the fetus. Large heads and thwarted limbs wait to float to earth, a fantasy of moon cyclops that evolve into human forms.

On the phone Glee and I discuss the irony of me defending her. "Just think. I might have to bring my art work into court. Della at the Art Pod will go wild over the publicity. We can turn this into a media event."

"Not what I had in mind. I just want it to be over."

"Don't worry so much. Everything will turn out all right." Where have I heard that before? "Besides, if it doesn't, this will make a great book. You could go off somewhere and write." She has no concept of working for a living.

And, speaking of work, I'm an anathema at school. Megan greets me with a sneering sniff and the other professors ignore me, worried that their positions are threatened too. I felt like a pariah at our last department meeting.

Tuni calls after dinner one evening. The call is for Rivka. After she hangs up, Rivka turns to us and says, "Tuni is giving me a raise! Twenty dollars an hour!" I've never seen her so enthused. Her face beams above her seventh-month-basketball- belly.

"It's way more than the minimum wage you were earning at the law library," says Michael. He looks up from his torts book. "What do you have to do for it?"

Rivka puts her hands on her hips. "I'll be working on investor reports and production schedules instead of mailing lists. She thinks I'm very efficient." Why is she looking at me with a crumpled brow?

"Steve told me about the subpoena for a deposition. Are you okay? That Flora woman's crazy." April's voice sounds concerned.

"I'm okay," I say without enthusiasm. "My face is breaking out from stress and the tic near my eye won't stop, but I'm fine."

My attorney, Steve's associate, explains to me anyone can sue about anything. It has nothing to do with right or wrong. And we have to defend it. To the tune of three hundred dollars an hour.

"Got to run," April says. "My Prada sunglasses broke. Don't worry. Glee's going to call you. We've got an idea. Bye, honey."

The phone rings an instant later. Glee's breathless voice announces, "I found the perfect thing to take your mind off your troubles."

Has she noticed the tic? What now? During Lara's wedding Glee, who embraces every new weird idea, suggested coffee enemas to soothe my nerves. Mocha lattes or double espressos?

"Glee, whatever it is, I don't have time for it."

"No, you'll love this. Ted and I are going to Shangri-La and we want you to join us. April and Steve have agreed to come, too!"

The last thing on my mind is an exotic trip. We said no to Glee and Ted's Galapagos Islands sojourn a few years ago when they celebrated their twenty-fifth anniversary. We were recovering from a wedding hemorrhage of our own at the time. "Is this the Shangri

La in Nepal where you need sherpa guides? I don't think my knees will make it and I know Maury would rather golf."

"Jean, listen." Glee can be persuasive.

"Rivka needs to be picked up from TuniEl. I've got to take the Volvo in for a tune-up. And my mother's called me three times in the last hour." I stare at clean clothes in the laundry basket that need to be folded. "And I have chores to do."

"That's precisely why you need this. You're too stressed out."

"You're a dear, but I don't think Shangri La is for us. Take pictures," I say as I reach toward the basket. "We'll have a dinner party when you return."

"Shangri-La is right here. You don't have to travel," Glee says.

"What?" I fold a T-shirt of Maury's that says *Workers of the World, Unite*.

"Jean." Glee's voice is determined. "You're coming with us to Shangri-La. I've made the reservations. You can't say no."

"What's involved?" I kick the plastic basket.

"We'll pick you up at nine so we can stop for breakfast. Bring a towel."

"Wait a minute. What are you wearing?" All of Glee's activities require special attire.

"Shorts, sandals. It's cas." She doesn't finish the word casual so it comes out "cazsh".

Where could Shangri-La be in our hot dusty bowl of a Valley? Is there some green oasis that I've missed? Rushing waterfalls that empty into cool pools? Lily pads with bright green frogs who croak? Hanging vines with passionflowers, their purple eyelashes heightened by Disney animation? I pluck one of my imaginary oversized blossoms and place it behind my ear. A slim-hipped brown maiden in a sarong brings me a delicious drink in an iced glass while I lounge on a soft chair. *I want this*.

The alluring image carries me through a terrible week to Sunday.

22

"DO WE HAVE TO GO?" MAURY RUNS HIS HANDS up and down my body, preoccupied with our Sunday morning ritual. Once a week my sensual husband has the libido of the proverbial rabbit, a hot stud ready to rock.

"Honey, I promised Glee and we're already late."

He sighs, rolls off the bed landing on all fours. He's a football player ready to hike, scrambling toward the closet.

In minutes we're ready in shorts, tees and baseball caps. We race to the kitchen to grab bottles of water and lotion. I don't want to look like a dried apricot at the end of the day.

Rivka sits at the table, a bowl of Bing cherries in front of her, the pits and stems piled on a napkin, a dour expression on her face. With an elbow on the table, her hand props up her head. I skip the niceties. How can someone so beautiful be so sour?

"Rivka, what's the matter?" I ask while Maury searches for his glasses and keys.

"You're leaving? Michael's at the library. What am I supposed to do all day?" Her arm falls forward onto the table like a long whine, fingers puffy with fluid.

"What is it you want to do?" I ask, annoyed with the delay. I should probably invite her to come with us but I don't want to.

"I wanted to go to the mall to look for baby things." Her voice changes to sarcasm. "God forbid, you'd pay attention to me."

"Rivka, you can take my car. Otherwise, I'll be happy to take you to the mall next week. We made these plans a while ago. We have a life, too, you know."

"I don't want to go by myself. You don't treat me like a daughter," she says, her voice rising.

"Wait a minute. We've taken you into our home, put up with your religious rules, survived your spoiled attitude, bought you clothes. . ."

"Stop, you're sputtering," says Maury. He puts his hand on my chest to push me back, his sunglasses perched on top of his hat. He takes over where I left off. "Rivka, your attitude of entitlement is inconsiderate. You've changed our household, our eating habits. I've even given up my chair. We've been patient but you're ungrateful." The audience of righteous midgets in my head applauds as Maury's voice reaches a crescendo.

Rivka pushes back her chair to stand up. Her red face reminds me of Tuni's gargoyles. "I hate you both. You're horrible." She spews, "I'm moving out. If Michael wants to come, fine, but I'm going."

As much as she's annoyed me, the thought of them leaving upsets me. What about the baby? Will Michael think this is my fault? I start to cry, tears spilling down my cheeks. Then the anger wells up in me, a waterfall of emotion that's been repressed for months. As the family peacenik I don't get angry often, but now fury rushes to my head in a torrent.

I reach across the table and grab the bowl of cherries, the napkin with pits folded into the corner. It feels cold in my hand as I lift it above my shoulder and throw it against the refrigerator. The smashed mess slides to the floor with some of the fruit magnets and family pictures. It was either the bowl or her neck.

"Bitch!" I scream. It comes out of my mouth before I can censor it. I've used the word before but never to someone's face. It's the accumulation of all the recent events. A loud sob croaks from the back of my throat. In my anger I realize she has the power to take my grandchild away from me.

Rivka's eyebrows fold into a broken arrow, her mouth crumples. The shock of our rebellion makes her run to her room. The door slams. I collapse in Maury's arms while he pats my back, my wet nose dripping on his shirt. "Sssh, shhh," he murmurs. He sounds like my bubbe who'd say "shah, shah" over a skinned knee.

I break from the hug to look at him. "I can't go."

"Come on. Calm down. Let's get out of the house and let her stew. No point staying here. You could use some fresh air to clear your head." He looks at the debris on the floor. "Give me a minute to clean up the glass. He smiles. You've got some wallop. I'm glad you never threw anything at me."

I stare back, then retreat to throw cold water on my face. At least we all know how we feel. But I have a gnawing worry about the baby. Will he hate me, too? With reluctance I grab the water bottles and head out the door.

After breakfast at The Pancake House, we drive for what seems like hours in Ted's Range Rover. The vehicle wears a rhino pack, a bra that drapes across the front like Madonna in black plastic.

"How far is this place?" I ask Ted, leaning toward the front seat. I feel terrible about losing it and breaking a good ceramic bowl.

His hands grip the steering wheel. "It's near New River." New River? They have outlet stores. We can't be going there. April wouldn't be caught dead in one of those places.

Ted twists his body to talk out of the side of his mouth. "Maury Man, this Vatican deal is terrific. I hope you're glad we pushed you a bit to get in. This thing is a going to be ka-ching world-wide."

Maury, subdued from our confrontation with Rivka, says, "I want to see some money first before I get too excited."

Steve turns in his seat to look at Maury, a baseball cap turned backward on his head. "Hey, whadja think of the letter?"

"What letter?" says Maury giving me a glance. Uh oh.

"The one about the deal," says Steve.

Maury looks puzzled while I start to sweat. Steve's high-powered chatter saves me.

"You saw the caliber of people at the Ritz meeting. Half the guys in my firm are in. We did our due diligence. TuniEl's got the licensing rights based on the Vatican's art. There's a bazillion people out there who want *tchotchkes* like that." Steve drapes his arm behind Glee in the front seat.

"I know. This is the big one that's going to fund all the pension plans," says Maury, his voice more upbeat.

"How's the home front?" asks Glee. She reaches her hand back to me for comfort.

"Not great," I answer. "We had a giant blow out with Rivka."

"What happened?" asks April, her ponytail swishing.

"I don't want to talk about it. All I'll say is Rivka hates me and she's moving out." My voice is sarcastic bravado.

"How do you feel?" says Glee with her therapy voice. She knows I abhor conflicts.

"I'm better now." I smile at Maury. "At least I know where I stand."

"You should have seen Jean in her rage. She threw a bowl of cherries against the refrigerator," says Maury.

"Jean threw cherries? As in life is a bowl of?" Steve asks. "Our little Jeannie?"

Maury proudly puts his arm around me. "Yup. She threw the bowl, pits and all. Let me tell you, that was one surprised daughter-in-law. Yesiree. Jean even called her a nasty name," he adds, doing his Groucho Marx imitation and tapping a pretend cigar.

Glee's watches me. I know she sees the pain in my eyes. "Don't worry, honey. You'll get over it."

I nod. Maybe I will. But will Rivka?

Finally, we enter a parking lot. It seems like we've been driving forever. I wanted to ask, "Are we there yet?" but I know Glee likes surprises. Ted cuts the motor. Everyone in the car jumps out to Glee's sing-song "We're here."

Without warning, the group takes off their shoes, slips shirts over their heads, unzips shorts, pulls down their pants. April's breasts bounce out of her camp shirt and bra. Steve's tush is inches from my face as he fools with his shoelaces. I've seen a few naked bodies before--but my friends *in broad daylight?* Maury's speechless.

I ask Ted's hairy back, "What are you doing?"

Glee says, "Hurry up. Take off your clothes! We'll all run in together!"

"Run in where?" I ask.

"Didn't you read the sign when we drove in?" she asks.

Maury, scrunched beside me, turns to get out of the car. The man moves slower than a drugged hippo as our legs unglue. He offers me his hand, an elegant gesture among the chaos. We stroll over to the fence and walk around to read the sign in bold script letters, SHANGRI-LA NUDIST CAMP.

No! They didn't! I start to laugh. Then I stop. What if I don't want to show off my slightly plump body? Isn't my pudendum private property? How do I let these nuts pull me into these things?

"Maury, how do you feel about this?"

He shrugs. "Hey, it's okay with me. I see naked people all the time." He senses I'm uncomfortable and puts his arm around me. "If you don't want to go in, just sit in the truck. I'll stay with you."

"Oh, what the hell. Let's go in," I say.

The group waits for us, wrapped in towels, prepared to make their mad dash to the front.

I encourage them to go without me. "I need a few minutes. Start without me." Maury trails off behind them after I convince him I'm okay. I hear April and Glee giggling as they push through the large wooden door.

In the truck I think about Rivka, Michael and the baby. Will she make good on her threat? Can I patch my relationship with her? Will Michael side with his wife? My stomach gurgles with banana nut pancakes. I sigh. Time to put the family problems away until tonight.

Twenty years ago Maury and I skinny-dipped in the Barstow's new lagoon. Of course, I have lumps in a few more places now but so what? All right. I'll be naked for a day. I peel my useless sports bra over my head, drop my clothes on the floor, and glance around. With the towel around me I hurry in behind an older couple with dyed shoe-polish black hair and gold chains around their necks.

Inside, I find my friends studying the activity sheet at a redwood table and benches under a tree. The ladies sit demurely on their towels. "You're going to love this," says Glee as I join them. "They have horseback riding."

"Won't our bosoms bounce as the horse trots?" I ask with an air of practicality.

Maury whispers to me, "I wonder if there's a TV in the clubhouse. The Senior Open starts today."

"Hey, April, there's a Miss Nude Arizona contest at four o'clock. You should enter that," says Ted.

"Right. Just what I need," says April, examining her pedicure. The day turns out to be a relaxed one and anything but sexy. I've seen women at the spa in various sizes and shapes. Childbirth is not that kind to most of us so besides sagging, dimpled bellies, there are large boobies, small boozies, teeny tits, gazunta-size bosoms, sagging Suzies and even a mastectomy patient proudly displaying her scar.

"What an affirmation of life," says Glee with a shake of her head.

After an hour we tire of commenting on the bodies. The men's parts are not that interesting because either their penises loop to one side or their balls hang low. It's bad form for the men to have an erection.

We decide to participate in activities. The guys go off to play volleyball, April borrows a tennis racquet and Glee heads for yoga. I find a tree and the Sunday paper. I check on everyone periodically. At first I can't find anyone because nudity is the great equalizer, no clothes to judge by, nothing to distinguish them in a crowd. A gentleman who shares my paper says that nudists are more intelligent because they don't waste a lot of time on bullshit.

My formula for finding everyone is: Maury looks like a silver-backed gorilla, Steve wears jewelry, Ted has two magnets taped to his right knee, Glee sports a hormone patch on her hip outlined by black adhesive and April has the most perfect body anyone has ever seen. Almost everyone wears a hat and sunglasses.

The day lazes by. I abandon my watch on Sundays so I have to get up to find out the time. At a mini pow-wow we decide to stay for the Miss Nude Arizona pageant, then head home. Risers have been dragged to the outside amphitheater. Red, white and blue decorations adorn the stage, a leftover from July Fourth or Memorial Day. An overhead sign announces today's event. Potted palms are rolled to the sides where the contestants are going to enter.

"How long do you think this will take?" asks Maury as we find a long bench near the front. I know he's had enough of what he'll later call *mishegas*, another word for nonsense.

"Can't be long. There's no swimsuit or evening gown competition," I remind him. He smiles.

Glee reaches over Ted to tap me. "Isn't this fun? Take some deep breaths. You'll feel your troubles melt away."

My troubles are not going to melt away from being naked for a day or taking deep breaths. Yet I do feel better. Even Flora has taken a back seat for the afternoon. The Master of Ceremonies introduces the judges.

". . . and since this is informal, contestants may enter now," the MC blabs into the microphone, his chubbie waving in the breeze. With his lineless tan and shaved head he reminds me of a huge dark thumb. The absurdity of it hits me. I start to giggle. It isn't very mature of me, I know, but when I get the sillies, there's no stopping. I keep trying to suppress my laughter. The naked family with five kids in front of us turns around to stare. Glee raises her eyebrows to give me a, you're- embarrassing-me look. I still can't stop. My body convulses with suppressed hysteria. Maury looks at me the way he does when people talk in the movies. The couple with gold chains tells me to shush. But I'm over the edge. All the tension from this morning rolls to the surface. I gasp for air.

". . . so if you lovely ladies will proceed to the stage, we can begin our search for Miss Nude Arizona who will compete in the nationals in Kissimmee, Florida. Don't be shy," says the announcer. A few women move toward the stage. From the back of their bodies I can see this isn't much of a competition. One woman's ass is sadly dragging, the other has pimples on her shoulders, and the third has ham hocks bigger than mine.

Then a stunning, statuesque redhead makes her way to the front. A helper gives each of the women numbers on a string to hang around their neck. As a feminist I abhor beauty pageants. The quintessential meat market.

Ted and Steve start on April. "Come on, April. Show them what a body really looks like. You'll win. Hands down." April waits, her lips pressed together. Is she contemplating this? Another woman with short silver hair in a bob gets up on stage. She has a good figure for a mature woman. I never use the word *old*.

"When will you ever have an opportunity like this again?" Steve asks.

April, a determined look on her face, stands up, pulls off her visor, pulls back her hair to accentuate her Cherokee-high cheekbones and takes a deep breath. She has a magnificent non-surgically enhanced body. With shoulders pulled back, she squeezes out of our row and moves toward the stage. Contestant Number Seven has arrived.

The women line up along the apron of the stage. April and the red head stand out in the group. The MC goes over rules and regulations. The first prize is an all expense paid trip to Florida, a week's stay in a condo and a set of luggage.

The MC asks questions one-step up from the usual pageant fare of, "If you were an astronaut, where would you go and why?" The answers are better, too. "I'd help homeless children become nudists to learn about life."

Then the naked women parade, exiting to the right. While the judges tally their votes, an overweight teenager fills the interlude with a baton solo. Her body sports black and blue marks from the falling silver rod. Are there jobs for nude majorettes? The MC announces it's time for the new Miss Nude Arizona to emerge.

The second runner up is the silver-haired lady. It narrows down to the redhead and April. In pageant fashion, they hold hands and whisper good luck to each other. April stands, breasts high, long legs poised in a dancer's third position. The redhead, Darlene, has a beautiful body, too, and a bright red triangle. Did she dye it for this? Glee says, "That can't be real."

". . . and the winner is," a pause for emphasis and a drum roll for tension, after a long explanation about what happens if Miss Arizona can't fulfill her obligation, "Miss April."

We jump up and applaud while the MC places a banner around April and a rhinestone tiara on her head.

Our ride home in the descending desert darkness is quiet. The mountains fade. April, proud of her win, falls asleep. Ted and Steve talk sports, and I, less consumed with family problems, rest my head on Maury's shoulder. Perhaps being naked for the day has distracted me. Rabbi Turkletaub's words float back to me, *Yie tov*." It will turn out all right.

24

WE RETURN TO FIND A NOTE ON OUR KITCHEN TABLE. Rivka and Michael are gone. I sob with guilt at the havoc I've caused. No, it's not all my fault, but she's in her last trimester. I'm a mess so Maury calls the few numbers we have for Michael's friends. No one's seen them. I finger the missive written in Michael's immature handwriting. "Ma and Dad, we're outta here. Can't hack it anymore. M."

I cry myself to sleep. What if I don't get to see the baby? What if I lose Michael? Maury says, "Don't worry, they're not sleeping outside."

Monday passes. Tuesday. Then Wednesday. On Thursday Maury cancels morning office hours to wander the halls at the law school. No one's seen or heard from Michael. Most of the people Maury talks to don't know who he is. He's in a whole different world with a wife and a child on the way. Just thinking about it makes my heart clutch. What if they went to Mexico? I'm ill inside, the weight dragging my heart to my knees.

Thursday night Glee calls at eleven PM.

"Jean, has Michael called you yet?"

"No, and we're sick with worry."

"Oh." She pauses. I wait. "They're here."

"What?" My heart begins to race.

"They're here. In my pool house. They showed up a few hours ago, but Rivka's sick."

"OhmiGod."

"Ted and I are driving them to the emergency room. You and Maury should meet us there."

Maury and I tear out of our bed and pull on clothes. As I wrestle with my sneakers, the phone rings again. Why is everyone calling me now?

"It's me, April. Is Rivka going to be okay?"

"I don't know. We're on our way to the hospital. How did you find out so fast?"

"Glee said Rivka's been *ka-vetching* in the pool house for two days. I wasn't supposed to say anything."

"First of all, it's *kvetching* and second of all, what do you mean she's been in the pool house two days?"

"Oh, honey, Glee swore me to secrecy because the kids made her promise. Otherwise they would've left and gone back to that seedy motel with cockroaches. Please don't be mad at us. The kids were so pathetic when they showed up, especially with her big belly. Glee thought they were better off in her pool house than in some dive so. . ."

Maury stands in the bedroom door, his shirt buttoned wrong, the keys jingling in his hand. "Let's go. I want to get to the hospital. You'll call her later."

I hang up with mixed feelings. My friends conspiring against me? It feels like there's a concrete block chained around my head and I'm sinking to the bottom of a lonely, dark river. Maury hunches over the wheel speeding through red lights after a brief slow down.

We arrive at the ER to find Michael camped out on a burgundy vinyl chair. Glee and Ted in bicycle shorts and headbands are hovering over him. Michael acknowledges us with a small wave of a few fingers. His expression shows relief before his head falls into his hands.

She rushes toward me, her arms in an open gesture. "They made me swear I wouldn't tell you," Glee says. Without make-up she looks younger than when she's painted up. Ted stands aside with a sheepish look. Maury marches through the closed doors to assess the situation. I stare at Michael's bony, hairy legs that stick out of khaki shorts. What happened to the little boy who used to put his arms around me and tell me I was his best friend?

I bend down to comfort him. He looks up at me when I touch him, the small child inside pleading, "Mom, I'm scared."

He stands up and hugs me. I hear his stifled sob on my shoulder. I'm still hugging him when Maury pushes through the double doors. As we break apart, Maury says, "Bernie thinks she's got early signs of pre-eclampsia. Her blood pressure's high and she's got a headache. He's going to watch her overnight in ICU."

"Dad, are she and the baby going to be okay?" Michael asks, his unshaven face haggard. Glee and Ted rush forward to hear Maury's answer.

"I don't know yet. We'll know more tomorrow, but Bernie's got her hooked up to an IV drip with magnesium sulfate. She's resting. She needs lots of water and bed rest. I think we should go home and we'll come back in the morning. Michael, you look terrible. How 'bout some sleep in your own bed?"

"No, I'll stay here. I don't want Rivka to be alone when she wakes up."

For a moment I think we should stay and wait with him, but I realize having us sitting there when she opens her eyes might be more upsetting for her. Worse, I feel responsible for contributing to the upset that put them on the run. Just what I need: more guilt.

Maury and I hug Michael goodbye. "We'll talk later," says Maury. His hang-dog expression reminds me of Amber when her treats are gone.

The four of us leave. Glee gives me a grim look as they step on the plastic runner that opens the automatic doors. We don't speak as we walk to our cars. She looks at me pleadingly over her shoulder. I respond with my best how-could-you? look.

25

MAURY BRINGS RIVKA HOME FROM THE HOSPITAL Friday before Sabbath supper. She shuffles to her room, her face pale as a paper moon. Michael comes in behind her dragging plastic garbage bags of their stuff.

"Mom, we have to come back for now. Glee wasn't comfortable with us there anymore and the OB thinks we should be close to dad so he can check Rivka's blood pressure." Michael looks at me sheepishly. "Is it okay?"

I stop chopping radishes for the salad, my range of emotions exhausted.

I don't respond right away. I feel guilty I over reacted so now I want to make decisions with forethought. Also, despite the crisis and the worries, Maury and I appreciated our space alone for a short period of time. It's hard censoring what comes out of your mouth when you know others could be listening. And misinterpreting it.

"Mom?"

I place my paring knife on the counter to walk over to Michael. For a moment I look into his flooded eyes. Then I hug him. His fists still grip the plastic bags. His body sags into mine. "Welcome home."

Michael sighs with relief. "Mom, thanks. I'm sorry we worried you, but when I came home that Sunday, Rivka was hysterical and . . ."

I put my fingers on his lips. "Shah, shah." He drops the bags to enclose me in his arms. No matter how old kids get your youngest is still your baby.

"Let's not talk about it now. What about your classes?"

His words rush out. "I'm in trouble. I didn't go at all last week. I know I have two papers due, one on constitutional law. I haven't started either of them yet. Maybe I should bag this semester."

I return to the counter and shake the paring knife at him. "Oh no you don't. Your tuition has been paid."

"Oh no what?" asks Maury as he enters the kitchen. "She's asleep now. Herb says she'll be fine with some rest."

What, besides rest, has she been doing all along?

"What's for dinner?" Maury asks, rubbing his hands together.

I give Michael a look and add scallions to the salad.

Later when Rivka emerges from her room, hair pulled into a ponytail with a fresh face, we light the candles. She says the prayers from her chair and a resurgence of warmth flows over me. My little family is back and the baby's okay. Quiet conversation turns to environmental causes, a favorite topic of Maury's. I'm relieved not to discuss anything personal. Sometimes it's good to give things a rest. Rivka never says she's sorry, but when she makes an effort to clear the table, I shoo her away.

"Thanks," she says with a weak smile, putting her hand in the small of her back and waddling away.

Rivka's pre-eclampsia symptoms pass, her blood pressure returns to normal and the swelling goes does down in her hands and ankles. By the following week she's ensconced in her lounge chair again. Tuni phones to beg her to come in two mornings.

"Do you want to go? I'll drive you there if you do," I offer.

"Yes, I'll go. The doctor said I'm okay." She's not enthusiastic, but she's not testy either. The family dynamic has sobered us all.

On the drive to TuniEl Rivka asks if I've spoken to Glee yet.

"No, I'm upset that she never told us you were there. We were frantic to find you and she knew it."

"We made her promise. Please don't blame her. It was my fault because I was so angry."

My hands grip the wheel. I glance at her. Her pretty face seems gloomy, the perfect arched eyebrows angled darts. I don't respond. I feel betrayed by my friends. I'll savor my bitterness for a while.

When Rivka returns after lunch with Michael, she goes to her room to nap. I leave for my classes, a neglected set of papers in my brief case.

After dinner Rivka places a strange object on the table. "What's this?" I ask. I pick up a deformed gold-plastered cupid with a protruding tongue.

"Tuni gave me that for the baby's room," says Rivka.

"Yes, but what is it?" I turn it over thinking it might appear friendlier in a different position. The grotesque expression glares at me.

"It's from a mythology series." Rivka bends forward to stretch her back.

"This is what she's making? This'll scare the baby. It looks like a gargoyle that's been guillotined. I know mythology. This is from Hades."

"Oh no. They're not making these. All their production is done overseas. She orders from other manufacturers to see what the competition is doing." She collapses into a chair.

"Oh." I put it back on the table.

"She says that's how she gets inspiration and sees what the rest of the gift market is doing."

I start preparations for dinner with a freezer search. The blast of cold air from the igloo makes me sneeze.

"They're redecorating in a minimalist style using feng shui," says Rivka.

"What's that?" asks Michael coming in from school laden with his faded backpack and extra books. He's made the astute decision to talk to his professors and get caught up. He heads toward Rivka for a kiss.

"Tuni said it's an ancient Chinese art of manipulating your environment to make it better. Everything in a room has to be positioned a certain way to get the best energy. They put a fountain out front for prosperity. I'd like to do that in the baby's room. The sound of water is soothing."

"First, you need a baby's room," I add, aware that time is running out for our production. She's just begun her eighth month. My back is to her so she can't see my roll of the eyes.

Maury turns off the History Channel in anticipation of dinner, a human Amber without the panting and drooling. "What does Ellis do all day?" he asks Rivka.

"He's on the phone a lot. He meets with investors. He doesn't pay too much attention to me."

"Do the investors tour the facility?" asks Maury. He's more curious than I've seen him since I first petted with him in the back seat of his Plymouth Fury almost thirty years ago. He steals a radish.

"Oh no. He meets them for lunch because I hear Glory, the receptionist, making reservations at The Ritz and other nice places. Once in a while people visit the site."

"What's there to see?" asks Maury. He peeks under the top of the pot that's cooking rice.

"Not too much. Offices. Computers. A display of product lines. It's just a warehouse really. Lots of packing boxes." says Rivka.

"What's the receptionist like?" asks Michael. Rivka's mentioned Glory a few times because they take breaks together. We all hope she makes a friend. I think part of her surly attitude has been her loneliness. She misses her mom and sisters.

"She's funny. Glory started when I did. Yesterday on break she told me Tuni's ex-husband called. From prison."

We freeze in our positions of refrigerator search, feeding Amber, and mixing a scotch. "How did she know he was calling from jail?" I ask in high alert.

"Because it was a collect call. Glory said it was from Kansas."

Leavenworth? I assumed she had a husband or two before Ellis, but I thought maybe it was a female one. "Did she find out what he wanted?"

"Sort of. Glory said Tuni cried after the conversation. When she brought her a glass of water, Tuni told her she divorced him when he was in jail and he's never gotten over it."

"Did Glory ask her what he was in for?" asks Michael.

"Embezzlement."

26

"JEAN, DON'T HANG UP. YOU'VE BEEN IGNORING my calls for days."

I hear Glee's tentative voice as I stare into my magnified mirror with red, squinty pig-eyes. Should I let her off the hook or express how upset I am she sheltered the kids and didn't tell me?

"Yes?" My voice is cool with anger that transfers into hurt, a melted red crayon smearing across a page.

"I had to take them in. They put me in a terrible predicament. Ted didn't want me to do it. My therapist said I needed to behave the way I would have wanted someone to treat me when I was young. April said I was betraying you by not saying anything. I feel so guilty. Jean?"

I find it hard to find my voice, the one that will tell her how I feel. I clear it for courage. "Glee, in all the years we've been friends, I've never been so angry at you. I was upset with Rivka, annoyed with Michael, sick with worry about their well-being and the baby's. The fact that you were complicit in this made it worse. You've manipulated me into crazy vacations, making a fool of myself and silly schemes, but never have you so pointedly interfered with my family."

"Can you forgive me?" she asks in a small voice.

"I don't know." My nose looks huge in the mirror's reflection. "I'm not ready to do that yet. You and April plotted against me." My voice catches a sob in my throat as I hang up without saying good-bye.

The phone rings again and I don't pick it up. I'm already late for class. When I retrieve the message, April sounds contrite.

"I know you're still angry, but why don't you meet me and Glee for lunch tomorrow? Let's talk about it. Love you."

Am I being a jerk? How can I deny how betrayed I feel? I decide to moisturize and forget the sunscreen. I'm living a reckless life.

To: jeanrubin
From: lara47
Subject: babies

Hi Mom!

Hope Rivka is feeling better. I can't believe I'll be an aunt soon. Is she getting cool stuff from her job? I'm over the yucky phase of pregnancy and onto to the good part. My hair and skin look great from the pre-natal vitamins Dad sent. My boobs are huge! Does that last? The Rubin women are already amply endowed.

I'm thinking of painting Tangerine's room robin's egg blue. I don't want to lock her into all that sexist junk of pink. I read a book that said yellow in a baby's room makes them wishy-washy. I can't tolerate wussy girls. It's a tough world out there and I want her to be strong.

Don't you love her name? Everyone in California is naming their girls after colors. My friend's daughters answer to Ruby, Violet, and Teal. Cool, huh?

The Womyn's Center told us to start inviting people to keep us company in the birthing room. Will you and daddy fly out? You'll have to get your tickets at the last minute, but Gus will call as soon as I start labor. Let me know ASAP because we only have room for ten people and I want to invite some of my bridesmaids. Gus' mom, Lois, and his step-dad, Don are planning on being here. Do you think I need to invite his Dad, too? His third wife, BJ, drives us crazy. She wants to bring her parents to stay with us for a free vacation the week before the baby is due.

Can't wait to see you next month for Passover! Tell Glee I've got the perfect belly for the plaster cast. Ask her if the ring is a problem.

Love,
Lara

To: lara47
From: jeanrubin
Subject: birthing babies

Lovely Lara,

If you want us there, we'll be there. Your father wants to know when having a baby turned into a sideshow, but he won't miss it. He'll bring his camera.

Rivka can't wait until you get here to discuss pregnancy and babies. We're a little burned out on the subject. She wants to know if you've got the dark line yet from your belly button to your po-po, as she calls it.

Glee's ready for you. The ring's going to add individuality. If it turns out great, she might abandon her current project, cast Rivka's, too, and start another trend.

That's all for now.

Love you,
Momma

To: jeanrubin
From: lara47
Subject: reply

Mom, dad doesn't need to bring his camera. We've hired the professional photographer from the Womyn's Center. Video included.

Love,
Lara

Amber's hot breath on my thigh convinces me to share my English muffin. It's a rare morning that I'm alone. I relish it after Glee and April's calls. I don't want to go to lunch with them but they're still my buddies. We've been friends for so long. They watched Lara and Michael grow up. I miss them. I'm sure we'll mend the tension soon. I wouldn't want Lara to miss her belly cast. I sip my herbal tea on the patio listening to the birds singing. I read the paper instead of just glancing at headlines. Some days we never take the rubber band off of it.

Flora's on the front page of the local section. She's trying to drum up support for eliminating unnecessary curriculum, in particular, Women's Studies. Even though the motion died in committee last year, she's bringing it up for another round.

"Why won't this woman go away?" I say aloud. I rock my foot with anxiety.

"Jean, you okay?" asks my neighbor popping her head over the back fence.

"Fine. I'm just fine." She fades away while I deal with the fact that I've been having a conversation with my dog. I drop the local news on the ground in disgust and turn to the business section.

TuniEl Corporation of Phoenix, Arizona announces its distinguished Board of Directors. It's a great publicity piece with a smiling picture of Tuni and Ellis in front of their sign. I recognize the names of some of the prominent people in town, including the owner of *The Phoenix Courier* we saw at Glee's motorcycle mayhem, Malcolm Burgess. Also on the list are attorney, Steve Lefkowitz and developer, Ted Barstow.

The phone jars me from my thoughts of Malcolm with his fake ponytail and bulging biceps.

"Hi Honey. Ya busy?" I think April asks that because she never is. "I want to talk to you."

My voice turns chilly. "April, I'm still angry."

"I know. You didn't return my call. Will you have lunch with us?"

"No." I realize as I say it that I'm still on *it* and it's probably time to get off *it*. I change the subject. "I read about Steve. What does he do on the board?"

April sounds relieved. "They had their first meeting at The Ritz and the spices were invited."

I smile at her little joke for spouses. "What did they discuss?" A crow starts a rabble-rousing discourse with an unidentifiable brown bird in our eucalyptus tree.

"It was a preliminary meeting to go over financials, production schedules, and figure out how we could help."
"What do you mean help?"

"There were some influential people there so when they asked about getting a new computer system, the man who owns the Twentifirst franchises said he could get them at a discount. Or, they wanted to know if anyone had contacts in the Philippines to assist in exporting. Malcolm Burgess knew someone because he buys newsprint over there."

"What's he like?" I ask, thinking anyone involved in newspapers must be literary.

"He brags about his military service. Seems he was in Korea, Viet Nam, and called up for the Gulf War as an advisor. These macho types act so righteous and tough, but I know I could make them weep," April says in a rare display of ego.

"Did the board get much done?" The birds take their discourse to our grapefruit tree, laden with luscious fruit.

"Oh, yes. Besides covering business, they came up with fifty more investors. Jean, this is going to be the cultural icon for the twenty-first century."

"I thought that was Lady Gaga."

"It is, sort of. Only it's not religious."

"April, I don't understand how you're getting money back if the products haven't hit the stores yet."

"They've had so many people investing, the monies they haven't used yet are earning interest. The banker on the board gave part of the financial report. They've brought in millions. Everyone wants a piece of the action."

Any minor worries I have float away. Maybe Maury and I aren't sophisticated about investing, but our friends are. The guilt dragon looms large when I think about the letter I threw away. For once, we're in the right place at the right time. Without being greedy, we deserve a break. Won't it be great to help the kids and have Maury cut back at the office? Maybe we'll escape to the Costa Rican rain forest for the vacation we've talked about for years. I'd love to take the whole family on a trip to Disneyland. Nothing's better than watching a little kid's face when they meet Mickey for the first time.

April interrupts my reverie. "How's Rivka feeling?"

"Fine. She's back to work part-time."

"That's good. I want you to know how sorry I am. Please forgive us. We both feel awful. We miss you."

"What the two of you did was disloyal. I can't brush it off like it was nothing."

"Okay then. Just stew. I hope you're over it by the Phoenix Valley Hospital benefit next week. I've got to go. Time to walk Thelma and Louise. Bye."

The phone feels heavy in my hand and I feel empty inside. April's never been curt with me before.

27

THE PHOENIX VALLEY HOSPITAL BENEFIT IS THE one black tie event we attend. Beside the fact that Maury's on the staff and we're expected to attend, they raise money every year for one project. This year it's a neo-natal unit. At The Phoenician we saunter into a dimly lit ballroom with impressive tables, centerpieces and crystal chandeliers that send glittery sparks against the faux finished walls. We look spiffy, too--Maury in his tuxedo and me in my mother-of-the-bride dress from Lara's wedding. It's a bit over the top with its red ruffled sleeves trimmed in gold, but I'm determined to get more use out of my Carmen Miranda look.

As Maury wanders off to the bar to get me a glass of wine, I scout the room for familiar faces. I recognize some of the doctor's wives from the old guard when we first moved here. Back then a women's auxiliary supported the guys. It disbanded years ago after the grand poobah planned a fashion show using spouses and a male attorney and police officer showed up as models. The woman-in-charge couldn't deal with men in her women's auxiliary.

Maury, my handsome hero, albeit a bit craggy, brings my drink and wanders off to commiserate with some other kindred souls about the mangled managed care mess. I overhear one of them in a plaid cummerbund and bowtie say in a loud voice, " . . . last week one HMO filed for bankruptcy and left me high and dry for sixty thou. How am I supposed to pay my staff?"

I'm still smarting from Megan's admonitions that I should have changed Tiffany's grade while I had the chance. And weary from watching legislative proceedings on late night cable all week to monitor Ms. Boudreaux. I find an anti-social corner to bury myself. There's no chance of blending into the moss green drapes in this get-up, but maybe no one will bother me while I people watch. I sip my chardonnay.

Ted finds me. "Jean, what are you doing hiding in this corner? Let me see how gorgeous you look." The compliment reels me in. His hand with manicured nails and a diamond pinky ring pulls my arm into the milieu of the room, a swirl of tuxes, gowns, drinks, and laughter. Ted surveys me, the tan from his daily round of construction sites a contrast to his bright white teeth. "You look stunning all dolled up."

"Thanks," I say, also greeting Glee, April and Steve, and the ever-present Tuni and Ellis with a nod instead of our usual hugs. They all appear in a movie star glow, especially April in gold lame, her figure defying the laws of physics.

"Where's Maury?" asks Steve searching the room. With my drink I motion toward a clump of penguin-men and a few women. I feel awkward to have been preoccupied with my own professional crisis. "Did you all come together?" I ask.

Tuni looks elegant in an off-the-shoulder iridescent copper gown that compliments her hair. "Yes. We rented a limo so we don't have to concern ourselves with drinking and driving," says Tuni. "We love supporting such a good cause. It's amazing how they keep these wee babies alive nowadays."

"Speaking of babies, how's Rivka feeling?" asks Ted.

"She's doing better. We're in the home stretch. She's due before Passover, which is less than three weeks away, but first babies are traditionally late." I'm uncomfortable because I don't know how much Tuni and Ellis know about the recent upset. Glee and April hang back. I recover enough to add with a smile, "The babies must know how anxious we are to greet them."

Tuni says, "I must tell you what a delight it's been having Rivka in our office. She's quite efficient. I know she's been an immense assistance to Ellis with all his mailings. Right, darling?" The emerald and diamond bracelet on her wrist moves as she twirls her drink.

"Oh, yes," agrees Ellis, nodding.

"Is there going to be a baby shower for her? I'd love to get her a bassinette," offers Tuni.

"That's very generous of you, but we're superstitious so we don't buy anything beforehand. Maybe after the baby arrives, you--"

"Excuse me," says a tuxedoed man with a camera. "Could you all bunch together?" Tuni, April, and Glee spin into action to position themselves next to their husbands, angling their bodies into a three-quarter pose to look slimmer. I move to the side, not wanting to be in the picture without Maury.

"Could I get you to move in a little closer?" the photographer asks, his hands punching together, an accordion player in motion. The group squeezes into a tighter mold, smiles pasted on their faces.

"On the count of three, give me your best." Click.

When everyone breaks from the pose, Tuni noses next to the photographer who is searching his jacket pocket for a pen and paper to write down their names, "What publication is this for?"

"*Fashionista.*"

The following week the legislature goes into overtime. Representative Boudreaux's bill to ban funding for Women's Studies programs passes committee and goes to the floor. When it fails, she holds a press conference where she vows to introduce it next year.

". . . and if these feminazis, as my good friend Rush Limbaugh likes to call them, persist in trying to ruin our young people and the moral fiber of this great nation, we will take stronger action. This is the sovereign state of Arizona. Our pioneer forefathers did not brave this desert land to have our children brainwashed with alternative lifestyles. Is that in the Bible? It is not! Why, if we allow these liberals any more leeway, you'll see condom machines in the bathrooms and porno in all the classrooms. My own daughter was subjected to a lecture in her college class by a woman who calls herself an artist and paints male body parts. This is ruining America."

I'm not off the hook yet. Even though Tiffany's problem was dropped, Megan, in her passionate desire to be rid of me, has pushed my contract into review, instigated a survey in my classes, and scheduled weekly meetings to review my lesson plans. The tortuous sessions in her fake English countryside office remind me what a little bit of power can do coupled with a large ego. I can forget about tenure. I'm hanging on by a thread.

"You know, Jean, in my day, I was quite the rabble rouser, too, but it's important to play within the system. That is, if you plan to stay here." She pauses for emphasis. "Megan, the Radcliffe undergraduate, was quite a firebrand in her day. Oh, yes. We were reading Kerouac and Ferlinghetti before the rest of the campuses had even discovered The Beat Generation."

Spare me. I bite the inside of my cheek. The fact that she refers to herself in the third person, as though Megan represents another far superior entity than the mere Megan who is trapped as the lowly head of a department, drives me nuts.

I imagine Megan, the buxom damsel in distress from another century, cone hat with veil trailing, landing on her round bum when a horse throws her. Megan, the knight, her sex disguised by armor, preparing for battle, sword held high. Megan, the Queen, jeweled crown on her head, an expression of disdain, glancing at her subjects below.

At the moment she looks at me as though an unpleasant sulfur smell wafts about her nostrils. Then she brushes crumbs of whatever she had for lunch from her hefty bosom.

I kowtow to the pressure and remove *Women As Lovers* from my reading list, but not others like *Sisters of the Soul*. Fortunately, she's not familiar with the titles. I know I'm taking a chance, but a part of me refuses to meld with her conservative views. Not only do I propose an education should expose students to a variety of philosophical thought, but I also think it's important for students who are wrestling with their sexual identity to know they're not alone.

Anyway, I make peace so I can keep my job. Besides the fact that I love the students and stimulation, I enjoy making my contribution to their intellectual awareness and a small financial contribution to our household, which, by the way, is in a flurry of activity. Pregnancy and Passover convene next week.

28

IT'S THE MORNING BEFORE THE FIRST SEDER, the symbolic feast to commemorate the Jews freedom from Pharaoh's slavery. We have not cleared all the bread, pastries, croutons, bagels, and bread crumbs from the house. According to Orthodox Jewish law all leavened bread must be removed. During the eight days of Passover we eat *matzoh*, a cracker-like unleavened bread that represents the Jews rush to leave their oppressors. In the past I cheated a little. I got rid of all the bread, bagels, and English muffins, and left the breadcrumbs for cooking and the salad croutons in the cabinets. One time I forgot hamburger buns in the freezer. However, with Rivka as my warden my household is going to be perfect.

Rivka, enthused about her first Passover, helps me, albeit in slow motion at full term. She shuffles from kitchen to pantry in her furry bedroom slippers, a corpulent sea lion in quicksand, who sinks into the lounge chair between chores. The other set of dishes for the service sits piled on the counter. We use sponges to wipe out the cabinets. Our numerous trips to the large garbage cans outside ensure that The Chief Rabbi of Israel won't find a crumb in my house. Or in my freezer.

I begin cooking the next morning while Rivka, sitting at the kitchen table, chops apples and nuts to be mixed with honey for the *charoseth*, our representation of mortar that held the temple together. The aromas set my salivary glands in motion.

I start the chicken soup and add matzo balls I bought at the deli. Whenever I've made them in the past they came out like hockey pucks, an excuse for family derision. No concrete jokes this year. Fluffy and soft, I nibble one to see if it meets matzo ball standards. The soft dough comes apart in my mouth fueled with flavor. The brisket and chicken are in the oven enhanced by packets of onion soup. Vegetable casseroles bake next to them. Only the gefilte fish needs to be put on plates decorated with a lettuce garnish and a slice of carrot for color. Some people don't like the beige-bland, molded appetizer made from a few kinds of fish, but Rivka and I share a taste test with horseradish. She likes it.

Rivka arranges the Seder plate with a little bit of all the symbolic foods. She's studied it all, the book closed on the table. The plate, a replica in Delft blue and white from one created in Czechoslovakia during the 1800's, remains one of my treasures. A pile of covered *matzoh* are arranged on a plate.

She surveys her work. "Let's see. The horseradish is for the bitterness of slavery, the egg symbolizes the offering in the temple and mourning, the shankbone's for the lamb that had to be sacrificed, the parsley reminds us of their poor nutrition. Also, we have to dip it in salt water to symbolize the tears. The *haroseth* made from apples and nuts is mortar. I read in another book that it also represents God's kindness. The *matzoh* shows what a hurry the Israelites were in to leave their oppressors. That's it. We're set." Rivka steps back to admire her arrangement of foods on the dining room table, hands propped into the small of her back, belly thrust forward. I'm impressed she's memorized everything.

While Rivka slips away for a nap, I leave to pick up my parents at their condo and Lara and Gus at the airport. The good moods are infectious. Lara looks adorable with her baby belly, a tie-dyed top and hair in pigtails.

"Grandma, have you made any new friends at your place?" asks Lara.

My mother ignores Lara's question. "Herm, should I tell them?" My parents, dressed in their blazers, hold hands in the back seat.

"Tell us what?" I want to know.

"Your mother doesn't want to tell you what happened," says my father with a rare bravado.

I turn around while I'm stopped at a red light. "Tell me what happened."

"Don't ask," says my mother making a shooing sign with her hand. Lara, who sits next to them, rolls her eyes. Gus slumps against the door in the front seat.

"I'll tell you," says my father. "We were invited to go to dinner with a new couple. They still drive--"

"I'll tell it," interrupts my mother. She elbows herself forward on the seat. "So your father and I got gussied up and waited downstairs with a whole group. When I asked which restaurant they said, you'll see. I was in the back seat talking to another woman so I wasn't paying attention where we were going. Your father never notices anything. Before I knew it, we were giving the car to a valet."

"Where were you?" asks Gus, more alert.

"We were in front of Phoenix Metropolitan Hospital."

"Why did you go to the hospital?" asks Lara.

"Wait. Wait 'til you hear." My mother waves her hand at us. "So everyone gets out, walks to the lobby elevator and goes to the basement. I kept asking what they were doing or if any one was sick, but they ignored me. We just had to follow."

"Florence, get to the point," my father urges.

"They took us to the hospital cafeteria for dinner! Can you believe it? And I got all dressed up! They even had half-price senior citizen cards for us. I was appalled. I'm never going out with those people again."

"Oh, Florence, it wasn't so bad. The food was okay and we only paid four dollars and fifty cents for two dinners with coffee and dessert."

The joys of senior living. I laugh as I pull into our driveway.

Before dinner I wake up Rivka. I sit next to her on the bed. She doesn't move from her frog position. I rub her back as she starts to stir, smoothing out the maternity top we bought months ago at the mall.

"Rivka, everyone's here and we're ready to start the seder." I stroke her arm. Through the open shutters I see it's almost sundown. My stomach churns in anticipation of our feast.

"I don't feel well," she says, rolling onto her back and bending her knees.

"Is this it?" I ask in anticipation.

"No, I don't think so. I just don't feel well. And my back hurts.

In fact, I'm really uncomfortable."

"Why don't you freshen up a bit and Maury'll take a look at you."

"Okay." I leave the room wondering if Baby Rubin is going to make his entrance on this momentous evening.

Rivka emerges with her hand on her lower back, a weak smile on her face. Maury concludes after some questions that she's fine. "Nothing a bowl of chicken soup with a *matzoh* ball won't cure," he says, his hair damp from a quick shower.

Michael rushes to her side and helps her with the dining room chair. There's no food on the table yet except for the Seder plate with the ceremonial food, wine, and a plate of *matzoh*.

Maury begins the familiar story reading from the *haggadah*, the book at everyone's place that recalls how our ancestors were released from slavery in Egypt. It's a good story, but a long one. We sip wine at the appropriate places and sample some of the items from the Seder plate. When we come to the Four Questions, Rivka is the youngest so she reads them.

"Why is this night different from all other nights?" She shifts in her chair. I can tell her back is bothering her. I flash back to Michael as a little boy asking the same question and sipping his grape juice, a replacement for the Manischevitz on the table.

The service continues for an hour. When I hear my stomach gurgling, I excuse myself and go into the kitchen to get the first course ready. Finally, Maury closes the *haggadah* and says, "That's the story of our celebration of freedom for this year. Let's all join hands and say a silent prayer." After a brief interlude, he asks,

"Who's hungry? Better yet, who's a little tipsy?"

"I am," says my mother as I put a plate of gefilte fish in front of her. "Michael, do you remember when you were ten or eleven and we let you drink wine instead of the grape juice for the first time? You pretended to be drunk and called the holiday Passout."

Michael shrugs, embarrassed by his grandmother's kid story. My father, sitting next to him, fork in hand, says, "These holidays are all the same. We were persecuted. We survived. Let's eat."

"Herm, shh," my mother says to quiet him.

"Why can't I tell the truth? I'm hungry. When my orthodox grandfather did the Seder, it took three hours."

I interrupt with his plate of gefilte fish, which the rest of the family finishes in minutes. Lara helps me clear the plates and bring in the soup. From my place in the kitchen, ladle in hand, I hear my father remark, "Who made the *matzoh* balls this year? It couldn't have been Jean. They're very good. What happened to the rocks?"

We devour the courses as a mound of dishes piles up in the kitchen, an ancient campground whose inhabitants haven't washed plates in years. I wish we could throw them over our shoulders into a mound like ancient tribalists. The conversation is lively and baby-oriented.

At the end of the meal we have more to read from the *haggadah*. It's a good thing one of our directives on this holiday is to recline in our chairs because my father is dozing and my mother's eyes are at half mast. Michael's rubbing Rivka's back. Lara and Gus are sitting with their heads resting against each others shoulders. I hustle to the kitchen to bring out chocolate and plain macaroons, the traditional dessert without flour. Rivka's experimental cake made earlier from *matzoh* flour sits on the counter. We decided not to serve it. It wasn't as hard as last year's *matzoh* balls, but it wasn't edible either. As if anyone has room anyway.

The evening comes to a close when Gus drives my parents home while the rest of us pitch in on the kitchen. I urge Rivka to lie down because she looks miserable. She and Lara curl up together to talk babies in the family room. As I wrap the leftovers in plastic wrap for tomorrow night's Seder, I hear a moan.

"I ate too much. Even the baby is full. *Aaugh*! My back is killing me," yells Rivka.

Lara jumps up. "What can I do? You want a heating pad?" We all rush to stand around her. Michael falls to his knees at her side, placing his hands on her belly.

"Ay Dios mio, my back is so achy and then I had a sharp pain. Too much brisket and *matzoh* at my first Seder." Rivka gives us a weak smile.

"Rivka, show me where the pain is," says Maury. The doctor takes charge. "In fact, let's go in your room so I can examine you better. Everybody back to your posts." I return to my job of scouring the brisket pan. Bits of onion soup and gravy have baked to the sides. It may have to soak for a few days.

Maury emerges with a grin. "Michael, call your OB. This is it."

"Aaaaah," I scream. "Tonight? This is so exciting!"

I peel off my yellow rubber gloves as the Rubin scramble begins. We run in different directions, keystone cops looking for a perpetrator. Everyone wants to go. Lara grabs Rivka's packed bag.

Michael rushes from room to room looking for his hairbrush. The father always loses his focus. I run to change shoes. The new baby can't see me in my around-the-house moccasins, can he? Maury yells for all of us to get in the car. Gus returns from grandparent delivery to chaos.

"Hey, guys, what's happening? I left and y'all were so mellow," says Gus, his Charleston accent pronounced.

"Rivka's having the baby tonight!" Lara screams, lassoing his arm and jumping up, down pogo-like.

"Honey, calm down. You'll hurt yourself," he says. Lara continues bouncing, pigtails flying.

"I can't find my keys," says Maury.

"Maury, this is not funny. Where's your spare set?" I ask.

He sounds dejected. "I don't know. I thought I had them yesterday, but when I went to look for them--" His hands plunge into his pockets.

"Never mind. We'll take my car." I rush past Michael and Rivka, parents-to-be in slow motion. I need to clear my rolling office of papers and files. The phone starts an incessant ring. Who would call on the first night of Passover? No one we know. Must be a telemarketer trying to sign me up for another mortgage, which I may need. It continues to ring as I race out the door.

We load into my last-legs Volvo with Maury driving and Rivka in the front seat, her legs stretched in front of her. The rest of us squish into the back seat. Rivka holds her belly and moans. "Ay, mi Dios. Oy, this hurts. Miguel? Miguel? I need you. Aaaah." Michael passes her his hand from the back seat.

"It's okay. Breathe deeply. You're going to be okay. Remember what they taught you in class. Whoosh whoosh. This is what we've been waiting for." Michael leans forward toward Maury, "Dad, I'm so glad you're driving. I'd be too nervous."

"Oh no! I'm all wet. This is terrible. My bladder's given out," screams Rivka. No matter how many books you read on pregnancy some of the details slip away.

"All right. Stay calm. It's only your water breaking," says Maury, aiming to put the key in the ignition without success. I'm glad I moved all the student term papers off the seat and into the trunk.

"Let me go in and get a towel," I say opening my car door. I run into the house, my heart fluttering. I rustle through my linen closet, towels falling on the floor as I try to grab one. I'm so nervous. As my clammy hands land a maroon velour bath sheet, I hear the phone ringing again. No way. I'm on a mission.

I plow back into the car almost throwing the towel into the front seat to the moaning Rivka. She elevates herself to unstick her pants from the wet mess. Maury helps her slip the towel onto the seat so she's not sitting in dampness for our ride.

"Daddy, hurry up. She'll have the baby in the car!" screams Lara as she slaps the seat.

"She won't have the baby in the car. We have plenty of time to get to the hospital," counters Maury, again aiming the key at the ignition. He turns on the lights. We blink like bats in the brightness. The roar of the engine rewards us. "Okay. We're off." The vehicle begins to roll.

Maury stops and turns to me in the back seat. "Jean, how many times have I told you not to let the gas get so low the light flashes empty?"

"Dad, just go already!" shouts Lara. "I'm going to have my baby too if you don't hurry up."

Michael reaches for me in the backseat, a reminder of long ago when his little hand warmed my palm.

Lara and I giggle as Maury squeals out of our driveway. He keeps it up around corners, driving safely but in a rush. We're off! The baby's coming tonight!

I can't wait to meet Jacob. A serious name for a little guy. His Hebrew name will be after Maury's grandfather, Jacov, who used to take Michael fishing as a kid.

We're having a *bris* at our house! The *mohel*, a religious person who does the circumcision, has been on call for months. I need to order food and wine. Where's Glee when I need her? I remember being a little tipsy when Michael had his so many years ago. It's more traumatic for the mother while the men stand around the table looking nervous. Later they head for cigars outside, hitting each other on the back.

Maury manages to call ahead, handing his elephant cell phone to Gus. The hospital alerts Rivka's OB.

Our arrival at the emergency room entrance looks like clowns emerging from the proverbial circus car in slow motion. When we're all clear, Michael and Gus hold Rivka's arms and aim her for the waiting wheelchair. She's upset about her wet pants, alternating her complaints between Spanish and English. Maury parks the car in a doctor's space, one of the last perks left in our healthcare system gone awry.

Rivka disappears with Michael behind closed doors. The rest of us sink into chairs deflated. All that excitement and now we have to wait. We stare at each other with no interest in the *Good Housekeeping* magazines piled next to us.

I'm so anxious. "Maury, can't you find out what's going on? Why hasn't Michael popped his head out to tell us what's happening?" Maury uncrosses his ankles, lifts himself from the chair, and saunters off to find his OB friend. He returns after what seems hours. "Rivka's resting, but she's got a long way to go. The labor started in her back. Bernie says we should go home and come back in the morning. Michael is with her and she's doing fine."

"No. We don't want to," says Lara, voicing our feelings. We want a baby. And we want it now.

Maury holds his hands out to pull me from my chair where I've made camp with water, notebooks, and phone. "Come on. She's in good hands. Let's all go home and get some rest."

Dejected, Lara, Gus, Maury and I slump toward the exit. I glance at my watch. Two-thirty in the morning. I'm tired, yet I don't want to leave.

We don't say much in the car. Once in the house Maury finds his keys on the bathroom sink. I crash on the bed with my clothes on. I don't even remove my make-up, a cosmetic sin according to the lady in the white jacket who sold me cream to erase my crow's feet. It's too late. The birds are marching all over my face and leaving droppings behind. No problem sleeping tonight.

29

THE CALL COMES AT SEVEN-THIRTY. JACOB HAS ARRIVED! We're so excited! I don't remember eating anything, but I know I did. We pile into Maury's car to behold the newest Rubin.

Rivka, in a blush nightgown, her face beaming, props herself up holding the precious addition to our family. He's wrapped in a blue blanket, his tiny pink face peeking out under a cotton hat. I think he looks like Michael when I first laid eyes on him. I lose it and start to cry. Maury gets misty, too. Lara and Gus, inquisitive observers, ask clinical questions about the delivery and labor including whether Rivka was shaved or not. Do I want to know? Seems pubic landing strips are popular. Michael's megawatt smile stretches from ear to ear, his athletic body lounging at the end of the bed. As if he did any of the work.

"Dad, I'm a dad," he says. He gets up to hug Maury first and then me.

I can't describe my feelings when I sit rocking Jacob. The continuity of our family, the honoring of Maury's granddad, the relief that he's healthy, all flood over me. I'm in a new phase: grandparent. I spend the rest of the day phoning friends and family, ordering deli trays and organizing Rivka's room for the baby. A bassinette and changing table show up, courtesy of an internet purchase a month ago. Flowers arrive. Neighbors send over an array of desserts. Maury buys cigars and stinks up the patio. Amber lopes from room to room with an occasional bark, loving the excitement and the snacks.

Rivka comes home from the hospital tomorrow. Her parents arrive in a few days and then the *bris* is on the eighth day, a tradition set by the ancient rabbis to make sure the baby survived one Sabbath. I send Lara and Gus out twice to buy diapers and a diaper genie, a device that turns diapers into sausages and kills odors. What did we do with all the stinky stuff years ago?

As I aim for my bed I realize I haven't heard from Glee and April. Even though things have been cool lately I left messages for them about Jacob. I'll call in the morning. I fall asleep like a bowling ball sailing down a well.

The phone rings the next morning. I feel for Maury, but he's already left for the office so I pick it up. "Jean? I know it's early, but I wanted to tell you before you saw the paper. I tried to get you night before last, but you didn't answer the phone."

My mind trailing behind a dream stays foggy. "It was the first seder. Who is this?"

"It's April. Congratulations on the baby. Is everybody healthy?" She sounds so serious, unlike the April that's in a perennial joy fest. "Everybody's fine. Jacob is adorable. So precious and tiny. What's the matter? You sound awful."

I'm sorry to call with bad news, but I thought you'd want to know."

Uh-oh. Bad news? I'm awake now. I scramble to sit up.

"What's the matter?"

"Tuni and Ellis are gone."

"Where did they go?" I'm in a fog. My world has been about dancing elephants and singing birdies the last few days.

"They've disappeared. The warehouse is closed. It's over."

"Wait a minute. You mean they're gone and our money's gone, too?" My cottonmouth tastes terrible.

"That's what I'm telling you. Steve and Ted didn't get a check last week. They tried to reach Ellis, but he wasn't available. The next day a recording said the number was disconnected. They hightailed it over there the night Rivka went into labor. I tried to call you a few times, but there was no answer. Anyway, the warehouse is abandoned."

"Of course it was closed up at night," I say, not wanting to accept the inevitable.

"No. They snooped around, looked through windows, checked out the waiting area. They went around to the loading dock in the back where they used to park their TuniEl van. Everything is gone."

"What about that cute cottage and the mansion they were building?" I shift my position to sit up and digest the bad news.

"There was no mansion and the rental is empty. Steve talked to the landlady and they owed her months of rent. They left with a U-Haul in the middle of the night."

"How did they pay for that slumber party with Oprah?" I ask.

"That should have tipped us off. Buffy Brinker—she's in charge of the charity--told me their credit card wouldn't run through. They did it twice. Tuni explained they charged Ellis' Vatican trip and were at their limit. They brought over a check the next week after some excuses about transferring money. That bounced, too. I knew something was up. I should've listened to my intuition."

Oh no. This is bad. I start to calculate in my mind how much money we've lost. Whatever it is, it's not as terrible as what the Lefkowitzes and the Barstows took a hit for. "Has someone called the police? What are we doing about this?" I swing my legs over the side of the bed. Can I brush my teeth and talk on the phone at the same time?

"The police are on it. That's what you'll see when you read the headlines this morning. *Glamorous Couple Scams Socialites.* Steve knows some detectives downtown and they said these guys are professionals." I hear the heaviness in her voice. "Honey, we've all been taken."

A burst of air escapes from my lips. Socialites? Please. We're not even living on the right side of town. I think about the gifts she kept showering on all of us. Why didn't I listen to that silent red flag waving? Why were we so greedy? "Okay, let me go so I can figure out how terrible it is," I say, heading for the bathroom.

By the time I'm dressed for combat, stirring my tea and reading the article, Maury appears. "What are you doing home? Don't you have office hours?"

"I came home to talk to you."

I stare at his craggy, worn face. The man I love. My hero who tried to take a short cut, a warrior who's supporting all of us financially and emotionally. He must know, although the newspaper still had the rubber band around it. Or does he? Jacob's arrival has diminished everything. April mentioned before she hung up that Steve turned a gray putty color when he found out. Losing large sums of money makes people ill. I hope no one jumps off a building or has a heart attack. I know I'm catastrophizing, but why is Maury home at this hour?

"Don't be upset. I've got to talk to you. I did a bad thing," he says, his mouth turned down at the corners.

"What are you talking about? What bad thing?" I can't imagine what it is he's done. We've already lost our money.

He pulls out a chair to join me, lowering himself with deliberation, hands spread out on the wood surface. "Please don't be mad at me. I'll make it up to you and the kids."

"What is it?" I ask. My heart races. Oh. No. He put in extra units even though I destroyed that letter and we're wiped out? Oh no. And just when I was starting to think about Michael and Rivka leaving and getting us back to our middle-aged honeymoon. "You didn't. Did you?' My voice rises a pitch. I know my eyes are wide with fear.

"Don't get excited. It's going to be okay. I'm going to see about taking on another HMO with more participants. Just hear me out. Initially, when I sent the first check in to TuniEl, it came back. I wrote it on the wrong account and there weren't enough funds in that one. You know I've had to shift some things around because of cash flow in the office. And, I admit, I get things mixed up sometimes with all the confusion around here and your job problems and stuff happening at the office. Anyway, Ellis called me and I had every intention of replacing it from my pension account, but I got busy and forgot. I'm a little absent-minded. Have you noticed?" He closes his eyes for a moment, his mouth crumpled.

Noticed? Last week he wore two different shoes and blamed it on the dark closet. If it involves keys, glasses, or errands, *fuggedaboutit*. I skip the sarcastic brain game and resume listening.

"Anyway, Ellis called again a few weeks later to tell me the first phase was closing. I meant to go to the bank. Then I had an emergency. Remember the guy who had an embolism in the office? The one with the brassy wife? He's going to be all right." He looks at me with sad-dog eyes. "I never got the money in for the first phase." I stop breathing. In no way can I get a word out. He's determined to take advantage of a full confessional.

"Ellis called me for the second phase, which was $50,000. By then everyone was getting checks. Honestly, Jean, I went to the bank because I had to sign papers to move such a large sum out of our pension and trust account. My beeper went off while I was there. Mrs. Goldfarb's grandson swallowed something. Also, I got sidetracked with Margo, the office manager, leaving and the HMO that left all the patients high and dry and I forgot again. I'm not like you. I can't do two, three, four things at once. I felt guilty because I knew I needed to get back with Ellis. He called me a few days ago to tell me how much money I was passing up, but I never got around to it. Something stopped me from following through. I've been worried Rivka would see our name missing from those lists since she works down there so I figured I'd better come home this morning and come clean. Are you mad at me? I never keep secrets from you, but—-"

I let a long big breath.

"Why are you smiling? This isn't funny. We've probably lost out on thousands."

I push back my chair so I can fling my arms around Maury's neck, pressing my lips against his. "Honey, that's the best bad thing you ever did. It's also the smartest thing you ever screwed up. I'm thrilled you didn't give them any money." We kiss, holding it longer than the usual morning peck. He pulls me onto his lap, holding me tight around the waist, his face quizzical.

"If I knew messing up was going to get you this turned on, I would have told you sooner." He gives me a little hump, a vestige of slow dancing years ago when our bodies used to touch in anticipation of a sexy night.

"You didn't mess up. Tuni and Ellis have flown the coop. They're gone. Adios. It's today's headlines." I reach to the table for the paper.

"What are you talking about?" His eyebrows pop up in surprise. "You're not mad at me?"

"No, my darling, we didn't lose any money. Tuni and Ellis were phony scam artists who took half of the Phoenix area." I hold the paper across my chest.

Maury's expression changes from worried to hopeful, the scowl lines between his brows fading. He glances at his watch. "I don't have to be back at the office until eleven. Time for a celebration quickie?"

Men and their priorities. "I adore you. I'm glad this all worked out for us, although I feel for our friends and others who lost so much money, but Jacob's arriving today, Rivka's parents have to be picked up, the *mohel* needs directions for the *bris*. And, this place is a mess. It's probably not a good time." Amber echoes me with a bark and a jump up onto her hind legs placing her paws on our arms. She doesn't like to miss out on any random affection.

His face breaks into a smile. He says, "Okay, but don't say I never tried to change our Sunday morning routine." He gives me another little hump. "You still get me going, you know." I look into his crinkly, dark eyes.

"I hope so." My hands run up and down his back, before I break away and get up. "Let's make a date for later."

I re-read the scandal and look at the picture of our friends and the crooks at the hospital ball, smiling in their beautiful clothes. I'll tell Maury later about the letter I tore up.

30

BABY JACOB STEALS THE SHOW WRAPPED IN A SOFT blue blanket sent by Glee from Saks. Our guests, most of whom have never attended a *bris*, admire him as his momma shows him off cradled in her arms. He's a small, fragile bird, blue veins showing through his translucent skin. The wonderment of his perfect tiny fingers with paper-thin nails amazes me. The center of attention, Jacob and his mother, Michael, the grandmas, grandpas, my father, our male guests and the *mohel* move in a line down the hallway into our cluttered office. Rivka hovers near the door holding Jacob. Worry bathes her face.

I cleared the desk. Why didn't I dust the bookshelves? An errant thread from a spider web hangs across the top shelf. I only clean as high as my height, which is almost a foot taller than the cleaning lady I let go when Michael moved back into the house. Dust particles dance in a light beam spearing through the shuttered windows. No one will notice my lackadaisical cleaning habits except my mother, and lucky for me, she's not in the room. My mother's standards even beat Aunt Yetta's who's known for pushing a pin through every miniscule square in her screen door to attack the *schmutz*.

The *mohel*, an Orthodox rabbi with a bushy dark beard and a wide brimmed black hat, passes the red *yarmulkes* left over from

Lara's wedding to the men. He looks out of place in my secular living room but Rivka wanted the official deal. Maury offered to get one of the docs who does it as a sideline but she declined.

Rivka's father, Tomas, turns over the skullcap in his hands, reading the inscription inside before he places it on his head. Maury reaches behind him and adjusts it to his crown.

The *mohel* unpacks his black battered briefcase, the handle worn to white in places. I view it as a sign he's experienced in his duties. Then he turns to instruct us on protocol.

"Grandmothers, you stand here next to the grandfathers," he says in a deep voice. My heart skips a beat at the reality of an outsider recognizing me as a grandmother. Do I look like my *bubbe* of years ago, her belly covered in a flowered dress, gray hair pulled into a bun and the slight smell of herring on her breath? I pull my stomach muscles in tighter with a vow to get back to the gym. Glee's been trying to get me to go to her karaoke spinning class for months, but I'm more apprehensive about singing than lasting an hour on a bike where I can't sit down.

"Maury, you're going to be the *sandek*, the person who holds the baby," says the *mohel*.

"Tom?" Tomas pulls himself taller, his dark eyes watching the *mohel*. What's he thinking? That his daughter has married into a bunch of crazies? "Your job is the anesthesia. Just put a little wine on the gauze and hold it to the baby's lips." I'm not sure Tomas understands everything, but the *mohel*'s hand movements are self-explanatory.

The circumcision ritual, a permanent physical sign of the oldest covenant between a Jewish male and God takes thirty seconds, but it feels like hours to the mother. Rivka hands the newborn to Michael and exits the room. Michael hands Jacob to me. I smile and kiss his diminutive forehead leaving a slight lipstick imprint. I pass him to Elphidia, Rivka's mother, who does the same. She hands the baby wrapped tight as a burrito to her husband. He gingerly hands him to Maury, a special torch of our heredity. Maury's experience as a doctor makes him a bit more confident handling the precious package. He places Jacob on the desk the *mohel* has prepared.

"It's time to unwrap him," says the *mohel*, placing a miniature *yarmulka* on Jacob's head. Maury takes apart the blue blanket, then the flannel receiving blanket underneath, peeling back the layers like a banana. Jacob's legs start to flail and he sends up a wolf-like wail. Does he know what's next?

"Don't worry. Don't be nervous," says the *mohel*. "All babies cry when you take their diaper off. They like being wrapped up. It's like the mother's womb. Grandpa, it's time for the *vino*."

When Tomas steps forward to soak the baby's lips with wine, the women exit the room. I pull Elphidia's arm through mine to guide her down the hallway. I glance back at Jacob, his pink lips sucking the gauze with wine.

We gather in the living room, a bit nervous. I call it The Bohemian Salon with its eclectic decor.

Elphidia and I sit on either side of the new mommy. I hope the mother hangs tough. Part one of the three-part ceremony has begun. My parents and some neighbors and friends shift around in the awkward silence. No one wants to talk about what's going on in the other room.

We hear Jacob cry. Rivka jerks and we hold her hands. Her mother whispers something to her in Spanish. "Is it over yet?" Rivka asks me, a mother's anxiety on her lovely face. With her hair pulled back in a bow and wearing the lace dress Elphidia brought for the wedding, she's an angel without wings. She and I have had our troubles, but the arrival of Jacob leads me to believe we're on a different track now. I know she'll make a good mother, her focus resolute.

"Is it over yet?" Rivka asks again.

"No, probably not," I answer. "They say prayers."

"Would you go and see? I'm worried," says Rivka.

I let go of her hand and get up to check, standing in the doorway looking at the men's backs. Their vertical bodies and heads dotted with red remind me of the upside-down Spanish exclamation points I see Rivka write. The *mohel* picks up the cup with red wine. Jacob must be drunk by now from the ancient anesthetic. His precious face screws into a red, loud wail as the *mohel*, prayer shawl draped over his shoulders, his black *yarmulka* balanced on the back of his head, deftly cuts the unwanted foreskin. His back is to me so I can't see anything, but I know the deed is done. Jacob starts a slow cry, more like a wounded animal.

I leave the witnessing for Maury and Michael. In the living room Rivka holds hands with her mother as they make ugly faces at each other. She gives Elphidia a brief explanation in Spanish. I know this has been done for centuries, but it still gives me the willies. Of course it's better than waiting until he's older. Can you imagine announcing to a thirteen year old, as some African tribes do, it's time for your circumcision?

I break the silence spouting one of Maury's obscure facts, "Did you know the British royal family trusts their sons to London's most skilled *mohel*?" I announce this to no one in particular when we hear shouts of *mazel tov*. Thank Goodness it's over. Rivka, whose fingernails leave teeth-like marks in my hand, jumps up. "It's over. He's okay," I reassure her.

"Can I go in?" she asks, her face expectant. Michael brings Jacob, a blue bundle with a red face, into the living room before she can leave.

"It's done?" she asks as she takes Jacob from him and coos to his little face.

"It's done. This guy is a trouper," says Michael, his face relaxed. "I'm so proud of him."

Everyone comes into the living room. Jacob quiets down as she retreats to her room to offer him her breast. Maury pours wine into glasses for the *Kiddush*, the blessing over the wine and the second part of the ceremony. We're all beaming, especially Michael, the new poppa. The rest of the relatives and friends banish the colored cellophane wrappings on the trays of food set on the dining room table. The party to welcome Jacob begins.

31

I INVITED MY TWO DEAREST FRIENDS TO MEND OUR RIFT. Glee arrives after the ceremony, sidles up to me with a plate of deli meats and a dollop of chopped liver sans rolls. "Leave it to you to have a penis party. I wish I had thought of it. Why didn't I bring my camera for a head-shot? I could have used Jacob's little one as a before and after for my last art show."

Then, her happy expression fades. "This TuniEl debacle has set us back. Ted says we can't take a vacation this summer and we've canceled our two weeks at Esalen. We've even bagged the plans from the landscape architect for a Japanese meditation garden. I'm upset, but not as much as I thought I'd be, although firing Lars, my personal trainer, wounded me." She lowers her voice as she looks around to make sure the next part is private. "I can live without the trips and trappings. I mean, I have my art and yoga." She swishes her hand through the air. "But never mind that. Ted was so consumed with TuniEl, then worried about it and now he's so depressed that we haven't had sex in weeks. I don't know if you've ever felt like this about Maury, but Ted doesn't turn me on anymore. The sparks aren't there."

She looks so forlorn, my dear friend who makes life perfect most of the time. "All couples go through phases where their desires wane. Be patient. It'll come back." I sip my wine.

"No, you don't understand. I'm totally turned off. I can't paint or sculpt if I don't have my sexual energy electrifying me. If I don't create, then I have nothing." Her arm gestures toward the ceiling and the sky beyond.

I glance around to make sure no one is listening, "What would turn you on?"

She sets her plate on an end table. Her large brown eyes focus on me, intent on her thought. "Lars. He'd be great for a roll in the hay." She pauses. "Except he's too dumb. I need someone I can talk to, someone with spiritual depth, like my art instructor, Professor Strickland. He's brilliant. Traveled to the Hermitage, knows art history." She pauses. "But he's overweight and smells of paint remover. And his teeth are yellow. I can't understand why people don't go for bleaching."

"Be with Ted, but pretend you've invented a Mister Potato Head," I tell her.

"How do I do that?" She sips more wine, her expression open for a solution.

"Take the trainer's body and Professor Strickland's mind. Put them together for a fantasy."

Her eyes open wider, the caked-mascara lashes almost hitting her brows. Her dark curls shake as she moves her head back and forth in wonderment. "You're a genius. I can handle losing the money. I can give up some of our perks, but I can't stand losing my orgasms." Her mouth sets in a firm line. "I'm going to try it."

Our conversation ends because my parents want to go home for their afternoon nap. The young ones and the old ones stay on the same schedule. They leave with a neighbor who agrees to drop them off. We hug good-bye.

April arrives late wearing a conservative-for-April black dress that covers her best assets. "How's the baby? I came late because the first part sounded too painful." She accepts a glass of wine from Maury, kissing him on the cheek. "Congratulations, Grandpa." She lifts her glass to toast us.

"Thank you. You're looking pretty spiffy for someone who's been through a disaster." April breaks into a weak smile.

When Maury returns to the bar, April leans in to speak in her conspiratorial tone, "I'm just sick about this whole TuniEl thing. How could we have been so naïve? I never had a clue. Although I did get some funny feelings about them."

Glee stares into the bottom of her drink. Guilt consumes me like a boa wrapping itself around my neck and squeezing. We didn't lose any money and they don't know that yet.

April continues, "It's just so damn easy for anyone to get into society here. Not like other places where you have to work your way up through the charity committee ranks. In Phoenix anyone who can afford a ticket attends events." Realizing she sounds elitist, she adds, "I feel terrible that we were influential in getting those people involved."

"You? I can't leave my house without my neighbors giving me the finger," says Glee, moving deli meat around her plate with a fork.

"Do you think we'll ever see any of our money again?" April asks without a shred of hope in her voice.

"I think those phonies are gone forever," I say. "They were romancing everyone for months like turkey vultures flying concentric circles."

"The DA's office is going to charge them with a felony," says April, proud of her insider's knowledge. "Maybe they'll get caught and return the money." She fluffs her hair with her hand.

"Come on," I volunteer. "It took less then a year to set up a sting that netted almost twenty-five million dollars. Let's face it, we were very profitable suckers." The guilt monkey nudges me after I used "we". When do I confess to my buddies we missed out on the scam? I recover in teacherly fashion to finish, "Something must have scared them to move so quickly. If they'd stuck around a bit longer, they would have done better than the Baptist Foundation that scammed the parishioners with the affinity fraud."

Glee shakes her head. "I've lost faith. In human beings. We were so gullible. Ted says he has egg all over his face because we got so many people involved." Then she giggles. "When I told him I'd like to lick the egg, he said he'd rather it was his sausage." She brightens a bit. "Maybe that means he's interested again."

April looks confused as we do a group hug. "I'm glad we're friends again," says Glee, her eyes glistening at me. "That you're not mad at us anymore."

A snake of blame creeps closer to my heart. Should I tell them? Not the right time. Rivka returns with the baby in her arms. After more cooing, the guests drift out the open front door.

Before cleaning up, I sprawl on the shabby chic sofa, legs propped on the cocktail table, head thrown back into the cushy pillows, to reminisce about the significance of the day. A new life has entered our family circle. I reflect backward to my parents and grandparents, and stories they shared about their grandparents in Europe. I land in the middle of the continuum, my mind racing forward to my married children and now their children. My perspective shifts to the future. Will little Jacob and I be friends? Will he be spirited like his momma? Or laconic like his dad? I can't wait to hold his little hand in mine and take him to the library.

32

"JEAN? MAURY?" RIVKA KNOCKS AT OUR CLOSED bedroom door. "Can I come in?"

"Sure, honey. Everything okay?" I ask. Maury sits up straighter in our bed.

"He's sleeping on Michael's chest. The *bris* knocked him out today. It's been so hectic with the baby that I haven't had time to talk to you. Between learning how to breast feed and my parents coming and the circumcision, this week--" She hesitates. "I want to say thank you for all you've done and--" She stops again, smoothing down her dress.

My expectant face urges her on. "I just wanted you to know I suspected something was going on at TuniEl near the end, but the money was so good and Tuni was so sweet to me, I--"

"Like what?" I ask.

"Like I overheard the computer programmer tell the receptionist he couldn't find any purchase orders. I know I should have said something, but we were getting ready for Passover and then labor started and--"

"Do you think they suspected you knew something?" Maury asks.

"I think they saw me whispering with Glory and were suspicious."

"Was there anything you could have done?" I ask.

"Not really. I was just trying to keep my job. Well, goodnight."

"The police will want to question her when they do the investigation but she doesn't have anything to hide."

"Really?" My mind races to a jail visiting day.

"Naw. It'll be okay. If there's a problem we'll get a good lawyer."
Oh no.

I reach for an article I've saved from the paper for Maury, handing it to him with his reading glasses.

REPRESENTATIVE INTRODUCES BILL

Students picket
By Madison Brandi Sparks and
Theodore Pomerantz
The Phoenix Courier

Representative Flora Boudreaux (Republican, District 435, Phoenix) introduced controversial bill number 45 to the Senate today. Bill 45 excludes members of the opposite sex from visits in dormitory rooms in all state universities. It has passed all rules committees and the House floor.

"Mixing young people in the rooms promotes sexual activity and inhibits learning," stated Boudreaux to a group of protesters with signs lining the capitol steps. "We must take action to stop the high level of fornication on campus."

Should the bill pass, Arizona will be the first in the nation to institute such restrictions. Although universities are cracking down on alcohol consumption, no state university has restricted visitations from the opposite sex.

The protest by students at Arizona State in Tempe was uneventful. Jennifer Tiffany Glass, a 19-year old recreation major, stated, "This is so ridiculous. It's totally out of line. What if I'm studying with a guy and the library is closing? If we can't come back to my dorm room, where are we supposed to go? So what if we do it? It's not the state's business." Jennifer Tiffany hails from Blue Lip, South Dakota.

"This is a bold step for a state legislature to institute. The entire country will be watching Arizona to see if student's horniness can be curbed through the regulation of dormitory restrictions," stated Luther Schlump, executive director of the Association of College and University Housing.

Megan in a puff of talcum took away my Women and Lit sections in anticipation of Representative Boudreaux introducing another bill to ban Women's Studies. She's not going to give up.

When we met for end of the semester review, Megan said in her haughty voice, "I have to give you credit for standing your ground. However, the Dean and I will not be issuing you tenure this year. We're going to transfer you to our satellite campus that's on the way to Gila Bend. A bit more driving, perhaps, but the community colleges feel an outreach program is important for our rural students."

I know she thinks I'll bag it, but I like the idea of a commute two days a week, listening to tapes in the car, and gearing up to mess some minds.

Doris calls late one night to say she's been accepted at the University of Texas so she's moving. I wish her well. "Ya know, Miz Rubin, I learned a lot of lessons, but the most important one was what Doctor Blackhead taught me. My life's a movie and I'm the director." Right. And I hope the sequel is *A Star is Born*.

Six months pass in a flash when you march zombie-like through days without much sleep. Jacob is precious but the nights he's up, no one gets any rest. Many times there's a few of us up watching "I Love Lucy" reruns.

This Saturday Rivka, in one of Michael's white shirts and a red bandanna, stands next to an orange U-Haul backed into our driveway, doors open, boxes piled next to it. The extra set of dishes and the family room furniture are already inside. Since it's a Saturday Rivka can't work, but like a rabbi, she can officiate. Michael and Maury file in and out of the house while she admonishes them not to break anything. Her baby weight hasn't melted away because she's still breast-feeding, but the perky figure is still there. The lactation Nazis continue calling to keep her involved.

I hold Jacob, bouncing him gently, watching from the doorway. I never thought I'd feel conflicted about Michael and Rivka moving to an apartment, but I'm going to miss this little guy. He must know because he reaches up to grab my face, his throat emitting a chortle. Jacob won't be too far away. I've committed to some babysitting after I teach a straight literature course on Tuesdays and Thursdays, enabling Rivka to continue her degree. I've come to a truce with my daughter-in-law. I make an effort not to do the things that bug her and she makes an effort not to be difficult. She says she appreciates the extra hands to change a diaper and give the little guy a bath. We've both made adjustments and compromises. I've learned to love and tolerate Michael's wife. Did I have a choice? I'm older. I had to be the emotional giant instead of the mental midget so our family could move on.

Michael's clerking at Steve Lefkowitz's law office. Even with a major financial setback, attorneys don't go out of business. Maury'll flip if Michael goes into personal injury though this last year has sobered Michael. He's a papa with a family to support and more responsibility than he's ever known. I love watching him cuddle Jacob. "Mom, ya think he'll be a sports fanatic like me?" he asks. I know he's matured because he doesn't wear his baseball cap backwards anymore. Only to the side.

On the business front, the civil suit against TuniEl consumed most of the last six months for the Lefkowitzs. I haven't seen their lifestyle change much, but April says her shopping budget has been curtailed. "Retail therapy is what keeps me going," she confesses. I'm sure her shoe addiction can be satiated with a smaller dose of Blahnik, Choo, and Prada. The truth is April's got enough clothes to last until 2045. She won't be naked for eons.

Glee and Ted, on the other hand, have put the semi- finished Sedona house on the market for twice what it cost to build. Financial recovery looms. That decision was so productive they've decided to downsize and put their Scottsdale home on the market, too.

"It'll give us cash flow while I get my coaching certification," Glee says. With all the therapy I've had, I can coach others to success. You know," she tells me in her most serious voice, "life isn't about collecting things. It's about the evolution of the soul." This week. In preparation for her new career, she becomes a platinum blonde. It cost less than surgery. And, she confesses, "My sex life's back in the groove, too."

Lara, Gus and Tangerine arrive next month. The Cecil B. DeMille production consumed thirty-six hours of intense labor, accompanied by a dancing *doula*, a merry midwife, a few stoned witnesses, a loud videographer, an annoying nurse, a fat photographer and two sets of appalled parents. The result? A baby and tasteful black and white photos. Yes, they really put Tangerine on the birth certificate. Tangerine Louella after Maury's mom. I hope the kid has a sense of humor.

Gus' latest entrepreneurial idea for financial stability involves a website entitled Alibi.com, a place for cheating spouses to hire a service that prints fake invitations and concocts alibis. Secretaries answer the phone with various business or hotel names to cover for the offending parties. Maury and I think it's crazy, but Gus swears the guy in Australia who conceptualized the idea is making millions. I should have known it started there considering that's where Tuni and Ellis came from with their scam.

As for the errant Sterlings, not a word or sign of them anywhere on the planet. I'm not worried. I'm sure they'll try it all again. How can one possibly budget twenty-five million? Their outrageous lifestyle and social climbing will reveal their shining faces in a society picture somewhere, sometime.

And, finally, Maury and I research Costa Rica on the worldwide web. The rain forests and retirement communities have such appeal. We can't consider the option yet, but we dream of a democratic government in a foreign land where I can write and Maury can play golf and we can both learn Spanish. Our dreams keep us alive.

We finally have our house back. Maury and I curl our naked bodies under the covers, our ceiling fan singing a repetitive rhythm. I wrap myself into his warm back. His hairs tickle my chest. We stopped wearing pajamas years ago because our first apartment lacked air conditioning. The elderly landlord, who wore suspenders and a belt, swore the swamp cooler, a weird contraption with a fan that cools water, worked just as well. Ha. We've been naked at night ever since. Sometimes I remind him of how much money I've saved not purchasing nightgowns.

"I have a confession to make."

He stops my hands on his furry chest, a part of his body I adore.

"What is it?" he asks, a slight sound of concern in his voice. "Don't tell me. You're *schtupping* the Dean and you want to run away to live in Gila Bend." Gila Bend, a city whose welcome sign greets visitors with "Home of 1700 Friendly People and 5 Old Crabs," remains a family joke.

"Be serious for a minute. I have to tell you something I did. I'm not proud of it, but it turned out all right in the end."

"I know. You finished all the cheesecake and you didn't become bloated." His attempt at lame humor when he knows I'm worried about my weight and night sweats isn't funny.

"Maury. I read a piece of your mail and tore it up," I whisper to his back.

He untangles our arms and legs from the spoon position to face me. "What mail?"

"You got a letter from TuniEl before the disappearance asking for more money. I read it and then made an executive decision to destroy it."

"Jean." His voice doesn't sound approving. Destroying letters remains a sore subject after what his mother did. I think it's more of not wanting to be controlled by a woman than what's in the letter. Men like to think they're in charge, and we try to fool them, but we know who's being managed.

My rush to confess tumbles the words together. Maury doesn't get angry too often. I don't want him to raise his voice. I turn into a wuss when people yell at me. Except for Megan Trumboldt. She makes me mad.

"I felt it was addressed to both of us even though your name was on it and I didn't want to show it to you because we already, or so I thought, had given them so much money. I kept seeing us old and poor and drooling on a front porch with Rivka taking care of us.

That thought is really scary. I know I should have discussed it with you. It's been gnawing at me for months. I'm sorry." I say this as I touch his face.

He's silent, his lips pursed together. I can tell he's not pleased. I've ruined our Sunday morning fun.

My voice registers little girl. "It turned out okay in the end. We didn't lose any money." He remains silent. Maybe I'll change the subject. "Our friends weren't that upset when we told them but I felt so guilty. I couldn't go on pretending we lost money, too, just to share in the camaraderie."

"Jean, the truth always works. They didn't stop being our buddies. Steve and his firm are putting together a civil suit besides the criminal charges that are pending. We're not going to be part of that." He pauses, then sighs. "Thank Goodness."

He reaches over to pull me close to him again, his lips find my neck and the crevice of my collarbone, his fingers creep into my armpits for a tortuous tickle.

"Are you mad at me?" I ask, gasping for breath through my laughter.

"Promise not to throw away mail I haven't read." I nod and he releases me to move closer, kissing me on the lips. I sink into his warm body. Another kiss, his tongue probing, lasts longer.

"Hmmm. What got you turned on?" I ask, pushing the covers away.

"The thought of not having to deal with all those lawyers," he says as he drops small kisses on my naked breasts. Let the games begin. I put Vaseline around the lens of life. *Yie tov.*

Acknowlegements

Even though writing can be a lonely art, it becomes a team effort. My heartfelt thanks to my Scottsdale Writer's Group, Deb Ledford, Virginia Nosky and Judy Starbuck, for their patience, Denise and Joan Domning who pushed for perfection, and those crazy Scottsdale ladies who gave me endless material.

www.ingramcontent.com/pod-product-compliance
Lightning Source LLC
Chambersburg PA
CBHW020735250626
47155CB00003B/762